Unknown Name
Unknown Number

Unknown Name
Unknown Number

A Wimsey Reade Mystery

Robin Hardy

Westford  Press

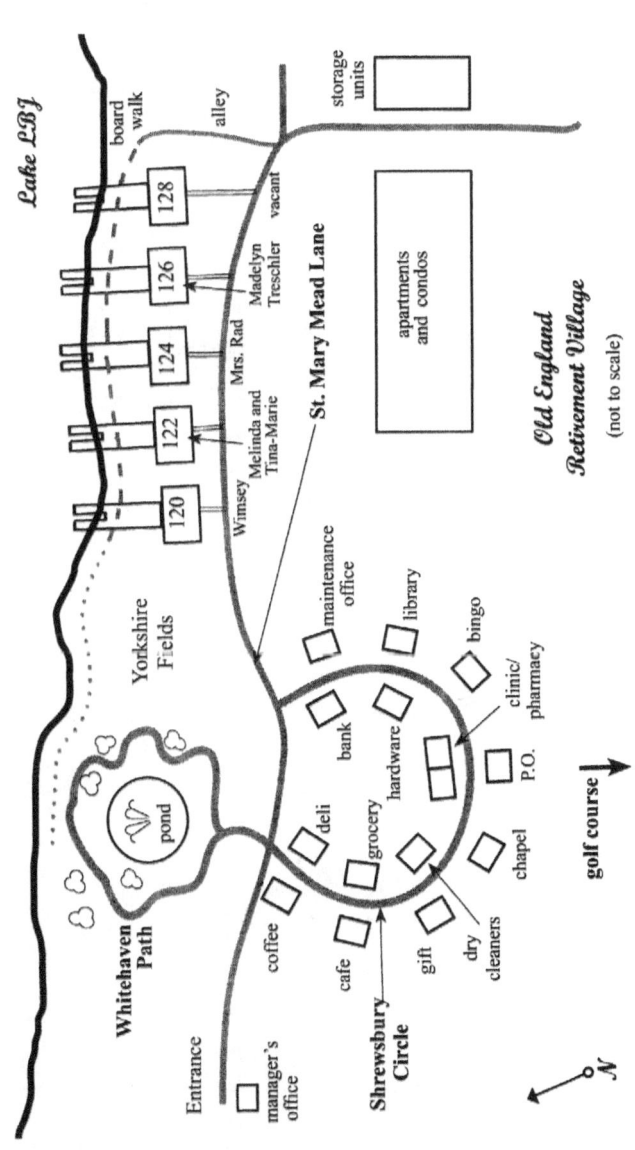

Lake LBJ

board walk

alley

storage units

128

126   Madelyn Treschler

vacant

124   Mrs. Rad

St. Mary Mead Lane

122   Melinda and Tina-Marie

apartments and condos

120   Wimsey

Yorkshire Fields

maintenance office

library

bingo

bank

hardware

clinic/ pharmacy

pond

deli

grocery

P.O.

golf course

Whitehaven Path

coffee

chapel

Entrance

cafe

gift

dry cleaners

manager's office

Shrewsbury Circle

N

Old England
Retirement Village

(not to scale)

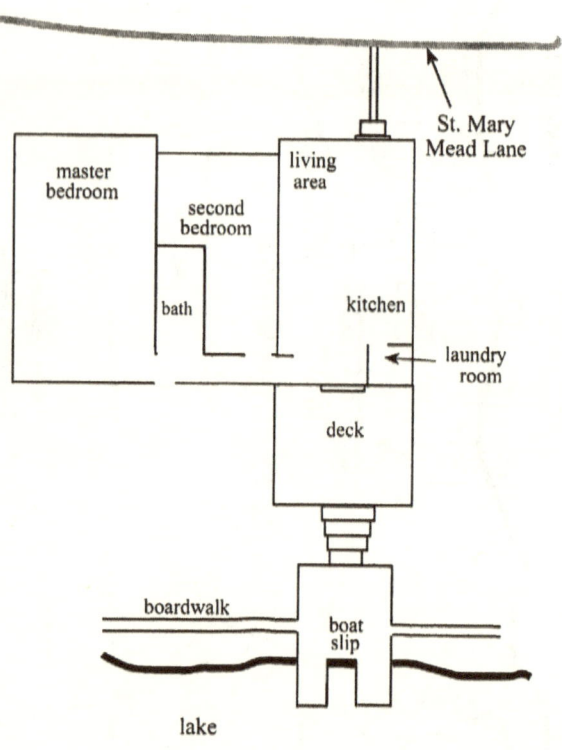

master bedroom

second bedroom

living area

St. Mary Mead Lane

bath

kitchen

laundry room

deck

boardwalk

boat slip

lake

Wimsey's house
120 St. Mary Mead Lane

(not to scale)

N

One

Wimsey Reade stood on the shore of Lake LBJ looking over the rolling green water. The mild sunlight of early October washed over the Texas Hill Country like a golden benediction. A Chinese pistache to her left shimmered in the afternoon; the hundred-year-old pecan tree behind her littered the ground with its bounty. An unleashed dog, a blond cocker mix, investigated the water's edge while keeping an ear cocked back to its owner.

Wimsey basked in the peaceful setting a moment longer, then began walking toward the house sixty feet away. Glancing over her shoulder, she called, "Cootie!" The dog lifted its ponderous ears and began loping up the shore toward her. Heading for the steps to the deck, Wimsey glanced aside with a wry smile at the boat lift. The house was nice, not too big for one person, but she really had no use for a slip, much less a lift.

When she had first brought her daughter Tara to see this vacancy in The Old England Retirement Village, Tara also questioned the need for a slip—or a house, for that matter. The village condominiums and apartments, not being on the water, were much cheaper. But pets were permitted only in the houses, and Wimsey could not bear to part with this dog, a bitch.

Her ex-husband despised the animal—"a pound dog," he called it—which probably endeared her to Wimsey even more. She would have paid extra for the house without regret, if she had to. But the previous resident had committed suicide here in such a violent, messy manner that the Village found themselves with a lakeside home no one would go near, much less lease.

A friend told Wimsey about it, and she, being neither squeamish nor afraid of ghosts, agreed to take it at a vastly reduced price. Glancing in satisfaction at the arrangement of nandina, mountain laurel, and yuccas around the deck, she mounted the steps with the dog at her heels.

Opening the French doors into the back living area, she heard her cell phone ring. Actually, the noise it made was more of a bleat. It was irritating, but since it was a new phone, Wimsey hadn't learned how to change the ring tone yet. It was an old-style flip phone; Wimsey was unwilling to sacrifice what privacy she had in order to get a smart phone.

Unhurried, she sat on the couch and reached over to pick up the phone from the glass-topped coffee table. Beside the phone lay that morning's newspaper with the lower-front headline: "ShaftCom CEO Indicted." Wimsey noted the Caller ID display on her phone before answering, "Hello." Cootie jumped onto the couch to nestle against her leg. Wimsey pursed her lips at the muddy paws.

"Mom! Where have you been?" said an exasperated female voice.

"Just walking along the lake, Tara," Wimsey said, stroking the dog.

"Well—did you get everything moved in okay? I wish you would have stayed with us longer."

"Thank you, Tara. I appreciate your putting up with me for as long as you did. But you need your space," *and I need mine*, she added silently.

"Well—Randy didn't mean what he said about Cootie being a 'flea bag.' We know she doesn't have fleas."

"I understand his concern, Tara. Randy's been allergic to fleas ever since your camping honeymoon," Wimsey said.

"Yeah," Tara exhaled. A toddler's voice rose in the background. The young mother hushed her, then came back to say, "Mom, have you seen today's paper?"

"I was just about to look at it," Wimsey replied, detached.

"Some news crew got hold of our unlisted number and called asking about Daddy. I was glad to be able to tell them that I hadn't heard from him since your divorce. Mom . . . are you okay?"

"Yes, Tara, I'm fine," she said truthfully.

"Well—I worry about you not having a car," Tara fretted.

"Why do I need a car?" Wimsey asked with a laugh.

"Everything is within walking distance. And if I need to get anywhere faster, I have a lovely bike with a basket."

Tara chuckled in return. "I'm glad you like your bike. Maybe you'll meet a nice old man."

Wimsey repressed a wry smile. "Darling, I don't even want to meet a *young* man, much less somebody *old* that I'd have to take care of." At 56, Wimsey's priorities had altered from those she cherished at 30. After coloring her hair for years, she suddenly stopped upon her divorce. It was a surprise, then, to see how completely gray she had become; she was now the silver-haired grandmother in the stories she had read as a child. When the reality of this had sunk in, she began to let go of other vanities: makeup became too much of a bother; clothes were chosen for functionality alone.

Tara replied, "All right, well—Randy'll be home soon. Will you call me if you need anything? I mean *anything*. We're only forty minutes away."

"Certainly. Don't worry about a thing. Cootie and I are enjoying the peace and quiet."

"Okay. I'll call tonight to check on you. Love you, Mom."

"Love you, too, dear. Bye." Wimsey closed the phone, then reached for the reading glasses that lay atop the paper. Donning the glasses, she focused on the front-page article below the fold that was headlined, "ShaftCom CEO Indicted."

"DALLAS, TX: Greg M. Corrister, CEO of international communications giant ShaftCom, Inc., was indicted yesterday on multiple felony charges of mail fraud and money laundering stemming from alleged efforts to hide the company's expenses and inflate profits. . . ."

Wimsey skimmed the financial details to move on to the second paragraph, which detailed Corrister's ascent to ShaftCom from the presidency of an insurance brokerage in Dallas that went bankrupt shortly after his departure. Wincing, Wimsey skipped that paragraph, too. The bankruptcy had not been Greg's fault. She was sure of that.

"Following the announcement of indictments against Corrister and CFO Drew Larson-Pettimore, ShaftCom stock plummeted to $7.62 a share from the previous day's high of $36.80. How much stock Corrister retained after secret sell-offs was unknown, but a substantial portion of his holdings in the company went to his wife Whimsy Corrister at the time of their divorce three years ago. Previously, the former Mrs. Corrister, who has resumed her maiden name Reade, had been the head supervisor at a competitor's customer service call center."

Wimsey reflected on that. It was a job she'd held long before Greg was hired at ShaftCom, and no one could believe that she enjoyed it. But she did. A far-sighted vice president had given her wide latitude in handling complaints, with the result that her department consistently won awards for customer retention.

But a month after Greg took the helm of the new communications company, she was laid off. Wimsey was neither surprised nor entirely heartbroken. Covered by her husband's salary and benefits, she considered herself relieved of the necessity of earning a paycheck herself. So she filled her time with volunteer work and a stream of pet projects.

Upon the dissolution of her marriage, however, she was forced back into the job market, and shocked when she was unable to find anything above minimum-wage level. She told herself it was because of her age and not because of anything Greg had done. Also, she discovered that she could not get health insurance for any amount of money—until she found this retirement center. Wisely or not, she had refused to relinquish her privacy to the government-controlled insurance portals.

She returned her attention to the article: "Whimsy Reade has been unavailable to comment on how the drastic devaluation affected her personal holdings, or if she expected indictments for her participation in the fraud. The Dallas County district attorney's office refused to comment further. . . ."

"If I had talked to the reporters, they might have spelled my name right," she mused. It was derived not from a personality trait but from her mother's deep appreciation of Dorothy L. Sayers. At any rate, Wimsey had sold all of her stock in ShaftCom shortly after the divorce (which, contrary to the information in the article, was not quite two years ago).

While she did not know of her husband's shenanigans with the company—and no one could prove otherwise—she knew of his shenanigans elsewhere, which prompted her to divest herself of anything having to do with him as soon as possible. At the time she sold her stock, it was selling at $58.10 a share.

This led everyone to believe that she had more money than she did. In fact, Greg had managed to hide millions from discovery, so what he offered her at the time of their divorce was a fraction of what was rightfully hers. But since Wimsey was as anxious for him to be free to marry his girlfriend as he was, she accepted the offer.

Laying down the paper, she took off her glasses and murmured, "Let's go for a walk, Cootie." The dog was agreeable.

With her companion properly leashed, Wimsey stuffed her house key, her village identification card, and a few bills into one drawstring-pants pocket. She would continue to lock doors even here, and she carried a little money with her wherever she went. The other pocket contained a constant supply of poop bags.

Thus they embarked down a pleasant, birch-lined street. The developers of The Old England Retirement Village, striving to attract active, independent (i.e., moneyed) retirees, built it in imitation of an English country village as interpreted by Disney. The curving streets were flush with shaded walks, scrolled iron benches, and old-fashioned lamp posts.

While cars were permitted, residents were strongly encouraged to park them in a reserved lot near the business office and instead drive the village golf carts wherever they needed to go within the community. Since fender-benders were common, the carts created much less damage to all concerned. But for the residents like Wimsey who preferred to combine exercise with errands, bike racks and trails were everywhere.

Cootie trotted nose down, tail sweeping from side to side, tugging to go just a little bit faster, though Wimsey was walking briskly as it was. Her street, St. Mary Mead Lane, was the main street of the development, curving its way through the whole village before circling back to exit to the outside world. She nodded pleasantly at passersby as she passed them by, for Cootie's pace made it difficult to stop and talk to anyone. It made for a good excuse, anyway.

St. Mary Mead Lane twice intersected Shrewsbury Circle, the social hub of the village. All the shops and meeting places were here, centrally located between the office to the west (where visitors were received for tours), the pond to the north, the lakeshore houses to the northeast, the apartments and condominiums to the east, and the golf course to the south.

Bypassing the circle for now, Wimsey came to a paved bike/walking trail leading to the large pond set in an expanse of silky green grass, and Cootie expressed the desire to go down that way. A whimsical signpost informed travelers, in large letters, that this was Whitehaven Path. (The village developers did not want their old folks getting lost.)

Letting Cootie lead down the trail, Wimsey admired the fountain jetting streams in the center of the pond. The dog stopped to hunch up and drop a pile; Wimsey also stopped to extract a poop bag with which to pick up the droppings, as dog-walkers were sternly admonished to do.

She tied the bag shut and tossed it in a lined trash barrel, then looked ahead at a fork in the path where it branched off to encircle the pond. Just past the fork on the right-hand branch a man and woman had stopped to talk. Not wishing to intrude, Wimsey headed for the left-hand branch. But approaching the fork brought her a little closer to the couple, and she couldn't help but observe several things.

First, they were arguing. Their voices were not raised—much less was there physical violence—but they were clearly disagreeing about something important. The disparity in their ages, and the familiar manner in which they talked, led Wimsey to assume they were mother and son. Mother was probably a resident here. She also had taken her dog out for a walk, and now indifferently held the leash of a mustard Dandie Dinmont terrier.

The two dogs spotted each other. Cootie jerked at the leash with an excited bark, but Wimsey pulled her back, ordering, "Stay!" The Dandie Dinmont, however, caught his mistress unawares. He pulled from her tentative grip and charged the interloper with furious barking. Wimsey watched his approach with mild amusement: he was a fine guard dog, zealous to protect his owner, but too small and too old to do much damage.

The antagonists met with a mutual show of teeth at Wimsey's feet. Hauling up on Cootie's leash with one hand, she bent to grab the smaller dog's trailing leash and separate the two. Cootie was content to sit and pant

—it was all in fun, you know—but the Dandie spun in circles on the end of his leash, enraged.

Wimsey held the dogs as far apart as she could and glanced at the Dandie's owner and son, about forty feet away. The pair were so engrossed in their argument that neither appeared to notice anything missing. Unwilling to trespass on private matters, Wimsey continued to hold both dogs.

She stood there for about three minutes, waiting for one or the other to look around for the dog, but neither did. "Hello?" Wimsey finally called. "I believe this is your dog?" The son shifted so that his back was to her; the mother, being smaller than he, was then obscured from her view.

At last the Dandie expressed his frustration by nipping at Wimsey's ankle, which reinvigorated Cootie to the fray. "Ow! Enough of this!" Wimsey muttered. Leading the dogs on either side of her, she advanced down the path toward the negligent owner.

"You're not thinking of us, or your grandson. You don't even—"

"Excuse me," Wimsey interrupted, and the son turned to her angrily. She coolly surveyed him—self-absorbed, thoughtless, a little cruel, she judged. Then, extending the leash, she addressed the woman. "I'm afraid your dog got away from you."

"Oh, I'm so sorry," the woman said, taking the leash. "Bad Reggie," she scolded ineffectively.

"No trouble at all." Wimsey paused to regard her tear-stained face. Though not very old—probably mid-sixties—the woman had the frail appearance of someone in delicate health. Nonetheless, her silver-white hair was perfectly coiffed, and Wimsey detected traces of powder and rouge on her cheeks.

Wimsey looked up at the son again, who was staring hard at her in an invitation to leave. He was in his early thirties, with styled hair and expensive leisure clothes—a late-in-life, spoiled baby, Wimsey deduced. (Years of mingling with her husband's friends and business associates had ingrained in her the habit of instant character assessment. While not always right, she seldom hit far off the mark.)

Lowering her head, Wimsey turned to lead Cootie in the other direction, toward the left-hand branch of the path. As she walked away, she heard the woman say, "I'm sorry, Norbert, my mind is made up. I just won't do it." Whatever spoiled Norbert had to say in response, Wimsey did not want to know. She kept walking.

She and Cootie had a pleasant walk. In landscaping around the pond, the developers had saved some large old Bur oaks while planting a smattering of Mexican plum and Texas redbud. The lake to the north was visible from almost anywhere in the community, as was the golf course to the south. The spray from the fountain added an invigorating scent of moisture to the air. It was the kind of day that made one glad to be alive, to be able to walk, to see only pleasant sights. On such a mild day, Wimsey was surprised not to see more people out walking.

Despite Cootie's straining at the leash, Wimsey

leisurely explored Whitehaven Path, which curved around small seasonal plantings, a sundial, and garden figurines. It was all quite charming, right down to the street lamps along the path. They were off now, being sensor-controlled, but no bench was without its own lamp post set in between the path and the pond.

After completing the circuit around the pond—about three-quarters of a mile—Wimsey and Cootie headed back toward their starting point at the fork in the path. Finding the path ahead unobstructed, Wimsey gave no thought to the arguing pair, other than fleeting relief that they had resolved their argument or taken it elsewhere.

Movement near the pond caught her eye, and she saw the woman standing at the very edge of the water by herself. She still held the leash on the Dandie, who was sitting quietly at her feet. But the man was nowhere in sight. Wimsey turned up the path without disturbing her.

Coming back to St. Mary Mead Lane, Wimsey hastened Cootie across the street, out of the way of a speeding golf cart (and holding no resentment toward the driver. The first time Wimsey had driven one of these on a visit, the accelerator had gotten stuck.) This brought them to Shrewsbury Circle, where the first building in sight was a coffee shop. So she stopped at its walk-up window to order a latte.

The attendant was a senior citizen who wore the shop's jaunty red apron over a white shirt and bow tie. "One tall decaf mocha latte coming up for the pretty lady," he repeated her order, whipping out a cup. She smiled thinly. While he mixed the brew, he said, "You must be visiting. You're too young to live here." His nametag read, "Chas."

Considering herself no longer "pretty," she didn't like being reminded that she once was. To hide her irritation, she restrained Cootie from darting after a squirrel, then put on a friendly face to reply, "Oh, no, I easily meet the minimum age requirement"—55. "I am Wimsey, and I'm a new resident."

"'As my whimsy takes me,' eh?" he said, dolloping whipped cream atop the coffee. "There you go."

Her irritation melted in cautious delight, and she took the latte. "Are you a Lord Peter fan?"

"Who wouldn't be?" he snorted. "My favorite's probably *The Unpleasantness at the Bellona Club*. But I have to admit I had a hard time getting into *Gaudy Night*. That's two-seventy-nine."

She dug in her pocket and pulled out a five. "I appreciated *Gaudy Night* a lot more the second and third times I read it. My favorite book is whichever one I happen to have read last. . . . Is 'Chas' short for Charles? Keep the change."

"No, it's just plain 'Chas.' It used to be 'Charles,' but I signed everything 'Chas' for so long, it stuck—like your mom always told you that if you kept making that face, it'd freeze that way. So you get a free latte next time you come in, Whimsy," he added, depositing the five in the register.

"Thanks, Chas," she said, allowing Cootie to pull her away. He waved, and she continued her stroll down the abnormally clean street.

Sipping the latte, she passed a deli, a café, a small grocery store, a dry cleaners, and a gift/recreation shop that carried seasonal decorations and games for lakefront residents and their visitors. Fall displays dominated the store windows, along with a few token, tasteful Halloween decorations.

Among these were orange and black placards that read, "Trick or Treaters Welcome Here," with the firm reminder that door-to-door trick-or-treating was allowed only at those premises that displayed the placard. Although Wimsey loved children (really), she probably wouldn't have trick-or-treating. A continually ringing doorbell got Cootie overly excited.

Finishing the latte, Wimsey deposited the cup in one of the ubiquitous trash cans and resumed her walking tour of the circle. For the first time, she noticed that the chapel was right across the street from the medical clinic with its attached pharmacy. There was something unsettling about that juxtaposition.

The bingo hall and library afforded a similar incongruence, especially with the large, exasperated sign on the library explaining that its tiny parking lot was for library patrons ONLY. Wimsey smiled, doubting that the village would resort to towing golf carts.

Next door to the pharmacy was an old-fashioned hardware store—a concession to the few men here, she surmised. Next to it was the bank with its walk-up automated teller machine, prominently located at the east intersection of St. Mary Mead Lane and Shrewsbury Circle.

Once Wimsey and companion got back to their street, the cocker knew where they were going and confidently led the way. On the right, across the street from the row of lakefront houses, were long beds of marigolds, pansies, daylilies, and fountain grasses, anchored by hardy hollies.

Cootie turned up the walk to the arched stucco entryway of the semi-Tudor house marked 120. Wimsey pulled out her key to unlock the door and bent to unleash the happy, panting dog. Cootie trotted to her water dish in the kitchen to lap noisily, then flopped onto the cool tile.

Returning to the couch in the living area, Wimsey sat to reach for a brochure beside the now-invisible newspaper. The brochure was titled, "Geology Field Trip for Lifelong Learners." It began, "The university is pleased to offer this bus tour along the Llano River. Under the direction of the head of our Geology department, tour members will study billion-year-old gneiss and granite outcroppings along the banks and riverbed. . . ."

Flipping to the back of the brochure, she picked up her phone to dial a number. When her call was answered, she said, "Yes, I would like to make a reservation for your geology tour of the Llano River this Saturday. Yes, that's for one. Yes, I do have a credit card—" She reached for her purse to retrieve the requested information.

When that call was completed, Wimsey looked toward her companion in the kitchen. "I'm sorry, Cootie;

you'll have to stay here Saturday. But it's only for four hours, so I'll wear you out with a nice long walk Friday." Today was Wednesday.

With that, she settled a contemplative gaze out the back window toward the lake. "We don't have much daylight left." Hooking her glasses on a chain around her neck, she went to the spare bedroom, where she scanned boxes. Her bicycle was also stored back here, as there was no garage. She moved two boxes and opened a third, withdrawing a sketch pad and drawing pencil.

By the time she reemerged into the living room, Cootie was waiting by the back door, tail in motion. So they started down the cedar steps. Wimsey's foot slipped; she grabbed the hand rail to steady herself and peered down at the steps—whatever finish had been applied made them slippery when wet, and Cootie had left damp prints coming up.

Wimsey cautiously descended, calling, "Stay close, or I'll have to leash you." Cootie scampered only twenty feet away.

Sketchbook underarm, Wimsey began to walk along the shore. She noted the spindly hydrilla just beneath the surface—a lake weed that Texas environ-mentalists were earnestly trying to control. There was also a generous colony of American Lotus, obviously introduced by the developers, and mostly benign. But then she spotted a plant that she didn't immediately recognize, even with her glasses in place, so she began a sketch of it to compare with those in her books.

Wimsey was neither an artist nor a scientist, just—

an amateur naturalist. She liked to study things. A few years ago she had run across a mysterious plant that she could not precisely identify; she took photos of it which turned out so poorly that she made sketches instead. These she mailed to a nature magazine with a polite request for identification. They got all excited and sent one of their regular contributors with an expensive camera to photograph her find. Then they published her sketch along with the photographs because the mystery plant turned out to be a new species. She still had the check they had sent for that. It was in one of those boxes. Somewhere.

Wimsey walked along the shore, taking notes in her sketchbook and occasionally calling Cootie back to her side until it got too dark to see well. So she whistled to get the dog back into the house.

Placing her open sketchbook on the desk in the second bedroom, Wimsey began pulling reference books out of boxes to check against her drawing. (The one time she had attempted to identify a plant by searching online had been decidedly unproductive.)

She spent far longer doing this than she had intended. After searching one book for her mystery plant and not finding it, she browsed the book lovingly before placing it on the shelf and reaching for the next book. The fourth book she picked up hadn't been read in so long, she had to blow dust off the top before opening it.

A compact disk in an envelope fell out of the back. Wimsey replaced the disk, flipping through the color photographs. She lingered over a breathtaking shot of

Big Sur, then that book, too, went on the shelf.

Finally, Cootie got her attention by pawing at her foot and whining. "Oh, dear." Wimsey glanced around for a clock that hadn't been unpacked yet. "You're hungry. I'm sorry, Cootie."

Leaving the plant unidentified, Wimsey went to the kitchen to pour Cootie her cup of dog food. Wimsey was taking a dinner out of the freezer for herself when her cell phone bleated from the glass-topped table. She selected a dinner and set it on the counter before retrieving the phone.

She checked the number display, then answered: "Hello, Tara."

"Hi, Mom. Is everything going all right?"

"Yes, dear, of course." Phone at her ear, Wimsey returned to the kitchen to set the oven timer and temperature while she talked.

"Well—I worry about you getting bored, being all alone."

"Bored?" Wimsey repeated. In a flash, she recalled the excitement of discovering that the brake line on her Mercedes had been cut. It was providential how she had discovered it right after pulling out of the drive—she had slammed on the brakes, remembering something she had left in the house. But instead of stopping, she had taken out the neighbor's brick mail box. Opening the hood, she had found the damaged brake line and, belatedly, the puddle of brake fluid in the drive where the car had been parked. Her husband Greg had been solicitously available all that day—he made sure everyone knew where he would be, and checked his messages with uncharacteristic frequency. Shortly after the car had been towed to a shop, he offered her the divorce settlement, and she had accepted.

"No, dear, I'm not bored in the slightest," Wimsey said. "I'm going on a geology tour this weekend that looks to be breathtaking."

"Oh, Mom!" Tara laughed. Since Wimsey always spoke in a deadpan, her daughter was never quite sure when she was joking. "Well—Halle, honey, not now, Mommy's on the phone"—Wimsey heard her granddaughter raise her voice in the background—"Are you sure you don't need anything?"

"Nothing, dear. I appreciate that you worry, but I wish you wouldn't," Wimsey said.

"Okay, well, I'll call tomorrow. Love you, Mom."

"Love you, too, dear." Closing the phone, Wimsey paused at the sound of sirens. An ambulance? Cootie raised her head from her food bowl. Wimsey looked toward the front door, listening as the sirens grew louder and louder, and then stopped. She waited, uneasy in the ensuing silence. Then she slowly unwrapped the frozen dinner to put it in the oven. But her hand rested on the oven-door handle for a long time while she listened.

She continued to subconsciously listen while eating, unpacking, and further arranging her books on the shelves. Even when she and Cootie went to bed, she lay in the darkness listening, and was disturbed that she never heard sirens from an ambulance transporting an injured but living person to an emergency room. "Then it wasn't an emergency after all," she murmured, closing her eyes.

The following morning, Wimsey left Cootie sleeping in while she biked to the grocery store for a few staples. Friendly as the village was, Wimsey couldn't imagine that they would welcome a dog in the shops. She scanned the area while she pedaled easily, then parked her bike in the rack and entered the store, where she picked up a half-gallon of milk, breakfast granola, lunch meat, bread, and fresh fruit.

When she took her purchases to the check-out counter, she was amused to see the woman in front of her toting a Siamese cat in a macramé shoulder bag. The cat hissed upon Wimsey's approach, so she was careful not to crowd him.

After paying for her groceries, she loaded her two bags in the basket behind the seat of the bike, then paused to look around again. The ambulance of last night had stopped somewhere close by, but everything looked serene and orderly this morning—nothing indicated an accident or mishap.

Of course, in an older population, health issues were probably more common. She wondered if they sent for a screaming ambulance every time someone fell down. Ruminating, she threw a leg over the seat to transport her groceries home.

An hour later, she was sitting in the second bedroom looking at her boxed computer and monitor. Then she looked under the desk at the jacks. She knew that somehow, the cables packed in those boxes powered the computer and accessories, but she had no clue how to set it all up.

While living with her daughter's family, she had used their computer for her infrequent internet needs. This computer, boxed since her divorce, had been bought and set up for her by Greg during the last year of their marriage, though she had expressed little interest in using it. Tara was the one who discovered that he had also set up an e-mail account in Wimsey's name, posting it on their alumni and social boards. Since Wimsey did not know it existed, he was also the only one with the password.

Her doorbell rang; Cootie scrambled to answer it with excited barking. Warily, Wimsey went to the peephole to look at her visitor: a man in a sports coat. A reporter, or a cop—neither of whom she wanted to talk to. He leaned over to ring the bell again, then knock.

"Down, Cootie," she instructed. The cocker stopped barking, but stayed close by with rapidly rotating tail.

With neither smile nor greeting, Wimsey opened the door. The man on her doorstep was in his mid-forties with thinning hair, a prominent nose, and bags under his eyes. "Wimsey Reade?"

"Who is asking?" she inquired.

"Detective Carter Lott. I'm an investigator with the Llano County Sheriff's Office," he said, extending a badge to her.

She took it to pretend to look at it, along with his photo identification card. "Sheriff's Office? You're not in uniform," she murmured, leaning against the doorframe to conceal her suddenly weak knees. She would not put it past Greg to attempt to implicate her in his troubles, or forge her name to documents she had never seen. She didn't have an attorney. She did not know any in the area—

"No ma'am; the county's investigators are plain-clothes." He noted the dog at her feet. "Are you Wimsey Reade?"

Evasion was futile, of course. "Yes," she said, returning his badge.

"May I come in?" He gestured behind her.

Reluctantly, she opened the door and stepped back. He entered, tucking the badge in his coat pocket as his eyes swept the living area of the small house. While Wimsey closed the door, he bent to pat Cootie. "Hey, fella. What's your name?"

"This is Cootie," she replied.

He straightened. "This was the dog you were walking yesterday afternoon?"

She blinked. "Yes. Why?"

"Do you mind if we sit?" he said, nodding toward the couch.

"I guess not," she said in resignation. While Detective Lott lumbered over to the sitting area, Wimsey appraised: Former athlete. Bad knees.

He spread out on the couch, Wimsey and Cootie following. The dog jumped right up on his leg and he began scratching her behind the ear just where she liked. *Dog owner*, Wimsey thought, sliding onto the opposite end of the couch.

"Now, then. Did you speak to anyone while you were walking?" He took a notepad from his shirt pocket and clicked a pen.

"Yes," she said.

When she did not offer further information, he prompted, "Who'd you speak to, Ms. Reade?"

"I passed several people, but just said the briefest hello. I couldn't tell you anything about them. When I came to the pond, there was a couple on the path—their dog slipped away from them to go after Cootie, so I returned him to them. Then on the way back from the pond, I stopped at the coffee shop window and talked to Chas about books. That's all."

He nodded, not having written anything yet. "Okay. The couple by the pond, with the dog. Describe them, please."

"An older woman; a young man I took to be her son," she said warily.

"Did you hear them talking?" He now leaned forward with his pad.

"They appeared to be arguing. The woman had been crying." Wimsey's heart began to beat faster when he put his pen to the pad.

"What, specifically, did you hear them say?"

She swallowed. "He said she was not being fair to him or her grandson. She said . . . she was sorry, but she couldn't do it. I did not hear what 'it' was. She called him 'Norbert.'" He blinked at this information; her heart was now pounding in her ears. "Excuse me, but—I heard sirens last night—"

He was pulling a photo from his breast pocket. "Do you recognize her?"

Wimsey looked down at the photograph. "Yes. That is the woman. Who is she?"

"Madelyn Treschler, a resident here." He replaced the photo in his pocket, leaning back.

"Well, may I ask—?"

"Two walkers found her body at the edge of the pond last night. She appears to have drowned."

Two

"Oh, dear," Wimsey breathed. "I'm so sorry. I can't imagine. . . . Two walkers found her? Not her son? Is Norbert her son?"

"Norbert Treschler is her son, yes," Detective Lott said, "but no, he claimed to have left her on the path by the pond and driven back to his home in Austin, which is where I reached him. He said he shouldn't have left her there the way he did, but he admitted to being angry."

"Well, that. . . . I'm surprised he would tell the truth about that," she mused.

Pen poised, he studied her. "Why?"

"It doesn't reflect well on him. But that's exactly what I would imagine happening after she said, 'I'm sorry; I won't change my mind'—the statement had such finality. And apparently he did leave. When we—Cootie and I—had walked all of Whitehaven Path and started back up toward the street, I saw her standing by herself at the edge of the pond."

He flipped through his notes. "What time was this?"

She looked off into space, faintly troubled. "I'm not really sure. I want to say—five o'clock? All the shops were still open."

He nodded. "And you didn't see Mr. Treschler?"

"No. She looked quite alone. So, if she was tired, or stressed, or ill, she could very well have fainted and fallen in," she said.

Detective Lott leaned back and tugged on his coat with one hand, the way undemonstrative men do when something interests them. "Her body was recovered from the north side of the pond," he told her.

"What?" she exclaimed.

"The opposite side of the pond from where you last saw her," he clarified, as if she didn't know exactly what he meant. "You don't think she could have walked that far by herself?"

Wimsey did not reply for a few seconds. The north side of the pond, closer to the lake, was much less visible to the rest of the village than the south side. Then she asked, "What of her dog?"

He flipped back a few pages in his notepad. "White terrier. Answers to Reggie."

"Actually, it's a mustard Dandie Dinmont, probably show quality. Where is he?" she asked.

Lott leaned forward, elbows on his spread knees. "Haven't found him. I've asked the village manager for a photo to circulate."

"You've checked around her residence?" she asked.

"Yeah, got our crime-scene guy out there now," he replied.

Again she paused. "You think it's murder."

"Don't know yet," he said flatly. "Ms. Reade, is there a number I can reach you at?"

"My cell," she said, and gave him the number, which he wrote in his pad. Then he stood, pausing as something occurred to him. "Would you mind walking back with me to the pond and showing me exactly where you saw them?"

"No," she said, standing as well. When Cootie hopped down from the couch and trotted to the door, Wimsey added, "I should take her. She may draw Reggie out, if he's anywhere around."

"All right." Lott nodded.

So Wimsey leashed her up and equipped herself for the walk as she did yesterday, then they stepped out into the bright morning. Although the thermostat was already creeping up to eighty degrees, occasional cool gusts presaged fall. Lott watched her glance at the ten-year-old sedan parked in the street in front of her house. "It's a county vehicle." He gestured a little defensively.

"I can tell," she replied.

"How?" he asked, amused.

"The police lights in the rear window," she said, progressing to the street.

He looked back to the car in concern. Yes, emergency lights were mounted in the rear window, but they were routinely obscured by clutter in order to catch speeders and other scofflaws unawares. The lights were so obscured now. Lott caught up to Wimsey in the street. "Hey, how did you see the lights?"

"I didn't; I just assumed they were there. No single man keeps a beach umbrella above the back seat in October," she said, looking around as if debating something.

His next question was, *How did you know I'm single?* but he decided not to ask.

Cootie, who liked routine, began tugging in the direction of the pond, but Wimsey held her back. "May I ask where Madelyn lived?"

"Three doors down from you." Lott waved east with his notepad.

Wimsey looked where he indicated. "There's no crime-scene tape."

"We don't know that there was a crime, Ms. Reade. We're still just trying to figure out what happened."

"In that case, may I see her house?" she asked.

He evaluated her, then decided, "Why not?"

So they began walking in the opposite direction from the pond, which Cootie accepted. Wimsey scanned the street: being a carefully planned development, the houses were similar in size and shape—only exterior moldings and colors, plus large numbers, differentiated one from another. They were also set close together, with small yards, most of which were planted with maintenance-free ground covers. The common back of the properties leading down to the lake was overall buffalo grass, which was so low-growing that village management could mow it only once or twice a year.

Approaching Madelyn's house, Wimsey glimpsed a small white blur out of the corner of her eye. She reflexively looked toward the back of the house but, unsure of what she had seen, turned to regard the dusty sedan parked in front. "And this would be your crime-scene specialist's car."

Lott glanced at her, then the vehicle, which was not county-owned. "It's that obvious, huh?"

"It's not Madelyn's car because it's parked in the wrong place and it's not a Cadillac or a Lincoln Town Car. And it's dirty," she said, advancing to the front porch.

"You're right," he said in good-humored resentment. "Her Cadillac is parked in the residents' lot."

Wimsey nodded, hooking Cootie's leash over a finial on the porch railing. "Stay." Dejected, the dog flopped down. Wimsey opened the front door just as a man in glasses opened it from the other side. The two drew back in mutual surprise.

"Hup! Hey, Carter." The fellow recovered, pausing to reseat his glasses on his nose.

"Brooks," the investigator acknowledged. "Ms. Reade, this is Brooks Boltrain. This is Wimsey Reade, our dog-walker."

"Ah. How do," Brooks said, extending a hand. Then he turned to Lott. "I don't see anything exciting, Carter. It's all clean. Housekeeping was just here yesterday."

"Yeah, well, thanks for checking," he said.

Entering around him, Wimsey glanced at his modest crime-scene kit, his ungloved hands, his uncovered shoes, and concluded that laboratory work would not contribute much to this case. Then she turned to scan the living area, similar in size and shape to hers, and caught her breath. "Oh, my!"

The two men looked at her expression of shock, then glanced over the room themselves. It was neat as a pin— no blood, signs of a struggle, or even anything out of place. But Wimsey bent to take off her shoes, tiptoeing into the living area as if she had stumbled upon a shrine. "I would post security if I were you, Detective."

"Why, Ms. Reade?" Lott asked. Boltrain looked irritated, perhaps suspecting her of trying to show him up.

"Where to start?" she wondered. "Well, the pair of malachite and gilt-bronze candelabra," she said, and the men looked at the ten-foot-tall monstrosities with scrolled arms, urn-shaped bodies, and chariots on the base.

"Looks like a moving headache," Boltrain muttered.

"I'm sure they are, but together they are easily worth thirty thousand dollars," Wimsey said.

Two male heads swiveled back to the candelabra. "You sure?" Lott asked, whipping out his notepad.

"Oh, yes. I attended too many Christie's auctions in my time," she attested.

"They just looked like something from Home Expo to me," Boltrain said.

"I kind of like them," Lott admitted.

"The pair of parcel-gilt console tables," Wimsey went on, nodding toward the one at the end of the sofa closest to them. Lott dubiously studied the mirrored back and lion monopodia as Wimsey continued, "They're by

Thomas Messel; again, easily worth fifteen thousand for the pair."

"Someone would pay fifteen grand for that? It's like something my grandma would buy," Boltrain objected.

Wimsey glanced at him in dry humor, considering the age of the person who had owned these articles, but Lott was writing rapidly. "Messelle . . . ?"

Wimsey spelled it for him, then pointed at one of a pair of objects resting on the tables. "The verde-antico jardinières—"

"The flowerpots? Are they gold?" Boltrain interrupted, belatedly bringing out a digital camera to photograph the containers with lion handles and swags at the top.

"No; they're gilt-bronze. Oh, that's auction-house verbiage. But again, the pair would bring eight to ten thousand at auction. And the rug you're standing on—"

She knelt to lift a corner and study the weave, then said, "Well, I can't identify it exactly; I'm not an expert, but it definitely looks like a Mughal millefleurs rug of North India. The last one I saw like this sold for over two hundred thousand dollars."

Boltrain jumped back off the rug. "You're putting me on, lady! How would you know all this?"

"She used to be married to Greg Corrister," Lott replied, still writing. He looked up to meet her eyes.

"The ShaftCom crook?" Boltrain said in interest, then caught himself. "No offense."

Wimsey did not reply. Punctuating a point in his pad with the pen, Lott said, "So Mrs. Treschler, being wealthy, brought to her retirement home a few of the objects she had acquired over the years, that she was most fond of."

"Exactly," Wimsey said.

"Which, if nothing gets stolen while we're investigating her death, should go to her son," he went on.

"Normally," Wimsey said cautiously. "But then, I don't know what they were arguing about. . . ."

"Ah," he said, pulling out his phone.

While Lott called in his findings thus far, Wimsey took a short tour through the rest of the house, identical in layout to hers. She saw more beautiful objects, little clutter, and a lot of dog paraphernalia—all the indications of the ordered life of a mature woman in full possession of her faculties.

Wimsey took special interest in the second bedroom, filled with trophy cases, photographs (many with Madelyn), and framed awards, all for AKC Registered Dandie Dinmont terrier Reginald Atticus Treschler. Wimsey studied these at length, noting that the earliest award was eleven years ago, the latest four. Like his mistress, Reggie was getting old.

She looked at the plethora of dog toys—terriers liked to chew—and then returned to the mounted, framed photos. Something about them bothered her, but she couldn't pinpoint what that was.

From there, Wimsey stopped in the bathroom. Opening the medicine cabinet, she was momentarily dismayed by the array of medications—there were at least twenty prescriptions here. She methodically went through them all, opening bottles and looking at dates on the labels. All these concurrent medications certainly created the possibility of side effects, disorientation, or blackouts.

But . . . the woman Wimsey had seen yesterday did not appear to be drugged, only distressed. Much depended on the time of death. However, Wimsey agreed with Boltrain that nothing looked to have happened here in the house.

When she returned to the living area, she paused in front of the back French doors, which were slightly ajar. She reached out, then withdrew her hand without touching them and turned to ask, "Did you open these doors?"

Detective Lott was on his phone, but Boltrain glanced up. "Yeah, I stepped out back to look around. Noticed that the doors don't latch very well."

Had Reggie somehow got back in after Madelyn had drowned, so that the crime-scene guy inadvertently let him out again? "Were they open like this when you got here?" she asked bleakly.

"No," he bristled.

"Did you happen to see a small white terrier—?"

"No," he said again, hoisting his equipment bag.

So he hadn't let Reggie out. But doors with faulty latches could let someone in. What if someone came here looking for Madelyn, then left to find her at the pond . . . ?

She regarded the detective tentatively replacing his

phone. He glanced at her and shrugged. "Ah . . . we're a small county office. We don't have the manpower for somebody to stand watch here while I investigate an old lady's death."

Wimsey nodded. "Any trucks that enter the village require a permit from the manager's office, and no one could cart off many of her possessions without one. I would just let the village know that they will be responsible for anything that disappears. You carry crime-scene tape, I assume. Use it," she advised. Lott brought out his phone again to scroll through the numbers.

She turned to Boltrain nearby. "You can protect the sheriff's office from accusations of theft by inventorying the house."

His thick brows behind his glasses shot up, giving him an unfortunate resemblance to Groucho Marx. "Inventory the house? I don't know what all this stuff is!"

She glanced at his camera. "Just photograph the rooms. Make sure you get clear shots of the furnishings."

"Uh, yeah," he acquiesced guiltily, seeing how he was standing there holding a county-owned digital camera. "What about jewelry and small stuff?"

"Photograph it, certainly, but I can almost guarantee you there isn't anything valuable. A woman like that keeps jewelry in a safe deposit box. She wasn't wearing any yesterday," Wimsey said. She slipped back into her leather loafers before heading for the door.

Lott and Boltrain exchanged glances behind her back. "Bossy old ladies," Boltrain muttered a little too loudly.

Lott coughed belatedly to cover him but Wimsey pretended not to hear either as she retrieved Cootie and went around to the rear of the house. Here, she let the dog sniff all around, clear down to the shore, to see if she could uncover any trace of Reggie. Cootie was most cooperative in finding all kinds of interesting smells, but unable to communicate anything useful to her owner.

The detective showed up to watch, then accompanied her to the front of the house again. "Uh, I just talked to a Sandy Schirm, the village day manager."

"Yes, she's lovely. Nothing will get taken out from under her. At any rate, the house will be surrounded by nosy old folks with a lot of time on their hands to watch it for you," Wimsey said, trying to sound cheerful.

Lott threw back his head and laughed—something he didn't do much, she sensed. But in her typical restrained manner, she did not react.

He collected himself and noted, "Okay, well, Brooks'll tape up the house after he's finished the photo inventory."

She nodded, letting Cootie have the lead toward the pond. "Detective . . . what time do they think Madelyn died last night?"

He flipped open his trusty notepad. "Ah, the two walkers called nine-one-one at eight-oh-six; paramedics arrived ten minutes later, no vitals, unsuccessful resuscitation. Medical Examiner declared death by drowning based on visuals; placed the time of death no earlier than five PM."

"Did they test for drugs?" she asked as they walked.

"Yeah, we're awaiting toxicology," he said. "Are you thinking something?"

Her brows gathered as she absently watched Cootie stop and nose in the grass. "She had a lot of prescriptions in her medicine cabinet, all current, in varying amounts. I didn't recognize them all, but there was Pilocar, which is used to treat glaucoma, Humira, for rheumatoid arthritis or Crohn's disease, and Capoten for a number of heart conditions. I have no clue how these may interact, but it's important to know what she was taking for several days before she died. The Capoten by itself can cause dizziness."

"Yeah, the, uh, the ME got on the phone with her doctor," Lott said.

"Which one?" she asked, looking at him. "The same doctor didn't prescribe all those medications. And he could only tell you what he had prescribed for her, not what she was taking."

The detective thought about this, then extracted his cell phone and thumbed buttons. "Yeah, Brooks? Listen, ah, Ms. Reade says that the lady's medicine cabinet was a pharmacy, so—yeah, go call in the prescriptions and fill dates to the ME's office. Yeah, that'll give 'em a head start. Okay." Putting the phone away again, he told her, "We would've gotten around to doing that."

"I know," she said. They walked in silence down St. Mary Mead Lane, passing a resident in a jogging suit who nodded curiously. They came to the intersection of Shrewsbury Circle to the left and Whitehaven Path leading to the pond to the right, and turned down the path. Wimsey eyed the spacing of the lamp posts every forty feet or so along the path. They were off, now, of course.

Far ahead by the pond, a lovestruck senior couple sat on a bench holding hands. Lott must have seen them at the same time Wimsey did, for he said inexplicably and without preface: "My wife left me for a sergeant out of Houston PD Homicide. We met at a forensics convention. He divorced his wife to hook up with her."

She did not respond, and the detective chewed his lip at his sudden unburdening. A few moments later, she casually noted, "Almost everyone thinks I have more money than I do. After paying the fifty-thousand entrance fee to live here, I was left with enough to pay for two years, then I have to—"

"Fifty thousand!" he ejaculated.

"Yes. That covers all medical care except prescriptions, which are discounted. Residents who want free medical care for the rest of their lives pay an entry fee of one hundred thousand. I couldn't afford that," she said.

Lott paused on the path to eye her. He could have asked why she felt the need to tell him that she wasn't rich, but then she could ask why he felt the need to tell her how he became single. "How long were you married to Corrister?" he asked.

"Twenty-eight years," she replied.

"Well, then," he said, "should anything happen to him, you're eligible for his Social Security benefits for all the years you were married, at least."

She smiled, murmuring, "Nothing will happen to Greg. Nothing ever does. He's the healthiest man I've ever known."

A sudden *honk honk* quickly drew their attention back to the street where a delivery truck veered up over the curb to avoid a resident who had wandered into its path. Lott observed, "Healthy people can still get hit by trucks."

Wimsey expelled a short laugh. "Yes, life is uncertain. But Greg is far more likely to be behind the wheel of a truck than in its path." Lott evaluated that, then unconsciously nodded.

As Cootie urged a resumption of the walk toward the pond, Wimsey redirected the conversation. "How did you find me?"

The detective blinked. "Ah, got here this morning to canvass for witnesses. Coffee shop attendant had your first name, so it was easy enough to find your address through the office."

"I see you read the newspapers," she noted, in reference to his knowledge of her ex-husband.

"Actually, I get most of my information online. But sure, the ShaftCom news is all over," he said.

By this time they had reached the fork in Whitehaven Path. Wimsey went down the right-hand branch about twenty feet and said, "Here. This is where Madelyn and her son were arguing."

"Okay, then," Lott said, looking around. "And where did you see her when you came back around?"

Deliberately, Wimsey left the path to walk to the water's edge—a distance of about eight feet at this point. The path meandered around the pond, varying from four to twelve feet from the edge. She held Cootie's leash taut, keeping her close by as she scanned the grass. Lott trailed her.

After a few minutes of looking around, Wimsey said, "It would have been about here." There were no trees at the waterline; there was nothing to obscure someone's line of sight from the path to the water. "I'm sorry that I can't seem to find her footprints."

"She was facing the pond?" Lott asked, gesturing with his pen.

"Yes. I don't believe she saw me the second time," she said.

They looked at each other for a minute. Lott regarded the tilt of her eyes and the downward slant of her mouth—thirty years ago, it would have been a pretty pout; now it looked as though she were perpetually displeased. Self-consciously, he smoothed his thinning hair from the effects of a sudden gust. "You want to see where the walkers found her?"

"Yes," she said, looking less displeased.

They walked at a companionable pace around the east side of the pond. Lott watched without comment as she let Cootie wander after her nose all along the path, and Wimsey did not bring up the obvious fact that his knees were bothering him.

"Is Norbert Madelyn's only child?" she asked.

"No," he said, referencing the ever-ready notepad. "Oldest son Trentham is an executive with DeGroot Diamond Company in South Africa. He and his family have lived in Cape Town for about seventeen years. Daughter Michelina divorced eight years ago and moved to Antibes on the French Riviera. Still there. Then there's baby boy Norbert, who's been struggling to establish himself in various business ventures for the last fifteen years."

"He lives in Austin?" Wimsey asked.

"Yes. Less than an hour away. So he was the one left to take care of dear old mom."

"She was a widow, I assume," Wimsey said.

"Oh, yeah," he said emphatically, and she cocked her head. "Sugar Daddy Number One, Marsh Dickers, owner of Dickers Construction Company, died almost forty years ago in a freak construction accident. Madelyn Dickers sued his company, got a multi-million-dollar settlement from the insurance company, then sold Dickers for another coupla mil. Trentham and Michelina were Dickers' kids, by the way. Then she married Dalton Treschler—"

"The real-estate mogul," she said in sudden apprehension.

"That's correct. Baby Norbert came along a year or two later."

"Dalton passed away—when?" she asked.

"About three and a half years ago," he said. "She inherited everything."

Listening, Wimsey assessed the placement of trees around the lake in terms of the obstacles they would present to anyone witnessing Madelyn's death. A handful of old Bur oaks remained from the pre-developed land, and a dozen or so ornamental trees were clustered in twos and threes. They would present some obstacle to sight, depending on the location of the viewer. The fountain in the center of the pond would present another.

But it was the land itself that provided the most cover. In the roughly 70 feet from the north edge of the pond to the shore of the lake, the land dropped about 30 degrees. Hence anyone south of the pond striving to see anyone north of it would get a view of half a person—assuming he could see around the trees and fountain.

"Did Madelyn move to the village right after Dalton's death?" she asked.

"Ah, within a few months, it seems. She was one of the first to move in when it opened three years ago," he replied.

It was unnecessary for the investigator to call attention to the point on the path where the ambulance had careened off into the grass at the water's edge. Wimsey looked at the tracks of the gurney in the turf, the muddy, confused footprints, the dragging trail, and the uprooted masses of water willow.

The path curved toward the pond, being only five feet from the edge here. This point was also nearly equidistant between two street lamps, each being about twenty feet away.

Cootie tugged on the leash to sniff all around the area. Letting the dog have her way, Wimsey surveyed the serene pond, then turned to gaze over the gray-green lake. Exhaling a sigh, she murmured, "She was murdered."

Three

"Murdered. What makes you say that Madelyn was murdered?" the detective asked. He sounded neither shocked nor skeptical.

"Where is the dog?" Wimsey reiterated.

"The terrier," he acknowledged, rubbing his neck.

Although she had no doubt he was aware of the discrepancy, Wimsey explained it anyway. "Madelyn had owned Reggie for at least eleven years, and brought him with her when she moved here three years ago. He was fiercely defensive of her. If it had been merely an accident, he would have stayed right by the body. The fact that he has not been found leads me to fear that he was a nuisance to someone."

"Yeah," Lott admitted, then sighed, "I guess I was just hoping this would be cut and dried—death by natural causes, or a plain and simple accident."

"It may still be. I may be making too much out of nothing. For all I know, one of the ambulance attendants may have taken the dog," she said.

He looked at her sharply, then pulled out his phone

again. Referring to his notepad, he began calling a few other numbers.

While he talked, Wimsey waited with Cootie. The dog nosed around the grass, found something interesting to pee on, and dug at a small mound near the water willows. Not caring to get wet, Cootie declined to venture into the water. But Wimsey watched her go repeatedly to the edge of the pond, tail rotating in excitement. Now and then she issued a confrontational bark.

Shortly, the meaning of this behavior sank in. "Oh, dear," Wimsey murmured in reluctance. Resigned to the obvious task in front of her, she bent to take off her leather loafers, along with her socks, and roll up her pants legs.

Futilely, she rolled up her shirt sleeves, too, then began cautiously wading into the pond, sliding her feet across the bottom so as to (hopefully) encounter broken glass—or any other object—with her toes rather than her weight-bearing feet.

Progressing inch by inch, she bent to feel in the water with both hands while Cootie stood at the edge, tail spinning. Wimsey was just really hoping there were no water bugs or snakes. Lott, phone at his ear, stopped talking to watch her.

About six feet from the muddy edge, in water that came over her knees, she stopped and lifted a sodden, dirty yellow mass from the water. Something was wrapped around it—something unwieldy.

Lott thrust his phone back into his pocket and

reached out with a wave. "Careful, now. Let me help you."

Holding the dripping bundle in front of her, Wimsey turned to make her way back to the edge while Cootie barked excitedly. Lott took her arm to help her out, but stood back for her to place her find on the grass.

While she held Cootie off, they looked down at the Dandie Dinmont terrier. Its leash had been wrapped around its body, along with a large pipe wrench. Lott scrutinized the head of the wrench without touching it. "A ninety-six. That's an eighteen-inch wrench, weighing in at six pounds. It would be part of a set. So we're looking for someone who'd be carrying around a pipe wrench?"

Shaking water from her sleeves, Wimsey rolled the poor dog over to get a better look at the wrench. "Not necessarily. It was stolen." She pointed to the engraving not covered by leash: "—perty of—tirement Village." "Which means," she added reluctantly, "that it was premeditated murder."

Lott got on his phone once again, first to summon his crime-scene guy, Brooks, and then to alert the Medical Examiner's office that a new victim was coming to their autopsy table. While Wimsey studied the dog, Lott asked the ME's assistant, "Do we have any test results back from the Treschler autopsy? Well, can we put a rush on it? . . . Okay, well—listen, with this pipe wrench we found—did Mrs. Treschler have any obvious head wounds? Uh huh." He listened a moment, then said, "Okay, I'll check back."

Stuffing his phone in his breast pocket again, Lott told her, "The ME's assistant said, no, she wasn't beaned on the head. But they don't have the toxicology report yet." Wimsey nodded distractedly, rolling down her wet pants legs.

She sat gingerly on the grass to reinsert damp feet into socks and shoes, thinking of poor Reggie. Much as she pitied him, she also felt it was appropriate, even good that he died, obviously, in defense of his owner. Old dogs who lost their masters usually never recovered; they pined away in grief. For this feisty showdog to go down fighting was an honor. She also hoped he exacted revenge—

Blinking, she got to her feet with something on her mind, but Lott cut her off. "I, uh, I'm going to be sure to mention in my report that you're the one who found the dog."

"I don't care about that. But you may need to look for someone with a bite wound. Reggie was a biter," she said.

"And baby boy Norbert is the first one I'll visit," he said, waving as Boltrain's Chevy came into view.

"Just to rule him out. Norbert didn't do this," she said.

He sagged. "Now why would you go and make this that much more difficult for me? How do you *know*?"

"The pond is the focal point of the village, between the lake and the golf course, visible from all over. While he is standing on the visible south side arguing with her, an eyewitness comes close enough to stare him in the face—so he takes his mother around to the other side and drowns her? Granted, he could have hired someone to do that, but he would have to have done that before he arrived, and he came with the intention of talking her into what he wanted. When she didn't cooperate, he threw a tantrum and left. By the way, what were they arguing about?" she asked.

"He . . . didn't specifically mention," he muttered. The look she returned was definitely disapproving, so he raised his hands. "I'll be sure to ask."

"Well—did anyone else see them?" she asked.

"A number of people, actually. Apparently the lady is well-known around here. But you were the only one to talk to her, and no one saw her go around to the other side of the pond. For sure, no one saw anyone stalking her with anything like a pipe wrench. Whoever did it just —slipped in and out."

"This was a crime of opportunity," she said. "Someone stole the wrench, and waited, and watched. . . . Someone was watching her. . . ."

By now Brooks had pulled up. He climbed out of the car and opened the trunk for a black bag. Then he knelt beside the water-logged little body. "Huh. They should've found this last night."

"Ms. Reade found it," Lott said quickly.

Boltrain glanced at her wet sleeves. "Huh." He proceeded to bag the body.

"If you don't need anything more from me, Cootie and I will go on home," Wimsey murmured, suddenly tired. She picked up Cootie's leash and then paused, turning back to Lott. He was watching her. "Detective, I would think that what's most important now is to know the stipulations of her will."

"I'll get on it, Ms. Reade," he said with a glimmer of humor.

Returning a faint smile, she began walking off with Cootie down the path, then paused again, tentatively looking back. Before she could say anything, he promised, "I'll call you with a report, Ms. Reade." She looked a little embarrassed, but nodded and went on.

East of the pond, between it and the houses, there was a large field bordered by a few trees. The village used this open space for numerous activities: picnics, open-air concerts, dog shows, spring kite-flying.

Wimsey intended to cut through this field to her house, as it was a little shorter than going back through the village. But after a few steps, she slowed to a stop. Cootie took advantage of the lull to sniff the lake air. Although the area was wide open, it was remote from the street, and somehow, Wimsey felt . . . exposed. Watched.

She looked all around—no one was in immediate view except Lott and Boltrain. Farther off were a few walkers who were obviously not stalking her. There were several craft on the lake within view, but she discounted them. Whoever murdered Madelyn at the pond didn't boat up—it wasn't possible except at a slip, and the only slips were behind the houses . . . of which hers was the closest. *"Whoever did it just slipped in and out."*

Wimsey eyed her house past the quarter-mile stretch of field. Out of curiosity, she determined to have a closer look at the empty slip. But . . . that creepy feeling of being watched remained. So she returned to Whitehaven Path and followed it to St. Mary Mead Lane. She felt the need to be around people right now.

At the street, she paused to regard the coffee shop, awkwardly named Coffee Au Lait. The walk-up window faced northeast, toward the pond. So, with an eye out for speeding golf carts, she crossed the street and leaned in the window. "Hello?"

Chas appeared at once. "Well, my Whimsy has taken me up on the free latte! Same as yesterday?" he asked, brandishing a paper cup. He seemed stuck on punning her name.

"Yes, that would be fine." She tried to smile engagingly, although flirting—particularly at her stage of life—did not come easily. "Sit, Cootie," she murmured in an aside, as the dog was impatient to explore. She turned back to the window. "Besides, you owe me for ratting me out to the cops."

Chas looked at her in quick alarm; seeing her smile, he relaxed. "I'm sorry about that, darlin'. You know the strong-arm tactics they use."

"No doubt. But I'm afraid I wasn't much help to them." She paused while he moved out of hearing range to fill the cup. When he came back shaking the whipped-cream can, she resumed, "It's so sad about Madelyn. Did you know her?"

He gravely doused the latte with whipped cream.

Wimsey regarded his deep-set, pale blue eyes. *Seen a lot of pain*, she thought.

"Just by sight," he answered. "La Madelyn was a little out of my league, what with my being a 'barista,' and all. Eh, I don't mind. Supplements the income and gives me something to do. The problem with most people here is that they've got nothing profitable to do, and, idle hands are the devil's workshop, you know. So there's a lot of intrigue and gossip. Lot of playing around. Friend of mine who volunteers at the medical clinic says that the STD rate here is three times that of the general population."

Wimsey tried not to register shock, but even she had not suspected a problem with sexually transmitted diseases in the village. The thought crossed her mind that she, of all people, may have been suckered by the developers' creation of a Disneylike fantasy. While sardonically noting the old-fashioned lamp posts and wrought-iron benches, she had still accepted them (unconsciously?) as the earmarks of a peaceful place— and what she wanted most, after her years with Greg, was peace.

Wrenching her attention back to the matter at hand, she murmured, "Then Madelyn—played the field?" Wimsey was dubiously weighing this possibility against the woman's frail appearance and full medicine cabinet.

Handing her the latte, Chas snorted, "Oh, there was fierce competition for the lady's charms. And the other ladies were mighty put out over her monopolizing the MMV men."

She took the coffee without seeing it. "MMV men?"

"The guys with Money, Mobility, and Viagra," he chuckled humorlessly.

"I see." Troubled, Wimsey sipped the latte. The range of suspects had suddenly expanded village-wide—over 300 residents occupying houses, condominiums, and an apartment complex. Chas himself was not exempt, despite his humorous acceptance of his working-class status in the village. His work ethic told her that he had been a powerhouse businessman in his day. "You owned a business," she observed.

He looked at her in surprise, then acknowledged, "For many years. A paper mill in Dallas—we supplied folding cartons, interior packaging, and corrugated packaging to businesses all over Dallas county. But competition, you know. . . . Well, I got a good price for it when I sold." This was apparently a painful topic, so he reverted to the previous one. "Were we talking about Madelyn or sex?" he asked mischievously.

"Madelyn," she said quickly. To soften the impli-cation that she didn't want to talk about sex with him, she held the cup in both hands and leaned casually on the window sill. He leaned on his elbows facing her. If he noticed her wet, soiled sleeves, he did not mention it. "Since you saw me walking Cootie yesterday, you must have seen her, too."

"Oh, yes," he said with a nod.

"Did you see anyone who was watching her, or following her?" Wimsey asked.

"Just the young fella she was with," he said.

Door chimes sounded, and she glimpsed someone walk into the shop behind him. "Oh, you have another customer. Thanks, Chas." She raised the cup and he waved before leaving the window.

Sipping the coffee, she walked Cootie on up Shrewsbury Circle. She paid more attention to the quaint design of the storefronts she passed today, especially that of the bingo hall, which was certainly an anomaly in an "Old England" village.

During her first visit to the village, her guide had apologized for the hall's very existence—*"It wasn't part of the original development. But the residents got together and demanded it." "What had the building been before?" "A movie theater. Turns out that no one here is interested in the movies they're making nowadays."*

Passing a few more free-standing shops, Wimsey and Cootie completed the circle to arrive back at the main street, and Cootie reliably led the way to 120 St. Mary Mead Lane. She strained at the leash clear to the cobbled walk and the arched front door.

Wimsey unlocked it and bent to release Cootie from her restraint. The dog scampered to her water dish in the kitchen. Following her, Wimsey glanced at the wall clock: just after one o'clock. (Unconsciously, she had begun to note the time of her movements.) She needed some lunch, but first she went to the bedroom to change out of her soggy clothes.

Impulsively, she decided on a rather fetching fall outfit of brown cotton pants with an autumn-leaf-print blazer. This amounted to an inner admission that she was going to start mingling with the residents. But she was still hungry.

She went to the refrigerator with the intention of making a sandwich, then stood with her hand on the refrigerator-door handle for sixty seconds. Pensively, she swung by the living area to pick up her glasses from the coffee table and hook them on the chain around her neck. Then she opened the French doors and went out. She wanted to have another look at that boat slip.

She descended the cedar steps to the slip. There, she examined the lift: it was raised, and the control box was locked. No one could have docked here yesterday, she realized in relief. As if to reassure herself, she patted the piling on the outer corner of the deck—then quickly raised her glasses to her face.

There were fresh gouges on the piling. Rope grooves? It looked as if someone had anchored a boat on the low piling while still in motion. This piling was, coincidentally, the closest anchor point on the lake to the site of Madelyn's murder. Faint, Wimsey sat right down on the deck.

"No," she murmured. "That's not possible. There would have been no time." She had seen Madelyn and Norbert some time around five o'clock, then had seen Madelyn again about twenty minutes later. She got coffee, spoke to Chas, then returned to the house and gone right out back. That must have been around six o'clock. Sunset this time of year was at seven. The walkers had called 911 shortly after eight. So did the murderer strike before sunset, or after? If he boated in, and tied his craft here, he had a quarter-mile to cover to get to his victim and back again.

It was incredibly risky, but—it could have been done. He would have had, perhaps, a 30-minute window of opportunity when Wimsey was not at the pond or at home; then another opportunity after dark—possibly as much as an hour. That was by far the most likely time to strike, under the cover of darkness. But what would possess Madelyn to cross to the other side of the pond at twilight? Did Reggie get away from her again? Or . . . was she lured by someone she knew?

Increasingly disturbed, Wimsey remounted the steps to the French doors, where she saw Cootie barking at the front door. Wimsey hurried to answer it as the doorbell rang, evidently not for the first time. She was formulating a question to Detective Lott as she opened the door.

Therefore, she was surprised, not pleasantly, to see two ladies standing on her front porch. One held out a beribboned basket of cookies. "Hello! Are you Wimsey? We're your neighbors in one-twenty-two right next door! I'm Melinda Chafe and this is Tina-Marie Pettengill."

"Oh—thank you," Wimsey stammered, taking the basket. "Please come in."

"Thank you," Melinda accepted. They came in and Wimsey distractedly closed the door. Cootie sniffed curiously at the visitors' legs; Melinda nudged her away with a foot.

"Please have a seat." Wimsey gestured to the couch. "I—haven't been able to do much shopping yet, but I can offer you ice water."

"That would be lovely, thank you," Melinda said. She and her housemate made their way to the couch, despite Cootie's assistance.

Wimsey set the basket on the kitchen counter and retrieved two plastic tumblers from a kitchen cabinet as Melinda turned to watch. "We noticed the moving truck yesterday, and called the office to find out who our new neighbor would be! We tried to come over then, but you seemed to be out all day."

"Yes, I was. Cootie and I went walking, getting the lay of the land," Wimsey explained, filling the tumblers with ice water from the refrigerator door. She caught sight of Melinda shooing Cootie off the couch. Quickly, Wimsey brought the waters to her guests, then sat in a swivel chair opposite the small couch.

"Thank you." Melinda took a sip before setting the tumbler on the table. Tina-Marie held hers in an uncertain grip without looking at it. She had a rather startling appearance: beautiful white hair styled in a short, contemporary cut, and loads of makeup. She wore thick, unnaturally white foundation, deep red lipstick, and heavy eyeliner. The effect resembled something out of a horror movie, and Wimsey determined to throw away whatever makeup she herself had left.

After a moment Melinda removed the tumbler from Tina-Marie's unresisting hand and put it on the table as well. Then Melinda asked conversationally, "Isn't the gentleman who came to your door with the police?"

Wimsey shifted her gaze from Tina-Marie to Melinda, who looked far more normal. Her iron-gray hair fell straight to her shoulders, and she wore no makeup under large glasses. Wimsey judged Tina-Marie to be the one with the money, based on her spotless white wool ensemble and the jewelry on both hands and ears. Melinda was the one who interfaced with reality for her.

"Yes, it was an investigator with the county," Wimsey replied. "I assume you heard about poor Madelyn. While I was out walking Cootie yesterday, I happened to speak with her, and the detective wanted to hear about that."

At her name, Cootie reasserted her right to the couch. "Oh, yes, that was so sad," Melinda said, not looking sad. But she scooted away from the dog beside her. "I heard she was murdered." She watched Wimsey for a reaction.

Wimsey shook her head. "Down, Cootie. I wouldn't know anything about that. The police don't tell you anything, you know; they just ask questions."

"I'm sure." Melinda's eyes flicked down at Cootie taking the next-best position at her mistress' feet. "You must have had your fill of that, with your husband's arrest."

Wimsey deliberated whether to correct her or not. In case the observation was aired as a test of her credibility, she chose to be candid. "Actually, my ex-husband. We've been divorced for two years. I knew nothing about his business dealings while we were married, so I know even less now."

"How terribly inconvenient for you, having to deal with the publicity," Melinda sympathized.

Wimsey shrugged. "It really hasn't been a problem. The few reporters I have talked to have been very courteous and too busy to waste time on someone who can't give them any information. And, it was such a godsend to find this place, and to know that my privacy would be respected here," she said with a smile, hoping to convey: *If you call the media to tell them I'm here, there's liable to be another murder in the village.*

"Yes, this is such a wonderful place," Melinda said, also smiling. "Though you do wish there were a few more men."

Wimsey shook her head again, emphatically. "That is one concern, thankfully, I don't share. I am not interested in meeting any men."

Melinda evaluated her. "The younger women usually are." She was probably six or eight years older than Wimsey.

"Which lets me off the hook right there!" Wimsey laughed. Melinda laughed; Tina-Marie was silent.

"Lot of women come here looking for husbands," Melinda confided. "And a few that hook up—the Failes and the Mattoxes, for instance. The Failes have been married for forty-six years, but the Mattoxes met and got married right here in the chapel just a few months ago, and already he's running around on her.

"Better warn you, though, that most people with the

same last name here are family, and ooh they hate being taken for married people. Don't ever make the mistake of asking George Trull about his wife Wanda! She's his sister. And Patsy Koehn just about bust her spleen when Bill Cassidy saw the nameplate on her door and asked if Gaylen Koehn was her husband. Gaylen's her aunt! But they're just four years apart and they pretend they're sisters and that it's still nineteen-seventy!"

Melinda hooted, but Wimsey's laugh was a little strained, and the merriment drifted off into an uneasy lull. Looking for a less prickly topic, Wimsey glanced out back to the lake. "I really love being right on the water, though I don't have anything to put in the slip out there. Do you boat?"

"No," Melinda said, shifting to see around Tina-Marie to the lake. "My husband was the fisherman. I still have some of the bass and marlin he caught and mounted, though I told him, 'Chafe, old man, when you die I'm getting rid of all this junk.' I'm going to do that, too, at the Garage Sale and Craft Show this weekend. Are you going to have a table?" She looked around the living area as if evaluating what Wimsey might sell.

Wimsey hesitated. "Um . . . I don't remember hearing about—"

"Oh, it's just THE fall event in the village," Melinda said. "People come in from all the surrounding communities to do their Christmas shopping. You can rent a table for ten bucks a day, or a tent for seventy-five bucks. It's Saturday and Sunday in the Yorkshire Fields right next to you here." Melinda pointed over her shoulder to the field. "But you have to register in the office for a space."

"I might do that," Wimsey said. "I just might."

There was another short lull, then she stood. "Well, thank you so much for dropping by. And bringing treats! I'm so glad to meet you. I know how valuable good neighbors are." Inwardly, she flashed back to the night that Greg locked her out of the house, and she had to go next door to call Tara to come pick her up.

Melinda stood, nudging up Tina-Marie by an elbow. "Then come by if you need anything. Oh, and don't mind 'Batty' Rad in one-twenty-four."

"Battirad?" queried Wimsey.

"Oh, I'm just awful," Melinda snickered. "Mrs. Rad. She won't tell anyone her first name because she doesn't want anyone to call her anything other than 'Mrs. Rad.' She also hollers out the window at anyone she thinks is too close to her 'property.' As if anyone owned anything here." All the houses and condos were strictly for lease, just like the apartments. "So 'Batty' just stuck."

Wimsey uttered a weak laugh, preceding her guests to the front door to open it. "Again, thank—"

"She was on a tear yesterday," Melinda mentioned, stopping at the open door.

"Excuse me?" Wimsey said.

"She got all excited, raising such a ruckus."

"Over what?" Wimsey asked.

"Oh, who knows? She's Batty!" Melinda chuckled, taking Tina-Marie by the elbow to lead her out the door and down the cobbled walk.

Wimsey waved after them. "Thank you! Have a good afternoon." Then she closed the door and leaned against it thoughtfully. 124? That was right next to Madelyn's residence. So why was Mrs. Rad raising such a ruckus yesterday?

The first thing Wimsey did was call the university and cancel her reservation for the geology trip Saturday —she couldn't afford to miss the village's fall event, not when most of the residents would be there. Then she put her house key in her jacket pocket and bent to stroke Cootie apologetically. "Sorry, old girl, you have to wait here for a while. I'm off to talk to a very particular lady who may not love you like everybody else does."

Four

Before leaving the house to talk to Mrs. Rad, Wimsey stopped by the kitchen counter for the basket of cookies. She took it with her out the front door, then paused. Melinda was almost certainly watching.

So Wimsey casually held the basket on her right side while she strolled down the sidewalk past Melinda's house on the left. At the next house, 124, Wimsey turned up the walk past profuse flowerbeds, mounted the porch, and rang the doorbell. She stood directly in front of the peephole with a smile and the basket discreetly held within view.

It took about three minutes, but, hearing shuffling noises on the other side of the door, Wimsey did not ring again. Then the door was slowly opened, and a lined, scowling face peered out. "Good afternoon. Mrs. Rad? I am Wimsey Reade. I moved into one-twenty yesterday, and just wanted to introduce myself." She held out the basket.

"Umph," the other grunted, turning from the door.

But she left it open as she moved away, so Wimsey took that as permission to enter, which she did, closing the door behind her.

She glanced around a clean interior, circa 1950. All the furnishings looked to be authentic productions of that decade—the blond wood dinette, the Empire Cinema sofa, the biomorphic chair—and she did not doubt that they were Mrs. Rad's original purchases. They looked rather incongruous to their owner now, but the lady, obviously, was once "cool."

Wimsey regarded her hostess, who was moving slowly toward the sofa by means of a footed cane. She was in her early 70s, with streaked gray hair pulled back in a clip, and wearing a Hawaiian-print muumuu. Although the temperature outside was pleasant— probably mid-sixties—the central heating system had generated a room temperature of eighty-five degrees. Wimsey placed the basket on the coffee table, then took off her jacket before sitting on the sofa. She waited, knowing better than to offer assistance, while Mrs. Rad laboriously lowered herself to the other end.

When Mrs. Rad was seated and settled, she turned thick glasses toward her visitor, who returned a vaguely pleasant smile while searching for something to say. Some moments passed before Mrs. Rad asked, "What do you want?"

Given that opening, Wimsey made up her mind to just tell her and see what happened. She leaned forward, elbows on her knees. "Mrs. Rad, you may have heard that Madelyn Treschler drowned yesterday. The police came to see me this morning because I spoke to her yesterday while walking my dog. Melinda Chafe just now told me that something happened yesterday to upset you, and I'd like to hear what that was."

Mrs. Rad leaned back with a mild, scoffing grunt. "She gave you the cookies."

Wimsey's face colored slightly. "Yes."

"They're unfit to eat. She's a terrible cook," Mrs. Rad said.

Wimsey's lips twitched. "Then perhaps you could feed them to the ducks."

Mrs. Rad's pale eyes sharpened in interest, then she shifted to look over her shoulder toward the back doors, identical to those in Wimsey's house. "You saw the bag of bread crumbs by the door."

"Yes. I also saw the Canada geese that stopped by yesterday. The mallards are probably here year-round, aren't they?"

"Yes," Mrs. Rad said. "But the Great Blue Herons are my favorites."

Wimsey considered this. "Too bad they don't care for cookies, do they? They prefer fish, insects, frogs?"

"They also eat snakes and mice," Mrs. Rad said. Wimsey smiled and nodded in acknowledgment.

"Eh," Mrs. Rad grunted, shifting on the sofa. "A young man was molesting Madelyn's house yesterday. He looked dangerous."

Wimsey sat up. "What exactly did he do?"

"He went from the front door to the side windows to the back, trying all the handles. He shouted the most obscene things at the house," the woman said.

"What time was this?"

"Three-twenty," Mrs. Rad said precisely. "When he could not get in, he went stalking down the street, that way." She waved west. "He did not walk on the sidewalk, mind you—he walked down the street as if it was all his."

Wimsey cocked her head at this appraisal. "Describe him."

"Young, brown hair, fancy-schmancy shorts," Mrs. Rad said as an indictment.

Wimsey chortled involuntarily, then passed a repentant hand over her mouth. "You've pretty adequately described Madelyn's youngest son, Norbert. He found his mother somewhere else and they went to the pond. That's where I ran across them."

"Well, he obviously didn't kill her," Mrs. Rad huffed, gathering her muumuu around her.

Wimsey was surprised at her assumption that they were talking about a murder. She said, "I agree, seeing how conspicuous he made himself. But—why did you describe him as dangerous?"

"You see how narrow these side yards are. He came within inches of my Chrysanthemums," Mrs. Rad said, affronted.

"Which is why you instructed him to be careful."

"I will not have my beds trampled," Mrs. Rad stated. "My garden help only comes twice a week, and I can't tend the babies any more like I used to." There was a note of bitterness here.

"Those are beautiful spider mums out front. . . . Kyoto?" Wimsey asked tentatively.

"Symphony," Mrs. Rad corrected. Then she conceded, "The two are similar."

Wimsey smiled at this show of generosity. Thoughtfully, she murmured, "Since he got your attention, it makes me wonder . . . who else noticed his behavior."

"Um hmm." Mrs. Rad leaned against the stiff sofa back. "Runs in the family. She's not made herself popular."

This was contrary to what Chas had told her about Madelyn—unless Chas was speaking for the men, and Mrs. Rad for the women. "How's that?" Wimsey asked.

The woman snorted. "Ask Melinda. She's the area gossip."

So Mrs. Rad was well aware of her nickname. "Is there any way I could persuade you to talk to the detective?" Wimsey asked.

"Certainly not," the other bristled. "What does he know about birds?"

"Probably not much," she admitted. Glancing around, she began, "I would like to leave you my phone number—"

"I don't have a phone." Mrs. Rad turned to peer over the back of the couch, toward the low kitchen window. The layout of her house was a mirror image to Wimsey's.

"No phone? Then what do you do in an emergency?" Wimsey asked.

"I don't have one." She began struggling to get up from the couch.

Wimsey stood, suppressing the strong impulse to help her. Seeing her hostess begin a lumbering trek to the front door, Wimsey took up her jacket and followed. "Well, thank you for talking to me. I appreciate your . . . taking the time. . . ." She bemusedly watched Mrs. Rad open the front door and shuffle out.

Wimsey followed at a respectful distance while the woman went around to the east side of the house, that facing Madelyn's. Scrutinizing the beds under the kitchen window, she said, "This Norbert of Madelyn's is going to get himself murdered if he keeps this up."

"What?" Wimsey looked at the freshly trampled Chrysanthemums under the window. "When did Norbert do this?"

"Just now," Mrs. Rad said in disgust.

"Norbert?"

"You said it was Norbert," Mrs. Rad observed.

"How do you know it was the same man?" Wimsey asked.

"I saw him at the window, but he got away from the old lady with the cane. I tell you, if I'm not right at the window, they'll tromp all over your beds and be gone. No one cares any more."

Extracting the feet of her cane from the soft earth, she began shuffling back toward the front door. "Pedro comes tomorrow," she comforted herself. "Dam' trespassers. Need me a gun. They took away my gun."

Wimsey stared down at the broken blooms. No

discernible footprints remained, but—was Norbert in the village? Was it Norbert? "I'm sorry about that, Mrs. Rad!" she called. The front door slammed, and Wimsey sprinted back toward her house.

Entering, she almost stumbled over Cootie waiting at the door. Wimsey retrieved her phone from the coffee table and scrolled to the village office number, which she called. Putting the phone to her ear, she heard the chipper greeting, "This is Sandy. How can I help you?"

"Hello, Sandy. This is Wimsey Reade. I just moved in yesterday."

"Hello, Ms. Reade! Is everything going all right?"

"Yes, Sandy, only—it's rather important that I know if Norbert Treschler is in the village right now."

"Oh, no, Ms. Reade. He's not. He's trying to take care of funeral arrangements for Mrs. Treschler in Austin. We're so very sorry about the accident, and our safety committee is putting a barricade around the pond to make sure nothing like that happens again," she said earnestly.

"Yes, all right," Wimsey said distractedly. "Thank you."

Terminating the call, she stood looking at her phone. Not Norbert? Then who was banging around Madelyn's house yesterday?

Her doorbell rang, startling her and sending Cootie into a barking frenzy. "Hush, Cootie," she chastened, hurrying to open the door.

Standing on her porch was a young man with brown hair and fancy-schmancy shorts—but definitely not

Norbert. Wimsey frankly stared; he glanced at Cootie sniffing his leg, cleared his throat and said, "Hello, ma'am, I'm Cliff Osborn. I'm a village-approved service technician." He paused to extend his laminated ID card to her view.

"I just wanted to introduce myself. I do a wide range of repairs and servicing, landscaping, moving, errands, shopping, basic car repairs, computer hook-ups—just about anything; and if I can't do it, I'll find somebody qualified who can."

Wimsey suddenly looked past him to the pickup truck with tool box. He continued, "I'd appreciate it if you'd take my card and give me a call if you need anything done. I charge very reasonable rates." Smiling tentatively, he held out a business card.

Wimsey took it. "What possessed you to trample Mrs. Rad's beds and look in her window?" When he looked ready to deny it, she noted, "Your Birkenstocks are muddy."

He groaned, sinking back. "Sh—, she saw me. Ma'am, I'm sorry about that. I tried to be careful, but—I try to catch the new residents before any of the other handymen—the competition is crazy. I knew you were new, and I thought I saw you go into her house, but I wasn't sure, and I wasn't about to ring her doorbell. Last time I did that, I got my head chewed off. I'd offer to replant for her, but—" He shrugged.

"So why were you trying to break into Madelyn's house yesterday?" she asked.

"Wha—?" His eyes widened. "Break in—with Batty

Rad standing watch over her precious flowers? Not a chance. Besides, I was hauling furniture from San Antonio for Guy Krenkel yesterday—he wants it set up for the big garage sale this weekend. Here—" He whipped his phone out of his shirt pocket. "I've got his number right here. You can call and ask him."

The name clicked in Wimsey's mind. Yes, she had met Guy briefly at the village office. He was also a resident, one of the first to move in. He had a grating, raspy voice and even more grating manner. "Yes; write it down for me, please," she said.

Somewhat grudgingly, Cliff scrounged a receipt from his pocket and copied down the number on the backside. Wimsey took it. "Thank you. I'll call you if I need you. Come in, Cootie." The dog obeyed and Wimsey shut the door in his face.

She took this new information to the couch, where she sat and collected herself for a moment. Cootie snuggled down beside her. Referencing the slip, she picked up her phone and keyed in a number. "Hello, this is Wimsey Reade. Is this Guy? How are you? Wonderful. Yes, I'm fine, thank you. You probably don't remember me, but—yes, that's right. Yes, I did take 120; moved in yesterday, as a matter of fact.

"Guy, I just got a visit from a young man named Cliff—" She stopped to listen. "Yes, that's him. Did he —?" Again she stopped to listen. "What time would that have been? I see. Well, thank you for the recommendation. Yes, I certainly will be at the sale this weekend—no, I don't really need any furniture, but I'll be sure to stop by and say hello. Thank you so much."

Pensively, she put down the phone. Cliff was telling the truth: his furniture-moving did indeed require most of yesterday. Apparently, it was Norbert after all who had been trying to get into his mother's house. And it was easy to see how Mrs. Rad would have mistaken one for the other, especially if her eyesight was not good.

Exhaling, Wimsey leaned back on the couch, and Cootie thrust her ear into her owner's hand for a scratching. Accommodating her, Wimsey thought, *If Mrs. Rad mistook Cliff for Norbert, might Madelyn have? Say, from across the pond? And if Cliff is shady enough to peep in people's windows, might he lift tools belonging to the village?* Then again, what if someone else noticed a resemblance between the two men and decided to exploit it?

She mulled over Mrs. Rad's advice to ask Melinda about what made Madelyn unloved in the village, but decided that the investigator should do that. Toying with the phone, she murmured, "I wish he had given me his number."

But she was still hungry, so she got up to open the refrigerator for lunch meat and lettuce. While she was distractedly assembling a sandwich (pausing frequently when a conjecture or theory crossed her mind), her phone on the coffee table bleated. She dropped the small jar of mayonnaise on the counter to run snatch up the phone.

When she looked at the number display, momentary irritation passed over her face. "Hello, Tara."

"Hi, Mom. Uh, how are you?" Her tone was strained.

"Fine, Tara. What's wrong?" Wimsey sat in anticipation; also in anticipation, Cootie waited in the kitchen.

"Well, I'm not sure." Tara forced a laugh. "Someone went through Randy's office early Wednesday morning when it should have been locked."

Wimsey blinked. "Someone ransacked his office?"

"Um, it wasn't quite ransacked, but . . . someone went through his personal papers and copied a letter he had sent to the village asking about their security," Tara said. "Randy wrote it right after you came back from looking at the house, and, we just wanted to make sure you'd be safe there, after all the—near accidents that kept happening to you. . . ."

It took a moment for Wimsey to process this. "How does Randy know that someone copied the letter?"

"Their section copier has a digital log that retains images of what's copied. His secretary just noticed today that something had been copied at, like, two AM Wednesday morning. She showed him the file and he recognized the letter. Someone broke into his office to find that letter and copy it," Tara said. "They didn't take anything else, and they put the original back when they were done. I asked Randy why somebody would be so stupid as to use the copier when he could just take a picture of it, and he thought they probably didn't want to turn on the lights."

"Does the letter mention my name?" Wimsey asked.

"Yes."

"All right, well, Randy couldn't help that," Wimsey said. "I don't really see anything that could come of it, as plenty of people know that I moved here. I appreciate your telling me about it, but I'm sure it's nothing."

"Uh huh," Tara said skeptically. "Mom, don't you think we should look at, um, protection for you?"

"Protection?" Wimsey laughed. "Why? Oh, good heavens, you should see the surveillance here—nothing happens without twenty people seeing it and talking about it. I'm as safe as in a kindergarten class." Neither of them explored the question of what, or who, might be a threat.

"All right," Tara laughed reluctantly. "It was just—weird, you know?"

"It looks that way, but there's probably some harmless explanation. Uh, Tara, could I call you back? I was just about to get something to eat."

"That's okay; you don't have to talk to me," Tara said in mock offense. "But I'm still going to check on you later."

"That's fine, honey. Bye, now." Wimsey put the phone down and returned to the kitchen, to Cootie's delight. But her sandwich-making continued in fits and starts. Why would someone go to such trouble to find out where she was? She had told a few of her close friends—and asked them not to tell anyone. And she had been careful not to let any of Greg's associates know where she was going after leaving Tara's. She could imagine Greg's sending someone to ransack his son-in-law's office—but not why. Greg never cared to know her whereabouts when they were married; why should he care now? All that had changed was . . . the indictments.

Wimsey paused again, and Cootie pawed her leg in impatience. Stirring, Wimsey dropped a sliver of lunch meat which the dog snapped up. Was he afraid of her testifying against him? There was nothing she could testify to; he should know that.

"Oh, this is ridiculous," Wimsey muttered. "It's a desperate journalist who's trying to scoop an interview." So she fixed her sandwich and ate it at the bar, tossing occasional bites to a politely begging Cootie.

When it was late afternoon, and prime walking time, Wimsey leashed up Cootie and equipped herself as usual for their walks. The moment she set foot outside the house, she spotted the activity in the field, so veered off the street to go have a look.

One village employee was using a tape measure, t-square, roll of string, and chalk to mark out booth spaces on the grass. While he made temporary lines with the chalked string, another employee went over the chalk with spray paint. Their activity elicited a great deal of interest from residents, who were all directed to a sign staked in the ground at the street edge of the field. It read: "Space numbers will be added Friday at 3 PM. Set-up may begin at that time. Absolutely no sales until Sat. 6:00 AM. VIOLATORS WILL HAVE THEIR PER-MITS REVOKED. NO REFUNDS."

Reading this, Wimsey wondered what had happened at previous sales to merit such stern warnings directed to old folks. Walking on by, she and Cootie intercepted Whitehaven Path. Immediately she saw the bright orange safety barricades encompassing the pond, and she paused in dismay. They looked hideous.

A pair of walkers she remembered from yesterday passed her in a huff, heading toward the street. The man was telling his female companion, "I don't care what happened there, that orange plastic is coming down! I don't pay six grand a month to look at prison fencing!" Wimsey let the storm pass, then turned back toward the street. She didn't want to walk next to barricades, either.

But on the way, she kept stopping. Something was bothering her, and she couldn't quite put her finger on it. Cootie made use of the opportunity to drop a pile; Wimsey absently picked it up with the bag, which she tossed in a trash barrel. There was something critical she was overlooking . . . somewhere. . . .

When they crossed St. Mary Mead Lane, Wimsey came alert to scan for golf carts. Then she paused at the coffee-shop window. Chas was not working now; there was a young woman behind the counter who had a rush of customers (all senior men), so Wimsey had to wait a few minutes to receive a sloppy latte. She took a napkin from the container on the counter to wipe spillage off the outside of the cup.

Seeing the mess too late, the young barista began a harried apology. Smiling sympathetically, Wimsey waved her off. "Don't worry about it; you've got your hands full." The girl smiled briefly and turned to her next customer.

Wimsey walked Cootie around Shrewsbury Circle while sipping the coffee and trying to ferret out whatever it was that was hiding in the back of her brain. It must have to do with Tara's call. Why should Wimsey be disturbed that a reporter was trying to find her? She knew that was going to happen.

No, that wasn't it. There was something else. But it was still related to Tara's call. If it was Greg who had someone go through Randy's office looking for her address, then it must be because he wanted something from her. What could he possibly think she had?

Money? No; he knew she didn't have any to speak of, certainly not what he would need for a high-powered defense attorney. Sympathy? A faithful wife standing beside a defendant made for good press. But no: if that was what he was after, he'd call on his present wife. If she wouldn't do it for love, she'd do it for cash.

What was left? Information? At that, Wimsey came to a standstill, spilling her latte. That's what it was. And she knew where it was.

Five

Wimsey tossed the half-full cup into the next trash barrel she passed and picked up her pace to a trot. Cootie thought that was fine, keeping the lead as if finally getting her way. Wimsey smiled and waved to everyone they met, so anyone watching would know this was all in fun. No urgency, or anything.

Both panting, they arrived on the doorstep of 120; after entering, Wimsey took care to lock the door behind her. She removed Cootie's leash, then went back to the second bedroom where she had begun to unpack books and her desktop computer.

Scanning the shelves, Wimsey removed a large coffee-table book, *America's Coastlines*. It was a collection of breathtaking photos from the National Oceanic & Atmospheric Administration's library.

Given Greg's professed love of the coast, Tara had given it to him one Father's Day, and had been somewhat hurt that he put it on a shelf and never looked at it. But Wimsey had taken it down time and again to pore over it. So, when the day came for her to move out of the million-dollar home she shared with him, she had sneaked into his library and taken the book.

Ashamed of the petty larceny, and unwilling to clutter her daughter's home, Wimsey had left it packed away for the few years she lived with Tara; last night was the first time she had looked at it since removing it from Greg's shelves.

Opening it now, she removed the CD in its unlabeled envelope that had been tucked into the plastic book sleeve. The disk had not come with the book. She had never seen it before last night. It had not registered as strange until she connected it with Tara's call.

Tapping the CD in her hand, she looked at the various computer components sitting around the desk. Then she went back to the living area to pick up Cliff Osborn's card and her phone.

She keyed in his number. "Cliff? Hello, this is Wimsey Reade, at one-twenty St. Mary Mead Lane. Yes, I called Guy Krenkel as you suggested, and he was most enthusiastic in recommending you. So I do have a job, if you're available. As soon as possible.

"Now? That would be wonderful. Well, I need my computer hooked up. . . . No, all the software should still be operable on it. . . . Eighty dollars an hour is very reasonable. I hope you'll take a check? . . . Okay, good. Yes, if you could, that would be great. Thank you."

She put the phone down and immediately removed the book and CD to a hiding place in her bedroom. Then she sat on the couch to wait for Cliff. It was risky using him, but riskier still to sit on anything unknown.

Minutes later the doorbell rang, and Cootie slid off the kitchen tile to beat her owner to the door. "Back, Cootie." Wimsey opened the door to a tentative but optimistic handyman carrying a small toolbox. "Thank you for coming, Cliff. It's right back here." He nodded, wiping his feet scrupulously before coming in.

Wimsey took him to the second bedroom—there were only two—and pointed him to the desk. "There is it. Or there are the pieces."

"Oh, yeah," he said. He looked over the equipment, checking the boxes in which the peripherals still resided. "Okay, looks like you've got everything you need. Let's give it a whirl."

Cliff placed the tower, monitor, and keyboard on the desk while Wimsey watched, trying not to look overly anxious. The printer/scanner went on top of a two-drawer wooden filing cabinet. Cootie attended him with diminishing interest until she finally left to go curl up on the couch.

"Nice set-up. It's a few years old. You might want to consider updating. I've got a friend who can get you a brand-new laptop for next to nothing," he chatted.

"Oh, let's see how this works. I probably won't use it much," she said, watching him attach a cable to the back of the tower and the monitor.

"What will you use it for?" he asked.

She paused. "Mostly Christmas letters."

He glanced up, smiling. "Not surfing? You have internet access already. All you need to do is create an account. Want me to do that for you?"

"Maybe later." She tried to smile, but mostly wanted to bark, *"Would you just shut up and get it done?"*

He definitely took his time, but even he couldn't stretch this simple job past his one-hour minimum. When everything was plugged in, he sat at the monitor and turned the computer on. Wimsey watched over his shoulder while the computer booted up as if it had been off only an hour.

"It all looks good to go," Cliff noted, but then a password prompt appeared. "You got a password?" He hit the "enter" key to attempt to bypass the prompt.

"Yes, I've got it written down somewhere. I'll have to find it," she lied.

He looked disappointed. "Don't you want me to make sure you can get online?"

"Oh, not right now, thank you. Let me get your check," she said. She left the room for thirty seconds to retrieve her checkbook from her bedroom, then returned to see him packing up unused tools.

She wrote out a check for $80 and handed it to him with a smile. "Thank you, Cliff. Let me see you out."

He followed her to the front room almost dragging his feet. "Nothing else you need done now?" he murmured, pocketing the check.

"No, thank you." She opened the front door.

"I can do just about anything," he mentioned.

"Yes, you told me," she said.

He paused at the door, and she restrained herself from assisting him out with a foot to his rear. "Just about anything," he said for emphasis.

She stopped smiling. "I'll keep that in mind."

He went on out to his truck; she shut and locked the door. "Was he offering . . . ? Nah."

She stood in the living area to compose herself, then went back to her bedroom to fetch the book along with the CD. Sitting at the computer, she typed in her password, a simple compound word of only six letters: "getout."

This opened her normal desktop window. She muttered, "It's probably nothing. I'm making much ado about nothing." Still, she extracted the disk from the envelope and inserted it into the CD drive.

A menu came on screen indicating that the files on the disk were spreadsheets. The files, about two dozen, were labeled by year and quarter—the last one being about six months before her divorce.

Swallowing, Wimsey opened the latest file. It was headed, "ShaftCom operating expenses," with the date. There was a visible watermark on every page. She scrolled through the entries without comprehending what she was seeing. She did not know if it was evidence of illegal activity or not. She did not know whether Greg had missed this, and suspected her of taking it.

Closing the file, she sat back to think. First, if this was anything incriminating, why in the world wasn't it password-protected? And, if Greg had any suspicion that she might have taken it, why had he done nothing in the past two years to retrieve it? The first answer that crossed her mind was that he simply forgot about it. He had a habit of hiding things and then forgetting where.

She remembered an early anniversary that had passed without recognition on his part; when she chided him about it, he righteously insisted that he had bought a gift and couldn't remember where he hid it. Some weeks later, digging dirty clothes out of his closet, she had found it: a teddy bear, custom-made out of mink. Years later she knew he was having an affair when she discovered charges for purchases from this same teddy-bear company, not for her.

This would also explain the lack of a password: Greg hated having to remember them—he never could remember the security alarm reset code. And why should he bother with a password on something hidden at home? Other than the maid, Wimsey was the only one there, and he always viewed her modest computer skills with contempt.

The second explanation for his sudden interest in finding the CD, or her—if it *was* Greg—was yesterday's headline: the indictments. Criminal charges would jog his memory about incriminating materials hidden at the house.

Wimsey considered this possibility, then puckered in dissatisfaction. Such an uninspired hiding place seemed almost beneath someone of Greg's imagination. That had been partly to blame for the difficulties in their marriage—his rampant imagination induced him to see infidelity in the most trivial things she said or did. Since he lied constantly, he suspected her of lying just the same; his own affairs made him assume that she was just as unfaithful. So, when it came to stashing incriminating evidence, surely he would have been more creative—

Unless he was in a hurry. She could almost picture him at the desk in his library, closing his laptop and swiveling in his leather chair to the bookcases behind him. He would grab the biggest, most prominent book on the shelf so that he'd be sure to remember it later. Then he'd drop the disk under its back flap, replace the book on the shelf, and walk away.

Wimsey stared at the blank wall above the computer. She should have known that keeping anything of his, even something he did not want, would come back to haunt her. So now the imperative was to get rid of it. She opened the CD drive to remove the disk and replace it in the envelope. All she had to do was walk down to the end of her deck and toss it in the lake, and her problem was solved.

And the indictments? In her heart of hearts, she had no doubt that he was guilty. Would the information on this CD convict him? Did she want that? Did she want to punish him for betraying her?

Not really, she thought, studying the silver disk through the cellophane window of the envelope. She didn't want anything to do with him. But . . . ShaftCom was a publicly held company. If Greg was guilty, he had betrayed thousands of people, not just her. She had no right to destroy evidence that could force the truth into the open and compel him to pay restitution.

Then again, if this simply contained back-up files of something the prosecutor already had, what she did with it made no difference. But—it was not in her power to determine whether it was useful or not. She had to go on the assumption that it was.

Sighing, she got up to rummage in another box for stationery and stamps. Withdrawing a box of Christmas cards, she paused. She did not want anyone to know this came from her. She did not want anyone tracing it back to the village.

Staring at the cheery Santa on the face of the topmost card, Wimsey suddenly flipped through the assortment to bring out a large card with a plain white envelope, and then a smaller envelope. She discarded the card that went with the smaller envelope. The CD with its protective sleeve was just the right size to fit into this envelope.

Then she sat back down at the computer to open the browser and create an account with the internet service provider. Once online, she looked up the address for the Dallas County District Attorney's office, where the ShaftCom case was being prosecuted. This she wrote in block letters on the smaller envelope—no return address, no note. She slipped the CD into this envelope and sealed it. Weighing it in her palm, she stuck on adequate postage, even allowing for the recent rate hike.

Then she opened the large Christmas card and wrote: "Hi, Artie! Merry Christmas! ☺ Hope all your crowd is well. Cootie and I are doing fine, getting acquainted with lots of interesting people.

"I found the enclosed in one of Greg's books—don't know if it is important or not, but thought I'd better turn it in. Please just drop it in a mailbox anywhere.

"I can't express how much I appreciate your kindness through these last difficult years. Your 3 AM counsel saved my sanity more than once. Some day you'll get payback! If you ever travel like you always said you would, you'd better make my place your first stop. I miss you. W."

This envelope she addressed by memory to Artie, inserting the card and the small envelope, then topping it off with an array of stamps. Belatedly, she realized it was possible to merely e-mail the files. But that would make it much too difficult for Artie to transmit the information anonymously. Best to send the original disk.

Before rising from the desk, she closed the browser window and turned off the computer out of habit. Then she went to the living area, where she took up her jacket from the couch. "Let's walk, Cootie."

With the dog leashed and the Christmas card in her jacket pocket, Wimsey walked briskly up the street toward Shrewsbury Circle. Cootie, sensing her nervousness, started at rustling trees and leaves skittering along the street. The wind was kicking up; it was twilight, and fifteen degrees colder. Although few people were out walking now, when Wimsey turned up the circle, she had to step lively to stay out of the path of oncoming golf carts. Worse, a light, misting rain began to fall.

Farther up the circle, she discovered the reason for the traffic: the bingo hall was brightly lit and open for business. A crowd of carts, even a car or two, filled up the modest parking spaces to the point of blocking the street. The little library lot was packed, as well. Of course, that did not impede someone on foot.

The post office next to the bingo hall was closed. But the street lamp illumined the drop slot under the green-striped awning. Wimsey glanced around, as she had been doing the whole way, and inserted the Christmas card into the slot. Turning away, she held her jacket around herself tighter to subdue the shivering.

As she resumed her walk down the circle past the bingo hall, she jumped at Chas' sudden appearance. "Well, my Whimsy has taken me here! You up for some bingo?" Out of the corner of her eye, she saw a few other faces glance at her. A woman near him looked Wimsey up and down, then took his arm jealously.

Wimsey tried to smile over chattering teeth. "Hi, Chas! Another time! I got Cootie out for a walk and didn't realize it had gotten so cold! And now it's starting to rain! I need to get her back in now. See you later!"

"Latte it is!" He saluted, going into the hall.

Shaking, Wimsey walked Cootie rapidly back down the circle. Did he see her mailing something? She had not wanted anyone to see that. Nothing to help it now.

Glancing at the shadows of twilight on either hand, she hastened Cootie the short distance to her new home. Although the misty rain had abated, even the dog seemed anxious to get back inside.

With relief, Wimsey unlocked the door and Cootie scooted in. Throwing off her jacket, Wimsey went to the kitchen to fill the dog's dinner bowl. Cootie settled down to eat, satisfied that everything was as it should be.

But Wimsey looked out back to the dark deck and

the dark water. She took a deep breath, then went to the bedroom for the book. Returning to the French doors, she paused with a hand on the scrolled handle. No, she would not turn on the deck lights. She did not want to draw attention to herself.

So she stepped out into the darkness to descend the cedar steps almost blindly, cautiously, knowing they were slippery when wet. With one hand grasping the railing, the other the large book, she went down to the deck surrounding the slip. Here, she looked over the water. With the nighttime lights reflected on the rippling lake, it was deceptively serene. What it would be to someone drowning out here was unimaginably different.

She paused as something occurred to her: Madelyn and her dog had been drowned in the pond because, obviously, the killer caught them there. But the shore was so much darker than the path around the pond, and covered so much more area, that had he at least tossed the dog into the lake not 30 feet away, poor Reggie would likely never have been found. What did this indicate? That the crime was impetuous, not pre-meditated, or that the murderer was stupid?

Snapping out of her reverie, Wimsey looked down at the heavy book she held. With intense regret, she tossed it into the water, where it landed with a plop and promptly sank. At the first opportunity, as soon as it was safe, she'd buy another copy.

Turning back up the steps, she glimpsed movement along the shore to her left somewhere. She looked, but it was too dark to see anything. So, maintaining a leisurely stride, she ascended the steps and let herself into the house.

She closed and locked the back doors, drawing the shades, then (just to reassure herself) went through the whole small house looking in closets, laundry room, and bathroom. There was no one hiding here, of course, so she went back to the kitchen to pull something together for dinner.

Tara called; Wimsey talked to her lightly about her walks with Cootie (not mentioning Madelyn) and her forays down Shrewsbury Circle (omitting that she had mailed anything). Tara worried a little about her getting bored; Wimsey replied, "Darling, I'm owed a little boredom. I've earned it, and I want to enjoy it." That satisfied Tara, but before going to bed, Wimsey checked locks on all the doors and windows one more time.

The next morning, Friday, Wimsey set herself to unpacking. Although she knew that she did not have anything else of Greg's, she meticulously went through all the rest of the books before shelving them, just to see if there might be any more surprises.

In passing through the master bedroom or the living room (both which faced the lake) she glanced out the large windows now and then; it was a wonderful view. Then she eyed the windows themselves with a little less appreciation. Larger windows made it that much easier for someone on the outside to see in.

When her phone bleated, she sprinted like a teenager to get it. Seeing the unknown number, she answered: "Hello?"

"Good morning, Ms. Reade. How are you?"

"Very well, Detective. How about you?" She was annoyed at feeling so relieved to hear from him.

"Eh, been better," he grunted.

"Bad news?"

"Not really; just long hours." He did sound tired. "All right. Toxicology found nothing in Treschler's body but traces of Valium."

"Valium?" she repeated. "Are they sure? That makes no sense. There was no Valium in her medicine cabinet."

He did not reply at once. Hearing paper rustle, she envisioned his flipping through his notepad. No, she realized, the sound was too loud. It was larger paper, probably in a file folder. "You're right. Brooks' list of her medications doesn't include Valium."

"Was it enough to knock her out?" Wimsey asked.

"No, lab said 'trace amounts.' Hmm." More paper rustling.

"What was the cause of death?" she asked.

"Drowning," he said. "They didn't find any contusions or defensive injuries to indicate use of force. That's significant, considering how fragile an older person's skin is. If you hadn't 'a' found the dog, they'd 'a' ruled it accidental death."

"What of the autopsy on Reggie?" she asked.

"Drowned," he replied.

"Did they swab his teeth?" she demanded.

"Eh, I don't think so. Being in the water, they said any traces of blood or skin from someone he bit would have been destroyed."

"I suppose so," she conceded.

He went on: "I talked to baby boy Norbert about the argument he had with her. He admitted he was upset that she was changing her will to the effect that each of her kids would get a token hundred grand, then the rest— some twenty million—would go to the North American Dandie Dinmont Association."

"Oh, my," she breathed. "And did she?"

"Yes, ma'am, that's exactly how her will reads. She had it changed about two weeks ago."

"How had it been previously?" she asked.

"Ah, her lawyer said some charitable donations, including the dog club, but the bulk of the estate was to be split three ways between the siblings," Lott said.

"You wonder what made her change her mind. How did Norbert find out?" she asked.

"She told him. Told all of them in letters. Said she didn't want them to be surprised. Her lawyer gave us a copy of the letter, if you want to see it."

"Can you just read me the pertinent parts?" she asked.

"You're rather demanding, Ms. Reade," he deadpanned. "Umph." She heard slight mutterings while he scanned the letter.

"Okay, here's the pivotal paragraph: 'I want you to understand why I am doing this. Marsh and Dalton were both self-made men, and they distrusted inherited wealth. They said it made people lazy, wasteful and ungrateful. So I am leaving you enough for a nice vacation to my funeral.'

"The interesting part," Lott noted, "is that maybe her second husband felt this way, in that he left everything to her and nothing to the kids. But husband number one, Marsh Dickers, went to some trouble to set up trust funds for his two kids. But since they were minors when he died, his widow took control of the money and just merged it with her own assets."

"I don't see how she could get away with that. If done properly, the trusts should stand up in court," she murmured.

"The kids never sued for it," the detective said. "They just grew up and went away. So far, we don't have any indication that Trentham or Michelina will be returning for the funeral."

Wimsey was silent, digesting this. "I assume she left a certain amount for funeral expenses?"

"Fifty grand," the detective replied, "which makes her bequest to her kids all the more insulting. She left notes with her lawyer with directions for her funeral, such as the type of casket, flowers, plot, etc., but since she didn't prepay, and didn't stipulate any penalties in her will for not following her wishes, Baby Boy Norbert threw her stipulations out the window to do everything on the cheap. As soon as the medical examiner releases the body, he's going to have it cremated. No burial plot. Don't even know of a memorial service yet."

"You would think that a woman who put that much thought into it would just go ahead and make the arrangements herself," she mused.

"Eh, seems she didn't figure on dying any time

soon," Lott tossed off. Then he elaborated, "Her lawyer said the notes were from their conversation at the time she came in to change her will. She talked in generalities, but didn't care to take the time just then to select a funeral home and nail down specifics. I think she was counting on the kids to do that."

"And Norbert resents being the one to handle the arrangements after her altering her will," she said.

"Sure. Wouldn't you?" Lott asked.

Wimsey sidestepped the question. "So, when Norbert received his letter, he was so upset that he drove out to talk to her about it Wednesday."

"Apparently," he agreed.

"A neighbor of mine saw him when he first got here. He went to Madelyn's house, didn't find her home, and went off looking for her," Wimsey related.

"What time was this?" Lott asked, muffled. This time she knew he was reaching for the notepad.

"Three-twenty."

"Who's the neighbor?" he asked.

"Mrs. Rad, in one-twenty-four. 'Batty' Rad." She repeated the highlights of her visit with Melinda and Mrs. Rad. "A curious detail, probably unrelated. . . ."

"Go on," he said.

"Mrs. Rad saw a village handyman, Cliff Osborn, looking in through the kitchen window while she and I were talking. She was furious that he trampled her Chrysanthemums. But she identified him as the same man she saw trying to get into Madelyn's house. I now know that's impossible—Norbert was not in the village yesterday, and Cliff was out of the village Wednesday. The significant detail is that they do look somewhat alike, and . . . Cliff drives a pickup with a toolbox in back."

"Okay," Lott said, and she could almost see his eyes darting up in thought.

"It may mean nothing," she emphasized.

"May not. But it's a handy place to carry around a pipe wrench. 'Osborn.' Spelled like Ozzy Osborne?"

"No, no 'e,'" she corrected him.

"Okay. All right, I'm going to check more on her other kids' contacts in the area. Call me if you find out anything else." And he clicked off.

Wimsey looked at her phone for a moment, not knowing whether to be amused, pleased or irritated that he talked to her as if she were a work subordinate. Free labor. After a moment's thought, she decided to be merely satisfied at being useful.

She returned to the task of unpacking. With so few possessions, it required little more than an hour to complete the job, collapse the boxes, and pile them at the side of the house for trash pickup, which was every Tuesday and Friday—the same days that Mrs. Rad's gardener came. Fortunately, the trash truck had not come by yet today.

Wimsey cut up an apple and heated some instant noodles for lunch, but she was thinking the whole time. After eating, she tossed the trash into the can and looked up to the kitchen clock, watching the second hand sweep around the dial to 1:34:15, 16, 17. . . .

"Let's go for a walk, Cootie," she murmured.

It was a typically gorgeous autumn day in the Hill Country—chilly enough for a light jacket, but sunny enough for sunglasses. This time Wimsey set out the back way to walk east along the lake toward her neighbors' properties. All had decks equipped with boat slips, as well as a boardwalk between them, so that someone walking down the boardwalk would pass over each deck as part of the easement. The actual shoreline, messy and irregular, was anywhere from five to ten feet out from the boardwalk. But since the walkway was at least sixty feet from the houses, not even Mrs. Rad could complain about traffic too close to her house.

Just looking, Wimsey walked Cootie as far as Madelyn's house, then retraced her steps west. She only glanced at the backs of houses that she passed, reserving the bulk of her attention for anything unusual along the shore underneath the boardwalk. She saw nothing suspicious, but any trespasser last night would not draw attention to himself playing in the water; he would stay on the walk. Except for the residents' deck lights, which they controlled, the boardwalk was unlit.

Immediately west of her own deck, the boardwalk terminated in a pebbled path that continued along the shore. Wimsey kept her eyes on the vicinity of the path, still just looking. Passing the Yorkshire Fields, she glanced up at the crowd gathering to impatiently await the assignment of lot numbers.

She kept to the pebbled path. Past the fields, it degenerated to a barely discernible footpath in the grass, since most walkers in the area preferred the paved Whitehaven Path around the pond. She surveyed this patch of ground carefully, canvassing back and forth between the shore and the pond. But there was nothing —nothing that she could see, anyway.

Just west of the pond, however, she uttered a small cry of dismay: a village maintenance worker was striding along the shoreline, stabbing trash with his pointed stick and depositing it in the trash bag slung over his shoulder.

Wimsey hurried to catch up with him. "Excuse me. You're doing a wonderful job—the shoreline is so clean! How often do you pick up along here?"

"Every other day, at least," he said, nodding. "It's easier if you don't let it pile up."

"I imagine so," she replied, and he resumed his route.

Exhaling, Wimsey turned back up the shoreline. That meant she was at least a day late, since he was obviously working his way from east to west. Had there been any telltale trash from Wednesday, it was gone, possibly before today. And she knew that Brooks hadn't searched for any.

Coming to the field again, she paused to watch. The magic hour of three o'clock was nigh upon them, for scores of senior citizens were waiting in an unruly line like so many first-graders. When one of three village employees sitting at a table determined that the appointed time had arrived, she waved at the first person in line, looked at his ID, and handed him a card.

Clutching it, he went off to investigate his lot, then promptly returned to the table to complain.

Wimsey watched a little while as sellers received their assigned places for the big garage/craft sale beginning tomorrow morning. Leisurely, she walked Cootie up the field in order to eavesdrop on the table near the street, where the woman in charge of booth placements was patiently explaining for the hundredth time, "I'm sorry, ma'am, lot assignments are first come, first served. Those who sign up and pay first get the prime spots. If you're unhappy with your location, you may trade with someone, as long as you let us know. No, there are no refunds." All this information, of course, was printed in large block letters on an easel-mounted board beside the table.

Shaking her head, Wimsey turned onto St. Mary Mead Lane to walk home. She let herself in the front door and bent to unleash Cootie. But instead of trotting over to her water dish as usual, Cootie lowered her haunches in alarm and barked aggressively. Dropping the leash on the kitchen counter, Wimsey took another step toward the back of the house, and stopped dead.

Cigarette smoke. She faintly detected the odor of cigarettes—not strong enough for someone to have been smoking in her house, but from the haze that shrouds a smoker. Someone who smoked had been—or was now—in her house.

Six

Staying right where she was, Wimsey looked around, but saw nothing out of place. She glanced back at Cootie seated on the kitchen floor. If anyone was in the house, Cootie would have been on him in an instant. Had someone from maintenance come in while she was gone? She hadn't asked for help with anything. And Sandy had assured her that they always called before sending someone out, and always left a note when they had been in a residence.

Warily, Wimsey went to check her phone on the coffee table—no calls since the detective's this morning. She placed the phone in her jacket pocket, resolving to carry it with her from now on. Glancing back at Cootie again, who had ceased her alarm, Wimsey checked the small kitchen and laundry room. Nothing. So she headed to the doorway of the second bedroom and looked in.

The odor of cigarettes was pronounced back here. On first glance, nothing looked to be disturbed. So she looked in the bath and master bedroom—no one was here, either. At that time she returned to the spare bedroom to look a little closer.

Sure enough, she spotted a desk drawer open an inch. The CD drive was standing open—and the computer was on. In a flash, she realized that anyone checking the recently opened files would see that she had accessed a disk containing ShaftCom financial records.

For the first time since her divorce, she felt afraid. She forced down the swelling fear and sat at the computer to see what had been opened.

The black screen indicated that the computer had been untouched for the last five minutes. When Wimsey hit the space bar, the password prompt appeared. Apparently, someone had attempted to look on her computer, but had been stymied by a six-letter password.

With trembling fingers, she typed in the password and opened the activity log. It confirmed that no one had accessed any files since she herself shortly after noon. Closing her eyes in relief, she laid her head on one hand. Then she deliberately turned to look at the shelves nearby. The books that she had arranged just so were now askew.

She stood at the shelves to pensively run a hand over the spines, straightening one or two volumes. Her classical music CDs on the shelf below had been thoroughly rifled. Someone had been looking for a particular book and a particular CD. Thanks to Tara's call, Wimsey had managed to rid herself of both in time. But . . . how did he get in?

The windows that opened were easy enough to check—all were locked. Thinking hard, Wimsey went to the back French doors and opened one. They were unlocked. She had left by these doors earlier—as careful as she always was, could she have forgotten to lock them?

After fetching her glasses from the kitchen counter, she knelt in front of the outside handle on one door and found minute scratches on the plate. From a pick? Not necessarily. Anyone who was careless with a key, including herself, could leave marks like that. She quietly closed the doors, locking them.

She sat on the couch, where Cootie jumped up beside her. Wimsey nestled her to think. It seemed clear enough what had happened: Greg had sent someone to see if she had the book in which he hid the ShaftCom data. Since she evidently did not, what would he do next?

Nothing, she decided—at least regarding her. He was not irrational; if she did not have what he wanted, he would not trouble her further. His utter silence over these last two years indicated his lack of vindictiveness toward her, and that would not change without cause. Now, should he discover what she had just mailed to the district attorney, matters could well change. But what was done was done, and she trusted Artie.

Wimsey looked outside at the golden late afternoon, and her fear evaporated. She stood. "Come on, Cootie; there's going to be some fun in the fields next door."

She made sure all doors were locked, then she and

Cootie trotted down St. Mary Mead Lane. The street was crowded with sellers transporting merchandise to the field. In the marked spaces of the field, village reps were helping residents set up tents and tables, and Cliff was practically torn asunder by demands for his services from all sides. Cootie, usually sedate, barked in excitement. Wimsey reached down to pat her. "Don't worry; we'll get a front-row seat in a minute."

She crossed the street to get a sandwich from the deli and a latte from the coffee shop. As Chas probably had a booth to set up, she was served by the young woman, promptly, with a smile. Returning the smile, Wimsey noted her name tag: "Lauren."

Wimsey took her dinner back across the street to a bench in view of the field activities. It was a double bench; one side faced the pond, the other faced the field. Poised to sit, she noticed that the orange barricades around the pond had disappeared. She nodded minutely before sitting on the bench facing the field. Cootie sat at her feet, torn between watching the action and begging for a bite of sandwich.

Wimsey ate while surveying the bustle. She wondered a little at the wisdom of setting up the day before, especially given the large sign that announced, "WATCH YOUR OWN MERCHANDISE. THE VILLAGE IS NOT RESPONSIBLE FOR THEFTS." Had she been more experienced with garage sales, she would have known that the most serious shoppers start early, and a sharp seller will be ready for them. The threat of rain only added to the excitement.

She watched one seller, a tiny woman, harangue two men on the erection of the fabric backdrop in her tent: "Are you an idiot? Are you blind? Two inches to the left! Not your left—what, are you stupid? To my left! Can't you see the gap? Can't you do anything right?"

The two managed to get the unwieldy frame positioned correctly, then walked off, expressionless. She shouted after them, "Be back here tomorrow at six and I'll give you ten dollars!" They kept walking. Suddenly Wimsey wondered why the village hadn't seen more murders.

She began to feel vaguely depressed. The residents here had reasonably good health—it was not a care facility for dementia patients or the terminally ill. There were a few confined to wheelchairs, but they had their own live-in caretakers. All the people who were now bickering over booth locations and set-up had sufficient means to live in one of the most desirable retirement communities in the country. . . .

And they were acting like spoiled brats. *Haven't we learned anything on the way to old age?* she thought. *At our time of life, seeing our bodies decay right in front of our eyes, shouldn't we be looking past the physical? Shouldn't we be looking for ways to do good, to make our lives count for something?*

She drank the rest of her latte and folded her empty sandwich wrapper into a tight roll. Twenty million dollars to a dog association? Sure, it was easy to ridicule Madelyn's choice of beneficiaries, but—*How have I done better with the resources I was given? I stayed married to a dishonest man for 28 years because of misguided loyalty. Now what do I have to show for my life? If I were to die tonight, what good would I have done anyone?*

The bench shuddered under the sudden application of additional weight. "You're not paying attention, Ms. Reade."

She glanced at the investigator who had plopped down beside her. "Good afternoon, Detective Lott." Cootie pawed his leg, so he reached down to scratch her ear with the hand that was not gripping a file folder.

"What the hell is this?" he said, regarding the field of battle.

She sighed, "The annual village Garage Sale and Craft Show starts tomorrow morning at six. I understand that it's the highlight of the year. People come from all over to shop."

He absorbed this, then squinted over his shoulder at the pond behind them. "The day manager told me they were putting barricades up so that nobody else would fall in and drown."

"They did, but took them down again," she said.

"You know why?" he asked.

"I believe the office got enough complaints to take them down, which is wiser all the way around. Barricades won't prevent another 'accident,' and you don't want to constantly remind residents or visitors where someone died." This is precisely the reason the village gave her a steep discount on her house—but she did not mention that to him.

"Huh. I guess so." He handed her the slightly bent file folder, jammed full. "Here's your copies of the pertinent paperwork to date—Mrs. Treschler's letter, and the will, the autopsy, contact info for her kids, and so forth. Also, prints of the photos Brooks took in her house."

She took the folder, eyeing him; seeing her encumbered with dinner trash, he relieved her of it and tossed it toward a bin ten feet away, missing. "Why . . . would you give me all this?" she asked.

He leaned forward, elbows on his knees, watching the senior citizens step up their assaults on the field as twilight approached. "I finally got hold of son Trentham in Cape Town—he hadn't received his mother's letter yet, but hearing the gist of it didn't surprise him. He makes good money and has no interest in the provisions of her will. He said he hasn't communicated with her for years, and has no intention of coming stateside for her funeral. But he wished me luck in finding her murderer. I'm not ruling anybody out offhand, but if I were, he'd be the first suspect I'd cross off my list."

"Besides Norbert?" she asked, smiling.

He frowned. "I'm hanging on to Norbert because I like him as a suspect. He's just really convenient."

She uttered a dry chuckle. After a moment, she asked, "Do the siblings stay in touch with each other?"

"Ah. A conspiracy. I like that idea, too," he said, then grunted, "Uh, he said he did e-mail Michelina and Norbert occasionally; she always responded and he seldom did."

When he fell silent, she listened to the tiny lady berate her lot neighbor for placing his tent on the dividing line between them instead of an inch inside. Their dispute grew so heated as to require mediation by a harried village employee. "Why are you shaking your head?" Lott asked.

"There is no motivation for murder," she said softly. "Her children had reason to be angry with her, but not murder her. If she were to live, she might relent and change her will back. But once she is dead, that can never be undone."

He looked shocked at the obvious logic. "Then we're looking for someone within the village."

"Yes," she said. "It must have been, still, a crime of opportunity. But until we know what someone had to gain from her death, we're shooting in the dark."

"Suppose there was no motive? Someone offs her for the senseless thrill of it?"

She turned to him. "In a retirement village? What thrill is there in taking out someone who already has one foot in the grave? That's shooting fish in a barrel."

"Eh, you're giving me a headache, Ms. Reade," he groaned. "Walk you home?" he said, standing. It was getting dark.

"Sure," she murmured. She stood, tucking the folder underarm and taking up Cootie's leash. Then she bent to pick up the trash and deposit it in the barrel. Lott shrugged.

They walked in comfortable silence up St. Mary Mead Lane until reaching her doorstep, where Lott said,

"You know, some people are murdered without a reason."

"Not Madelyn," she said, taking out her key.

"How do you *know*?" There was a twinge of exasperation, possibly feigned, in his voice.

She unlocked the door, then looked back at the glimmering orange sunset. "Because. . . ." She struggled to articulate the undercurrent of thought. "Because she was being watched. And if she was being watched, it was for a reason."

He nodded, glancing inside the house. "Let me know if you come up with anything."

"I will, Detective. Good night." She went in and closed the door.

First, she tossed the file folder on the coffee table to make a brief inspection of all rooms, doors and windows. Finding everything secure, she showered and donned pajamas, then retrieved the thick folder to take to bed with her. She turned on the reading light, turned down the covers, and propped up the pillows to sit back and open the folder while Cootie made herself comfortable at the foot of the bed.

Hardly had Wimsey focused on the first photo of Madelyn's furnishings when the thought crossed her mind, *Why didn't I tell him about the book and CD?*

She looked up as if staring down an invisible questioner. She knew the answer: she didn't want Detective Lott to know. It wasn't any of his business. She didn't want him feeling obligated to protect her. She didn't want to develop any kind of relationship with him other than that necessary to find Madelyn's murderer.

Besides—she settled her eyes on the photo again—that had all been taken care of.

Has it been? Do I trust Greg that much?

Exasperated, she closed the folder to lay it on the bedside table. "No, I don't. But I know him. He's utterly predictable. He won't bother me as long as I stay out of his way." With that, she clicked off the light and scooted down under the covers.

The following morning, Saturday, she awoke, dressed, and had breakfast early, but it was still seven o'clock before she and Cootie got out of the door. She took her wallet today, in case she found something worth getting cash for.

Exiting her front door, she was mildly startled at the number of vehicles all along the street either way. "My, my, Cootie. I guess they weren't kidding. I'm glad we don't have to drive anywhere." So saying, she began walking down the middle of the street to get to the field.

Although sunrise was still thirty minutes away, several hundred people were on the field, guiding themselves by flashlight where necessary. Most of these were vendors, many of whom were in the process of setting up. But a number of experienced buyers were already scrutinizing the booths. Wimsey joined them.

The smartest sellers had their booths all set up and brightly lit. In the dusky early morning, they attracted crowds simply because people could see the merchandise.

Wimsey walked down the rows between tents and

tables, looking over heads or around bodies to check the wares. She paused on the edge of a crowd to listen to one old geezer who turned out to be Guy. He had leased three spaces to make one long showroom floor of furniture, illumined by standing lamps.

She got close enough to hear him say, "Yeah, time to get rid of the heirlooms. Never had children, so nobody to leave these valuable pieces to. It's a shame, really—" He was interrupted by someone asking how much he wanted for the dinette.

He glanced at the furniture, wiping a tear from his eye as he invoked his darling deceased wife who had loved this set, babying it with weekly applications of linseed oil. But when he finally got around to giving a dollar figure, Wimsey stifled a laugh. Even at this distance, she could see that the furniture in question was department-store overstock.

She moved on, squinting at booths that were yet in the dark. Then she caught a glimpse of malachite and gasped. Hurrying to one dim booth, she gaped at the stately, ten-foot-tall candelabra from Madelyn's house. Straining to see the other wares shrouded in darkness, she just made out the Thomas Messel tables and—here she almost fainted—that magnificent Mughal Millefleurs rug rolled up carelessly on the ground like a bathroom mat.

Progressing farther into the booth crowded with Madelyn's treasures, she finally spotted someone reclined in a Chippendale chair, balanced on its back two legs against a sideboard that looked like an Emmons &

Archibald—but she couldn't be sure in the dark. "Excuse me." She tapped the figure on the shoulder, anxious to get him seated properly in the chair to avoid damaging it, if nothing else. "Excuse me?" She tapped a little harder.

"Uh?" The man snorted, almost lost his balance, righted the chair and stood, whereupon she recognized him as Norbert Treschler. "What do you want?" he muttered, coming awake.

Unsure whether he recognized her or not, she said, "Oh! Mr. Treschler. I'm so sorry about your mother's death."

"Uh huh. Did you want to buy anything?" he asked.

"Well," she floundered, knowing that she couldn't afford anything here, "what do you want for the rug?"

He hardly glanced at it. "Oh, a hundred bucks."

"A hundred—!" She caught herself. "Mr. Treschler, I don't think you should sell anything here till you get it appraised."

"Done that," he said briskly. "It's all junk. Mother just loved these knockoffs. Okay, eighty bucks for the rug."

Her mouth hung open for a moment. "Are you sure?" she asked weakly.

"All right, then, sixty. Look, give me a break here, okay? I have to get rid of all this stuff today," he said crossly. "Dealer from Austin was supposed to be here by now."

A light went on in her head. "Is this the same dealer who appraised the pieces for you?"

"Yes, one of 'em. But another gave me a separate appraisal, and it was right on the money. I'm not stupid," he added defensively.

"Of course you're not," she said soothingly. "I just don't understand. . . . Did they come out to see the furnishings?"

"Nah, sent 'em phone pics. Anderson had dealt with Mother in the past, and knew what she had. But if he doesn't get here quick—look, do you want anything or not?"

"Yes, I'd like—several things here," she said cautiously.

"Cash up front," he stated.

"Fine. I'll get cash and be right back." Careful to note the location of the booth in the dark, Wimsey quickly walked Cootie back to the street. Had she not known that the bank with the ATM was just across the street, a large sign to that effect stood at the edge of the field.

She patiently waited her turn at the ATM behind two other customers, then withdrew one thousand dollars cash from her account. All the while she was thinking, *Could I have been wrong? No, I know what I saw. Yes, I could have been mistaken. But if these pieces are such convincing fakes, that could be another motive for Madelyn's murder. Either way, it's worth the investment.*

Walking back toward the booth, she glimpsed Cliff lingering on the edge of the field. With most vendors already set up, he was evidently looking for business.

Without hesitation, she collared him. "Hello, Cliff. I need your help."

"Sure, Ms. Reade," he said, "but I'm waiting on—"

"I will pay you a hundred dollars an hour, cash, if you come with me now," she said.

"I'm right with you." He fell in beside her as she strode back to the dark booth, Cootie leading the way.

"Whoa. Whaddyou want here?" he muttered, squinting into the booth's shadowy depths. He jumped slightly when Norbert emerged.

"The rug," she pointed. "Mr. Treschler, please tell me also what you want for the candelabra, the tables, the sideboard—"

Norbert interrupted, "How much have you got, total?"

"A thousand dollars. That's the per diem withdrawal limit from the ATM. But I also promised Mr. Osborn one hundred dollars for carting if off," she said.

"Okay, nine hundred dollars for the lot," Norbert said, licking his lips nervously.

"All right," she agreed, much to his surprise.

She turned to Cliff, but he looked around and said, "Wait a second. The street's blocked. I can't get my truck through to your house."

"Where is your truck?" Wimsey asked him.

"At the office parking lot," Cliff replied.

She instructed, "All right, go get it. Drive into the field west of the pond, just past the welcome sign. Come around the north side of the pond, between the shore and the trees, and pull up as close as you can to this booth."

He hedged, "The village prohibits driving offroad anywhere but on this field. They'll fine me for it."

"I'll take responsibility, Cliff," she replied.

"Okay, then." He sprinted off.

She turned back to Norbert. "I want a receipt for everything."

He sighed in reluctance, then said, "Sure." Bending, he picked up an advertising flyer that had blown against a tent leg. He flipped it over to sign his name at the bottom and hand it to her. "'Ere you go. You can fill it in."

"I'll do that," she murmured, taking the sheet and folding it carefully. In return, she pulled out her cash and discreetly counted out nine hundred dollars. As he stuffed the wad into his pocket, she mentioned, "I don't suppose you have any padding or moving blankets."

"Yeah, I actually do," he said almost cheerfully. He opened the drawers of the sideboard to start bringing them out.

"Thank you, Mr. Treschler." With a little more daylight, Wimsey took stock of the items crowding the ten-by-twelve-foot booth: the Chippendale table and four chairs, the sideboard, rug, candelabra, and Messel tables. Noting the absence of some pieces she remembered seeing, especially the bedroom suite, she asked, "Where is the rest of your mother's furniture, Mr. Treschler?"

"At my house," he said. "We kept what my girlfriend liked. This is the junk she just couldn't live with. I mean, where're you gonna put those?" He gestured to the ten-foot-tall candelabra.

"In an art museum," she replied straightforwardly, and he laughed.

They waited in silence for the handyman to return with his truck. Wanting more information without appearing to pry, Wimsey noted, "I'm so glad I got here before the dealer. I hope he won't accuse you of breaking a deal."

"Oh, no way," Norbert scoffed. "I told him to get here early." He looked at his watch, then scanned for Cliff.

"I suppose you have a lot of loose ends to tie up with your mother's estate," she added.

"Nope. This just about takes care of it," he said.

Another small silence. She scanned the contents of the booth again. "I suppose you wanted to keep all the show memorabilia."

"Uh?" He looked at her blankly.

"Oh, all the awards and photos from your mother's showing her dog," Wimsey explained.

"Yeah, sure, all that stuff stays with the dog," he said.

"Pardon?"

"Well, why would we sell all that? It's proof of his value as a show dog, for stud fees and such," he explained.

She was momentarily flabbergasted. "Mr. Treschler, I thought—that the dog had drowned."

"Oh, that was somebody's idea of a sick joke— maybe the old bat who 'found' the dog in the lake. I've got Reggie," he said.

Seven

Wimsey was seriously taken aback. "Mr. Treschler —you have Reggie?"

"Yes," he said.

Since he offered no further explanation, she asked, "When did you get him? Where did you find him?"

He shrugged. "When I came out Thursday to start going through Mother's things, I found him waiting by the back door, so I took him home."

"Thursday?" she repeated. Sandy had said Norbert wasn't in the village Thursday. "What time?"

"Thursday evening. Why are you asking all these questions?" he said, irritated.

"I apologize. When I heard about poor Madelyn, I was very anxious to know what had become of the dog. I heard he had drowned, but I am very glad that's not so."

At this time—and not a moment too soon—Cliff pulled his truck right up to the front of the booth, to the irritation of visitors and surrounding vendors alike. Hopping down from the cab, he lowered the tailgate and brandished rope.

Since Norbert was eager to get out of there, he helped Cliff load everything up. Wimsey put Cootie in the cab and stood in the bed herself, arranging the pieces as they were loaded and swaddling them with blankets and padding. In the early morning sunlight, she briefly studied the objects as they came into her hands. She was looking for faked patina or telltale seams, but saw nothing that negated her first assessment.

When the tent was empty, Norbert waved, producing a nice fake smile, and quickly walked off. Cliff tied the merchandise securely down and hesitated with the tailgate open. From the bed of the truck, Wimsey waved. "Go ahead and close it; I want to ride back here. Just don't go over ten miles an hour."

"Uh. . . ." He looked toward the blocked street.

She pointed across the quarter-mile of field. "Turn at the end of the row of booths here and drive through the field to my house. You and I can carry these things in."

"Okay," he said, resigned. He climbed into the truck and started it while Cootie stood up on the seat to watch out the back window. First, he had to back up about fifty feet before he could maneuver the truck completely out of the booth area. Wimsey, watching patrons hasten out of the way of backing taillights, imagined there would be another rule added to the longsuffering garage-sale committee's list for next year.

Cliff turned the wheel toward her house across the field and sped up to about twenty miles an hour, knowing that she only had $100 left in her pocket regardless how long this job took. Wimsey rode uneasily with a hand on each swaying candelabrum, but he had tied everything down well enough so that they reached her front walk without mishap.

He backed the truck up to the walk, then climbed out to lower the tailgate, giving her a hand out. Wimsey let Cootie into the house, stopping long enough to see that the dog trotted in to lap from her water dish—apparently, there had been no unannounced visitors.

That settled, she brought in the smaller pieces while Cliff hauled in the candelabra first. This he was able to do easily enough with a hand truck. He paused in the small open foyer to ask, "Uh, where do you want everything?"

"Just here in the living room. I'll sort it all out later."

It took him barely a quarter hour to get everything unloaded into the house. When done, he paused at the door with his hand truck. "Well—"

"Thank you, Cliff." She pressed the remaining five twenties into his hand. "I appreciate your help. I imagine you're needed at the field now."

"Yes, ma'am." He saluted with two fingers and sprinted out to his truck.

Sighing, Wimsey closed the door and plopped onto the couch to eye her purchases. "I may have just blown a thousand dollars. Well." She reached into her jacket pocket for her phone. "I won't know till I tell someone what I've done." She scrolled down to the detective's number and pressed the call button.

He answered almost immediately. "Good morning, Ms. Reade. You're on the job early."

"Good morning, Detective Lott. I have just pur-chased some of Madelyn's belongings from Norbert at the garage sale this morning."

"What?" he said.

She explained the events of the morning, ending with, "He let them go cheaply because he said two appraisers told him they were knockoffs. I . . . still don't think they are, but I'm going to try to get hold of an expert I knew in Dallas. I thought you might want to—"

"I'll be right out," he said, and clicked off.

She eyed her phone momentarily. He had not given her a chance to tell him what Norbert said about Reggie. She reminded herself to cover that with him when he got here, then went to her computer in the second bedroom.

She turned it on, entered the password, and brought up a search engine to locate a phone number for the art and furniture expert she remembered from her wealthy days. Before leaving the computer, she logged off instead of shutting it down.

Number in hand, she called, glancing at the clock: it was not quite eight-thirty. On a Saturday morning, she was prepared to get an answering machine. She did, and when the beep sounded for her to leave a message, she said, "Mr. Zurita, this is Wimsey Reade—formerly Wimsey Corrister. My husband Greg and I were clients of yours about six years back. I have purchased some items from the estate of Madelyn Treschler, and I would appreciate someone from your store—"

A voice came on the line: "Mrs. Corrister, how are you?" It was a thick, heavily accented European voice.

"I'm doing well, Mr. Zurita; only it's Reade now—"

"I didn't know that Madelyn had died," he said.

"A drowning accident Wednesday. It was very tragic," Wimsey said.

"Oh, dear. So terribly sad. What did you buy, darling?" he asked.

She gave him a rundown of the pieces. "Hmm," he said. "Are any of them from Dalton Treschler's estate? Or did Mrs. Treschler purchase them?"

"I don't know, Mr. Zurita. Why?"

"Yes, dear. Hmm. Madelyn was a queer bird; she liked lovely things, and had the money to buy them, but she did not want to spend the money, so she had a terrible habit of having reproductions made of worthy pieces and passing them off as the real thing. Oh, yes.

"Mr. Treschler, now, invested in genuine pieces, you see, but she—the old dear—had copies made and then sold the originals. But she never let on till one of her friends who had received a pair of eighteenth-century Louis the sixteenth giltwood and rouge *languedoc demilune* console tables from her as a gift brought them to an associate of mine to have them appraised, and—oh, my—they were copies. Very nicely done, but worth perhaps one-tenth of the original, you see. Oh, the friend was quite put out. Quite put out. So."

There was a short silence before Wimsey said, "Well, I don't know what I have, then. Is it possible—?"

"If you have anything of Mr. Dalton Treschler's, yes, it would be worth knowing. Give me your number, dear—are you in Dallas?"

"No, Mr. Zurita; I'm at the Old England Retirement Village in Horseshoe Bay. It's about half an hour from Austin," she explained.

"Oh, well, then; I will have my Austin associate call you," he said.

"Thank you, Mr. Zurita." She gave him her cell number and he clicked off.

She put the phone on the coffee table and surveyed her crowded living room dubiously. Then she got down on her knees to upend one of the Chippendale chairs and look at the bottom.

First thing she saw was the uneven paint on the underside of the seat, and she wilted. Looking at the backs of the chair legs, she saw that they had been clumsily filed down to resemble wear from generations of men leaning back in it as Norbert had done. Just these two signs screamed, *"Fake!"* But Wimsey had not examined the table and chairs before shelling out her thousand dollars.

She plopped down on the couch, and Cootie joined her. Wimsey eyed the gaudy candelabra, not having the heart to examine them further. From where she sat, they still looked good. But they—like the Messel tables—were not antique, so copies would not have the clumsy antiquing that forgers used. Excellent copies could rival the originals in appearance.

Sighing, she pulled out the flyer from her jacket pocket. Turning it over to the back side with Norbert's signature, she wrote a detailed inventory and description of what she had purchased from him: the "Chippendale" table and four chairs, the sideboard, the rug, the candelabra, and the Messel tables. Then she dated it as of today: October 12.

When her phone bleated, she glanced at the Austin-area number before answering, "Hello?"

"Mrs. Corrister, please." It was a woman's voice, displeased.

"This is Wimsey Corrister, but I am using my maiden—"

"Mrs. Corrister, you have items for appraisal from the Treschler estate?"

"Yes, I do," Wimsey said.

"Fine. Then please bring them to our gallery at—"

"I'm sorry; that's impossible," Wimsey said calmly. "If you want to see them, you will have to send someone out to the Old England Retirement Village in Horseshoe Bay. If you can't accommodate me, I will have to call someone else."

There was some exasperated muttering on the other end, and Wimsey guessed that Mr. Zurita *really* wanted to see what she had. "Fine. Where is it?" the woman asked.

Wimsey gave her directions, then asked, "Who will be coming to view the pieces?"

"Daphne Zurita," she said, and hung up.

The detective was the first to arrive about thirty minutes later. When Wimsey let him in, he did a mild double-take at the garage-sale merchandise crowding her small living area, then bent to give Cootie her due attention. "Have a seat, Detective." Wimsey indicated a narrow path between the sideboard and the couch.

"Well, you've been busy. How much did all this set you back?" he muttered, wending his way through furniture and hitching up his pants legs to sit.

"Nine hundred for the lot and another hundred to transport it," she sighed. "And I'm pretty sure the Chippendales are reproductions. I don't know about the rest."

"The Chippendales," he repeated, glancing around.

"The table and chairs. Oh, and Detective—what was Norbert told about Reggie?"

"Eh?" His eyes flicked between her and the furniture. "Ah, he was notified that the dog's body was recovered from the pond."

"When was he told this?" she asked.

"Ah. . . ." He reached slowly for his notepad. "The day you found it. Thursday?"

"Yes, we found the dog on Thursday." She slumped a little wearily. "Norbert said *he* found her dog wandering around when he came to her house Thursday evening. He said he has Reggie."

Lott's expressive eyebrows contorted. "He claims to have found the dog alive?"

"Yes," she said.

He gazed into space, processing this. Then he blinked. "That makes no sense."

"It certainly doesn't, especially since he has told the truth about everything up till now, that I know of," she said.

"Well, he can't be telling the truth about this," Lott pointed out.

"It would seem not," she said, and her eyes suddenly glazed over. "Excuse me, Detective." She stood and left the room, then returned with the file folder on Madelyn.

Sitting again, she flipped the folder open to Boltrain's photographs. Lott leaned over to see what she was looking at, and Wimsey suddenly asked, "Detective, don't you have a partner to work these investigations with?"

He looked uneasy. "Ah, budget cuts, you know, with the economy the way it is . . . and me with a stack of pending cases ten feet high—" The doorbell rang. She put the folder down for the time being.

Accompanied by Cootie, Wimsey opened the door to an elegant, irritated, heavily made up woman carrying a briefcase. "What is with the county fair? My driver couldn't get through!"

Wimsey looked out to see a village employee in a golf cart pulling away from the curb. "I'm so sorry. Ms. Zurita? I am Wimsey Corrister Reade."

"How do you do. Let's see what you have," she said briskly. Detective Lott stood from the couch, buttoning his coat. She instantly dismissed him as a person of no account, then tossed her briefcase on the couch and began sweeping evaluations of the furnishings cluttering the small living area: "Reproduction"—addressed to the candelabra; "reproduction"—referring to the Messel tables; "fake"—snorted at the Chippendale set.

"Ma'am, you're not even looking at them," Lott protested.

Wimsey glanced at him for the defensive tone, but

he got Ms. Zurita's glaring attention—not for his questioning her knowledge, but for his unforgivable use of the honorific reserved for *old people*.

So she pursed her lips and walked over to stand in front of the sideboard. She studied it critically for twenty seconds, then placed a hand on it. Turning to the detective, she said, "And this. Is. A. Fake."

She stepped away from it impatiently, and her eye caught the rolled-up rug on the floor. At that, she seemed to stop breathing. She went to her briefcase for a pair of cotton gloves and glasses.

Then she got down on her knees (in dress and hose) to gingerly unroll the rug. Lott, showing considerable generosity, moved the coffee table aside so that she could lay the (approximately) three-by-five-foot rug out flat. Donning the glasses, she leaned over to examine it minutely. Wimsey and Lott glanced at each other.

Minutes later Ms. Zurita stood, briskly removing her glasses and gloves. Then she whipped out her phone and keyed in a call. The others watched as she was transformed into a little girl: "Hi, Daddy. I'm at Mrs. Corrister's. I don't think you want most of what she's got, but there's a lovely Mughal millefleurs pashmina pile prayer rug, late eighteenth century. Yes. I'm really sure, Daddy. Okay."

She closed her phone and turned to show her teeth at Wimsey. "Zurita's would love to put this rug up for auction for you, Mrs. Corrister—"

"Reade," Wimsey said. "I am going by Reade now."

"I'm so sorry. Ms. Reade. Since you're an old friend

of Daddy's, he really wants to represent you in this sale. There's a fifteen-percent commission off the top. May I take it for you?"

When Wimsey hesitated, Lott looked as though he was going to shake her. He turned to Ms. Zurita to ask, "What do you think you can get for it?"

"I will recommend a minimum bid of three hundred thousand," she replied, adding with a shrug, "It could go much higher."

Lott turned to Wimsey in threatening disbelief at her hesitation. She did not look at him before nodding. "All right."

"Do you have a bill of sale?" Daphne asked delicately. Wimsey showed her the flyer-receipt. Daphne looked it over, then snorted, "Norbert Treschler. What an idiot." Then she whipped her phone out again and jabbed a key. "John? Get the car up to 120 St. Mary Mead Lane right now. I don't care how."

Closing the phone again, she sat on the couch to take a document from her briefcase and smile (so to speak) at Wimsey. "Here's the contract, darling. We'll need to take the rug and the bill of sale today. We're having a major furniture auction in New York in November that I hope to make."

Wimsey sat to glance over both copies of the contract (one for her and one for Ms. Zurita), which was all standard verbiage. While she knew Mr. Zurita to be a sharp operator, he was protective of his clients. She signed, and Detective Lott signed as witness.

In handing over one copy of the contract, she

removed the receipt from Daphne's talons, saying, "Let me make a copy of this." Wimsey took it to the second bedroom and ran it through her scanner. Then she returned the original to Daphne's outstretched hand.

"Wonderful, darling." Tucking the contract and flyer into her briefcase, Daphne went to the front door to look down the street. From the couch, Wimsey watched her wave and hurry across the lawn, leaving the door ajar.

"Cootie, get back," Wimsey ordered, and the curious dog reluctantly returned to the couch to supervise from there.

Daphne returned with scissors and an armload of protective covering which she spread out on the floor and cut to size. Again donning gloves, she laid the rug on this padding, then covered it with another layer and rolled it all up.

Meanwhile, her assistant entered with a bundle of one-by-four-inch slats and a tool pack. While Wimsey and Lott watched, he constructed a custom box on the spot for the rolled-up rug. All of this prep took less than 20 minutes, then the Zurita workman packed up his tools, hefted the box under one arm and carried it all out.

Daphne turned to Wimsey with a limp hand. "Thank you, darling. We'll be in touch."

"You're welcome. Please give my regards to your father," Wimsey said, lightly shaking her hand.

Ms. Zurita even glanced at the detective in acknowledgment of his existence before she turned out behind her employee. Wimsey watched her walk to the SUV parked on the grass (where Cliff had parked his truck) and made a mental note to expect a bill from the village for resodding.

She closed the door and looked at Lott, who was staring at her worthless furniture, hands on hips. Nodding at it, he asked, "What're you gonna do with the rest of it?"

"I don't know," she sighed. "Put it out on the curb."

"Well, in that case, let me buy some of it off you. My mom would go nuts over the monster candle things, there. And the Chippendales. She wouldn't care that they're fake," he said.

"Take them," she said with a wave.

He looked at her in irritated incredulity. "Sure. Then tell me how to explain to my boss that I helped myself to the possessions of the deceased whose murder I'm investigating."

She relented. "All right. Um, fifty dollars for the table and chairs, and one hundred dollars for the candelabra."

"One hundred dollars each, or for the pair?"

She clarified, "For the pair."

"The pair is worth more than the table and four chairs?" he asked.

"Yes, in my opinion. The furniture pieces are shoddy fakes, but the candelabra are very good reproductions. And if you're going to dicker, then I *will* put them out on the curb," she vowed.

"One hundred fifty for the dinette and candelabra," he acknowledged. "I need to go rent a trailer, then I'll come back with the cash."

As he started for the door, Wimsey sat on the couch. "Detective."

"Ma'am?" He looked back.

She picked up the bulging file folder. "We need to talk about Reggie."

"Uh—yeah." His face reddened slightly at the reminder, and he returned to the couch to sit beside her. Cootie jumped up on his other side to paw his leg.

Opening the folder, Wimsey began going through the numerous eight-by-ten glossies that Boltrain had taken. She separated out one on the coffee table, then a moment later found another to place beside it. Lott leaned forward to look at them.

"I repent for any uncharitable thoughts I may have entertained about the quality of Mr. Boltrain's crime-scene work," she said. "He did an excellent job."

"I'll pass that along," Lott muttered, studying the two photos she had selected. "These are photos of her dog—that is, photos of photos of her dog."

"Yes. Mr. Boltrain took shots of the awards and photos she had up on the walls of her spare room. I noticed at the time how proud she was of them. He must have noticed, too. And his work answers the question of what happened to Reggie," she said.

"The dog drowned," Lott reminded her.

"Yes. But Norbert also told the truth, as he has consistently done from the beginning," she said.

"How could that be?" Lott asked crossly.

"There were two Reggies," Wimsey replied.

Eight

"Two Reggies?" Lott asked in astonishment.

"Yes," Wimsey said. "I should have guessed as much after hearing what she did with her other possessions. What's worse, I saw the second Reggie run away from her house Thursday—I just didn't realize it at the time."

"Two Reggies?" he repeated. "Why?"

She sighed. "Madelyn was very . . . duplicitous, it seems. She liked the look of expensive furniture, but not the cost, so had reproductions made of quality pieces—which is very easy for a skilled craftsman to do when he has the original to work from.

"There's nothing wrong with that, in itself—I would be perfectly happy with reproductions of fine furniture—but according to Mr. Zurita, Madelyn gave everyone the impression that they were authentic, going so far as to give them away under that pretext. And those who knew her financial standing, or her late husband's purchase habits, believed her."

"Finding out you bought an expensive fake would

provoke a lot of people to murder. But how does that relate to her dog?" Lott asked.

Wimsey began laying out other photos of Reggie's awards. "She liked showing him, and she especially liked winning. But Reggie was getting old and cranky—an ill-tempered dog will not do well at shows. So it appears she bought another mustard Dandie Dinmont and started showing him in Reggie's place. Look."

She pointed between the first two photos she had laid out. "Supposedly, these are both of Reggie—one is undated, but it's early. The other is among the last of her shows four years ago. But look at the shape of his nose in each. Look especially at the hind legs and the haunches."

"They don't even look alike! This dog's got longer legs!" he exclaimed.

"Yes," she said.

He sat back in perplexity. "Well—why didn't she just start showing the new dog under his own name?"

"Oh, Detective, I don't know," she mused. "It could be several things—it's a lot of trouble and expense to register a new dog to show. You have to start from scratch, and a beginner has a lot to prove. But a champion, you know, comes to a show with a reputation. Then again, at her time of life, Madelyn might have felt —entitled. That, or she thrived on seeing what she could get away with. There's just no way to know what she was thinking."

"Somebody would have noticed, 'Hey, this isn't the same dog,'" he pointed out.

"Certainly. There are stringent safeguards against counterfeits, especially when you get to nationals," she agreed.

He looked at her. "So how did she get away with it?"

Wimsey shrugged. "We may have discovered why she left the bulk of her estate to the dog association."

Lott nearly fell off the couch. "Twenty million for the privilege of cheating scot-free? At a *dog show*?"

"People develop strange priorities, especially as they get older," she said quietly. "Competitions of any kind can take over your life. What was important to her? We've already seen that it wasn't her children. Charity work? Benefits?" she asked.

"I haven't run across mention of those," he muttered.

"But we know she cared about appearances," Wimsey said, indicating the fakes surrounding them.

He absorbed this for a while. "What would happen, then, if a competitor found out? . . ."

"And complained, and no one did anything about it?" she finished his thought. "Winning at shows means higher breeding fees. For someone who had less money than she, this would be important. It was important to Norbert."

Lott's staid face suddenly contorted. "And he let this priceless rug slip through his hands."

"It's not priceless, Detective," she murmured. "Few things are." Her face changed. "But now that you mention it, I do want to go back by the sale."

He stood. "I'll go get a trailer and your cash."

"And . . . you might make inquiries with the Dandie Dinmont Association," she suggested.

"That, too," he said hastily.

He departed, and Wimsey again leashed up Cootie, who appeared to expect to be taken on outings at a moment's notice. Before leaving, Wimsey checked the back door again—and found it unlocked.

This disquieted her. She knew—or thought she knew —that she kept it locked all the time. Did it have an unreliable latch like Madelyn's? She practiced closing it and locking it several times, and it worked fine. Since Cootie was tugging impatiently on the leash, Wimsey just made sure both doors were locked before heading out.

It was approaching noon, and St. Mary Mead Lane was even more congested than it had been this morning, if possible. When the weather was nice, as it was today, an outdoor garage sale was wonderful. With the lake, the pond, and the beautiful trees as backdrops, people were moved to buy junk they normally wouldn't even look at. So Wimsey joined the crowds strolling and looking.

The merchandise was the same as that at garage sales everywhere. Wimsey saw a lot of worthless clutter and a few gems she was sorely tempted to beg for, such as a Black Forest standing bear clock that one gentleman had displayed along with some amateurish paintings. She introduced herself and attempted to strike up a conversation about the clock, but he answered in grunts. The most she learned was that he was asking twelve hundred dollars for it. Not trusting her appraisal skills after being fooled by Madelyn's reproductions, Wimsey nodded good-bye and moved on.

She came to another space with two tables, and a more disparate selection could not have been found anywhere. The table on the left held all kinds of fishing tackle and gear—rods, lures, nets—and an array of men's clothes and hats. Beneath the table were four- and six-foot mounted bass and marlin. The table on the right held exquisite costume jewelry, knickknacks, porcelain —all predominantly white and feminine. Wimsey promptly looked around for Melinda and Tina-Marie, but saw neither. A young woman sat in a folding chair beside the white table, reading a celebrity gossip magazine.

Two spaces down, she heard, "Well, Wimsey! See anything that strikes your—fancy?"

"Hello, Chas." She was so pleased he didn't make a pun on her name that she came over to seriously look at his merchandise. Boldly banking on no rain, he had a trio of tables set up in a U-shape in between tents on either side of him. Because he was offering nothing that aspired to being expensive, he was doing a brisk business.

"Oh, these notecards are lovely. They're just what I need." She flipped the package over to see the "$5" sticker, so dug a ten-dollar-bill from her pocket.

Chas was glad to make change for her. "I thought I saw you out here early this morning."

"You did. I'm afraid I'm not the savvy shopper I

thought I was," she said dejectedly. Lest he press for an explanation, she hurried on, "Oh, I love the candle. Will you let that go for five bucks?—seeing how that's all I've got left. Great. Thanks, Chas."

Tapped out for the day, Wimsey decided she had best quit the field. Chas lifted a hand as she waved goodbye, then he turned to take someone else's money.

With her purchases in a grocery bag, she walked Cootie down the wide aisle, careful not to get close enough to booths on either hand to be tempted. "One thousand ten dollars is enough for one garage sale," she told herself in mild disgust. She was skeptical of Daphne's aspirations for the rug. Like everything else, Wimsey would believe it when she saw it.

Not enamored of the crafts, she felt safe eyeing them from a distance. They appeared to be mostly crocheted pieces and painted wood. But when she spotted a booth of clocks created from soldered odds and ends, she slowed dangerously. Cootie saved her by dragging her on.

She came upon Norbert's empty tent, a loose edge flapping forlornly in the breeze. She smiled at the knowledge that he would not be back to take it down like he was supposed to. While Wimsey passed it by, the woman in charge of the show approached with a man in shirt sleeves talking anxiously in her ear.

Wimsey pretended to study merchandise in a neighboring booth when the pair stopped at the abandoned tent. The man in shirt sleeves was piteously complaining, "He was supposed to meet me here. We had an arrangement for me to buy his mother's furniture. It was all knockoffs, nothing valuable, but I had a buyer lined up and he stiffed me!"

The village rep looked over the abandoned site. "Do you have anything in writing?"

"Does a man always have to 'have it in writing'? Wasn't there a time when a handshake was good enough?" he whined.

"I'm sorry—"

"Can you find whoever bought his goods?" the dealer demanded—as that was certainly he.

"No, Mr. Anderson; you'll have to take that up with Mr. Treschler. And I have another tent to knock down," the woman muttered.

Wimsey watched while they departed, the dealer still complaining. *He must have realized the rug was genuine*, she reflected. He and a conspirator gave Norbert honest appraisals of his mother's possessions— with the exception of the rug. *Sometimes, crooks get their due.* She just hoped she was able to see the same happen for Madelyn's murderer.

She stopped by the deli for a late lunch, then she and Cootie went home. Upon entering, Wimsey first went through every room, as had become her habit. Nothing appeared to be out of place, and the back door was still locked. Uneasily, she reflected that if she really believed she was done with Greg, she would not keep looking over her shoulder like this. Unless . . . it wasn't Greg. This whispered suggestion she shook off.

With some time to kill before Detective Lott

returned, Wimsey surveyed her new acquisitions. She decided the faux Messel tables would do fine on either end of the small couch, and the sideboard could go back in the second bedroom. So she dragged all pieces of furniture to their new places. The notecards and candle went in her desk and on a bookshelf, respectively.

After positioning the sideboard against the wall, she paused over the computer to make sure it had not been tampered with. Then she told herself, "If you're going to be so paranoid, you'd better go ahead and tell the detective about the disk." But she didn't want to, so sat to peruse Madelyn's file instead.

An hour later her doorbell rang. Accompanied by Cootie, as usual, Wimsey opened the door to Detective Lott on her porch. Looking past his shoulder toward the curb, she said, "You got through to park on the street!"

He looked exasperated. "Now how did you know the pickup was mine? I told you I was going to rent a trailer."

She looked back out to the street. "The silver pickup is yours?"

"Yes. Isn't that what you meant?" he asked. "I thought, 'She'll be looking for a trailer, so I'll just bring the pickup and see what she says.' And you look out the door and know the pickup's mine right off the bat, even though there are trucks and trailers parked all up and down the street, and I just want to know how you knew."

She let him in, looking outside dubiously. Bringing cash out of his wallet, he said, "I would really like to know, Ms. Reade."

"I didn't know the silver pickup was yours, specifically. So . . . I must have picked up on the signs that you hadn't walked very far to get to my door. That's all I can tell you." She was most unnerved by the inner message, *See? Listen to your instincts. There might be a reason you keep looking over your shoulder.*

Skeptical of her explanation, he handed her $150 in cash. "May I get a receipt?"

"Of course." She went to the desk in the spare bedroom for paper to hand write a bill of sale with detailed descriptions of the furnishings.

Then she stood out of the way and held open the door while he hauled out his purchases. On one trip, he said, "Do you mind coming out to the truck while I tie this stuff down?"

"Not at all," she said.

To Cootie's resentment, Wimsey closed the door on her and followed Lott to his truck, where he climbed up into the bed and shook out a moving blanket. "Okay. I talked to the director of the North American Dandie Dinmont Association. He had been informed of Mrs. Treschler's bequest, and highly resented any suggestion that it was inappropriate or a waste of money—" He paused, grunting, to pull the nylon rope tight around the candelabra, and Wimsey reached out to adjust the blanket between rope and gilded bronze.

Lott resumed, "He informed me of a number of charities that the NADDA supports, including college scholarships, arts funding, and daycare, and said that her bequest would be divided among hundreds of applicants according to guidelines set by the board of directors. *And*—" he broke off to hoist the faux-Chippendale table up into the bed—"he was 'aghast' and 'appalled' at the suggestion that Mrs. Treschler had cheated at competitions, to the point that he threatened to sic lawyers on me should I whisper such 'irresponsible allegations' to anyone. Got to protect the good name of the association, of course. Our conversation pretty much ended there." Lott squinted down at her.

"Then, obviously, she bribed local judges. Finding out who, at this point, may not be profitable, if the bequest was genuine," she mused.

"What about, you know, disgruntled competitors who lost to her?" he asked, wrapping rope around the blanketed table.

"Yes, I've been thinking about that. Detective, what would you do if you had spent thousands of dollars preparing for a show, only to discover that your competition won by cheating?"

He stopped wrapping. "I'd blow the whistle. I'd tell everybody who'd listen. And if I didn't get any satisfaction from the association, I'd take it public."

"Of course you would," she said. "As opposed to murdering her and keeping quiet about the second dog so that her son could inherit it and reap the benefits of her forgery."

"You're right," he said, shoulders slumped, gazing over the top of the pickup. "Dam', she must've bribed a whole bunch of people."

"And when it got to be too much trouble, or

expense, she retired 'Reggie.' Her last show was four years ago," Wimsey pointed out.

He resumed tying down the table, then grunted, "You're the one who started down the rabbit trail of dog shows."

"You have to rule everything out, one thing at a time. 'When you have eliminated the impossible, whatever remains, however improbable, must be the truth,'" she quoted.

He quickly looked down at her. "Sherlock Holmes," he said.

"Correct, Dr. Watson."

He straightened, groaning, "Where does that leave us?"

"Well, let's go back to the beginning. What do we *know*?" she asked, handing up a chair to him.

He thought about that while tying down the chair. "We know that Madelyn was lured to the north side of the pond and drowned sometime between five and eight-oh-six PM Wednesday, and her dog drowned by someone wrapping his leash around a wrench."

She studied him. "Do we know that Reggie was drowned *after* Madelyn?"

"No, but—wouldn't that be kind of awkward, drowning her dog while she's standing there saying, 'What are you doing?'" He took out a handkerchief to wipe sweat from his face. "Hand me up another chair, would you?"

She did. "But again, that's something we don't know. Reggie got away from Madelyn to come after

Cootie when I was walking her, so it's possible he got away from her again to go after the murderer, who drowned him. Then when Madelyn came looking for him. . . ."

Lott stopped to think about that. "I see. Well, we also know that she changed her will; that she faked expensive furniture; and that she wasn't well liked in the village." He began tying down the blanketed chair.

"All of which is irrelevant," she murmured.

He stopped abruptly. "Ms. Reade, *how do you know*?"

She blinked, then shook her head. "I don't. Just guessing."

"'I never guess. It is a shocking habit,'" he quipped.

She smiled. "*The Sign of Four*"—also Sherlock Holmes. "Let me rephrase that, and say that we don't know how those facts come into play. The only other thing we *do* know is that she was being watched."

"I agree," he said with a nod.

He loaded the remaining chairs in silence, then hopped down from the pickup bed and closed the gate. "Thank you, Ms. Reade. I'll . . . be in touch when I know anything else."

"You're welcome, Detective. Yes, do." She smiled vaguely and re-entered her house. Cootie was not too resentful to stretch up lazily on her leg in a request for yet another outing. The golden afternoon beckoned.

Wimsey fetched the leash with a persistent air of distraction. The exchange of Sherlock Holmes quotations had recalled another to her mind: *"Where a crime is coolly premeditated, then the means of coverting it are coolly premeditated also."* And that troubled her more than anything yet.

It seemed clear that the murder had been premeditated. But the "coverting" of it was sloppy and almost irrational—which could only mean that there were critical facts as yet uncovered . . . or that she and Lott were wrong in what they assumed they knew.

With the garage/craft sale showing no signs of abating, Wimsey steered clear of the field to take Cootie up Shrewsbury Circle. On a Saturday afternoon, with the village focused on the sale event, almost all the shops were closed—only the deli and coffee shop were still open. But the chapel was, too. So on a whim, Wimsey went inside. Cootie went with her.

It was one of those modern interfaith chapels that carefully eschew any religious imagery to avoid offending someone of a different religion, producing a blandness that evoked no religious sentiment in anyone. Wimsey's only contact with churchgoers had been among Greg's friends and contacts, to whom a church was a business and fellow worshippers clientele. Seeing the power plays and subterfuge that occupied the highly paid CEOs of these organizations, Wimsey never attributed anything supernatural or altruistic to their mission.

She looked around the quiet, empty chapel, and Cootie sat to wait patiently till they should go back outside. It was just a room with padded chairs, a nice sound system with earphones for the hard-of-hearing, and an abstract stained-glass window at the front. There was a lectern off to the side, beside a piano. And that was basically it.

Wimsey lingered in disappointment, then wondered why she was disappointed. She came in here looking for something. What? Was she searching for what was beyond the edge of life that most of these residents stood so close to?—that they all drew nearer to everyday? Or was she hoping to find a deeper aspect of Madelyn's character? *That's it*, Wimsey thought. *I wanted to see that Madelyn had a spiritual side, to perhaps take some of the sting out of her murder.*

Since no one was here at present to answer any questions, Wimsey turned to go out again, and Cootie jumped up. Beside the door Wimsey saw a basket on the floor with a hand-lettered sign: "Donated Bibles. Take One."

Bending, she rummaged through the books. There were a Douay Bible, several King James Versions, some new translations, and even a Book of Mormon. She fingered one old cloth-bound book that had faintly printed on its spine, "Goodspeed."

Opening it at random, she read, "Do not store up your riches on earth, where moths and rust destroy them, and where thieves break in and steal them, but store up your riches in heaven, where moths and rust cannot destroy them, and where thieves cannot break in and steal them. For wherever your treasure is, your heart will be also." Wimsey blinked at this, then took the little book with her when she and Cootie left.

They walked back by the site of the garage/craft sale, but Wimsey was rather tired of it by now, and especially tired of the traffic. So they headed home.

Approaching her house and seeing that Mrs. Rad was out two doors down, Wimsey kept walking till she came within hailing distance. As she stuffed the Goodspeed in her jacket pocket, she called, "Hello, Mrs. Rad! Are you going to the garage sale?"

The woman turned to eye her. "No. Bunch of junk."

"Mostly, yes, it is," Wimsey admitted. She looked over the Chrysanthemums. "Your beds look beautiful. Did Pedro manage to salvage your poor crushed mums?" She stepped to the right side of the house to look. "Oh, he did a great job! You can't tell anything was ever wrong with them."

Mrs. Rad shuffled over on her four-footed cane. Wimsey noticed that broad rubber tips on the feet prevented the cane's sinking too much in the turf. "He did well enough, but they shouldn't 've been trampled to begin with." She directed a stern, appraising gaze to Wimsey. "And there you've got trespassers tramping around your house, too."

"I should explain all that," Wimsey said. "I bought many of Madelyn's furnishings that her son Norbert was selling—"

"I saw that," Mrs. Rad said.

"Well, yes, so Cliff—the handyman who trampled your mums —trucked them to my house—"

"I know him," Mrs. Rad said.

"And, I had an appraiser come out—"

"The snooty woman," Mrs. Rad said.

"—with her helper, but it turned out that most of the things were reproductions—"

"I could have told you that," Mrs. Rad said.

"—but the detective was interested in purchasing some of the pieces—"

"I know him, too," Mrs. Rad said.

This time Wimsey was silent a moment. "I'm afraid they did a lot of damage to the yard, but—"

"I'm not talking about them," Mrs. Rad said. "I mean the man who was prowling around your back patio yesterday."

Nine

Wimsey was too startled to reply at once. Then she asked, "You saw someone around my back patio yesterday?"

"Yes, late afternoon. I was watching my birds, and I saw him messing around your back door and then come down your deck and leave. He must've gone up to the street. If he'd 've come back this way, I could have got a good look at him. But I just saw that it was a man," Mrs. Rad said in disapproval.

Wimsey blinked. "Thank you for telling me. I'll . . . do something about security."

"I would," Mrs. Rad advised.

Wimsey started to walk away with Cootie, then paused. Looking back, she asked, "Is . . . there anything I can do for you today?"

Mrs. Rad shrugged. Reluctantly, she said, "The deli collects old bread for me, and I'm almost out."

"I'll go get it for you right now, while they're still open," Wimsey said. Mrs. Rad grunted.

Wimsey and Cootie set off at a brisk trot back

toward Shrewsbury Circle and managed to reach the deli just as they were closing their doors. She claimed the large plastic bag of old bread set aside for Mrs. Rad, then returned to ring the doorbell of 124, as she didn't see its occupant outside anywhere.

When Mrs. Rad eventually came to the door, Wimsey started to hand over the bag, then caught herself. "Would you like me to put it by the back door for you?"

"Yes." Mrs. Rad shuffled backward, opening the door.

Wimsey paused to hook Cootie's leash over the porch railing finial. She murmured, "Stay, Cootie," before bringing the bag through the living area and placing it beside the French doors. Noting the binoculars hanging on a hook by the door, she glanced out to the shoreline, then to the left toward her house. It was not visible at all from inside.

"Mrs. Rad, would you mind—showing me where you were when you saw the man on my deck?"

Grunting in return, Mrs. Rad opened the back door. "Take the binoculars," she said, lightly waving. Wimsey did. "Now sit in that deck chair," Mrs. Rad instructed, pointing. This Wimsey did also.

Sitting in the chair about four feet from the railing, Wimsey did not even need the binoculars to see past the back deck of 122 to that of 120. Moreover, with the binoculars, someone with good eyes could have descried details about the appearance of a man on 120's deck. But at this time of day—about the same time that the cigarette smoker rifled Wimsey's spare room yesterday —her back deck was in heavy shade. And, Mrs. Rad's eyes were not that good.

"I believe you." Standing, Wimsey handed the binoculars back to her, and Mrs. Rad eased herself down to the deck chair. She raised the binoculars to watch her birds, and Wimsey added, "May I get you a glass of that mint tea on the counter?"

Mrs. Rad glanced up at her. "With three ice cubes. No more and no less."

"Certainly."

Wimsey found a glass in the cabinet and filled it with the required beverage plus three ice cubes. Upon delivering it, she said, "Thank you for watching out for me, Mrs. Rad. I'll stop back by later."

"All right," she replied from behind her binoculars, settling the glass into the beverage holder in the chair arm.

Wimsey retrieved Cootie from the porch and went home. Immediately upon entering, she checked the back door, which was locked. Then she extracted the Goodspeed from her pocket to lay it thoughtfully on the glass coffee table.

Being curiously reluctant to open it again, she went to the kitchen to pour Cootie a cup of dog food and put a container of soup in the microwave for herself.

While it heated, she ruminated on what she had learned: So, her intruder had been seen. True, Mrs. Rad could not identify him, but he had been careless enough to let himself be observed on her back deck by at least one resident. He was cocky, and not overly bright. *I'm on to you*, she thought, raising her eyes coolly to the back doors.

Almost to Wimsey's disappointment, the evening passed uneventfully with only a check-in call from Tara. Wimsey assured her with unmerited exasperation that she was doing fine, and why all the unnecessary worry?

"Oh, the indictments," Tara groaned. "Dad's lawyers are playing hardball, coming out with all kinds of accusations against everybody for everything. You remember sweet Mr. Dwiggins?"

"Bill Dwiggins? Of course. He took me to the emergency room when I broke my toe," Wimsey said.

"Well, Dad's lawyers are painting him as this evil mastermind of the whole scheme," Tara said vehemently.

"Bill? That's absurd. He was only a department head," Wimsey scoffed.

"That's what they're doing! Aren't you keeping up with this?" Tara asked.

"No," Wimsey said stubbornly.

"Mom, *that's* why I worry! If you hide your head in the sand like this, you're going to be completely blindsided when they come after you!"

Highly unlikely, Wimsey thought. But to placate her daughter, she said, "All right. I've got internet hookup now; I'll keep up with it online."

"Okay. And, just—let me know if anything happens," Tara said.

"No problem, dear. Good night." And it never

crossed Wimsey's mind that she might be withholding anything from her daughter. But she did think a lot about Bill Dwiggins. He didn't deserve the suspicion, much less the blame, for what Greg had engineered. She wished she could help him, at least as a character witness. Given her professed ignorance of ShaftCom, however, Wimsey couldn't see her doing him any good.

Just to keep her word, she accessed the Dallas newspaper online, skimmed a few stories, and e-mailed a link to her daughter to prove that her mother did what she said she would do.

The next day, Sunday, the garage/craft sale was still going strong. Wimsey knew this because, even though her bedroom was back from the street, traffic noise woke her before seven o'clock. Cootie started barking in anticipation, so Wimsey got up to dress, have breakfast, and go look around.

Against her better judgment, she stuffed Lott's $150 in her jacket pocket, then stepped outside to discover that it was a little cooler this morning—probably 55 degrees. So, much to Cootie's alarm, she went back inside to dig a suede hat out of her closet. Then she and Cootie set out, stopping by the coffee shop for a fully caffeinated latte. Since Chas was no doubt manning his tables, Lauren served her again. "Going to the garage sale?" she asked.

Wimsey made a face. "Yes, though I shouldn't. I spent way too much on junk yesterday."

"That's what they're for!" Lauren laughed, then quietly sighed at the entrance of an elderly suitor who demanded some attention with his coffee. Equipped with her morning caffeine, Wimsey took Cootie out to the field in the early morning sunshine.

She hardly thought it possible, but there appeared to be more people out here today than yesterday, even at this time of the morning. Then she saw why: On the second—and last—day, sellers began discounting their merchandise so that they could pack up early. Chas had sold so much yesterday, he was able to consolidate his tables down from three to two. Even so, he had someone helping him with customers today.

Stopping to look out of courtesy, Wimsey saw a majolica frog pitcher that she was sure was not here yesterday. Either she was still stinging over Madelyn's reproductions, or the passage in Goodspeed hit a little too close to home, because she handed over the $10 that the price tag requested without even looking at the manufacturer's mark on the bottom to see if the pitcher was worth what she thought it was.

Chas took her money and began wrapping the pitcher in newspaper, observing, "If I didn't know better, I'd think you kept coming by to flirt with me, Wimsey."

She puckered her lips impishly. "Think whatever you want, Chas, but I'm sure I didn't see that pitcher here yesterday. Did you go shopping last night?"

He glanced around to make sure his helper wasn't in hearing range. "Sort of, I did. A few other vendors didn't want to stand out here all day again today, so I bought the best of their stuff."

"At half price?" She took the bag he held out.

"Gotta pay the rent," he said with a wink. After a pause, he added, "Couldn't help but notice—since you live right next to the field—that you unloaded some furniture yesterday. Something you bought from somebody here?"

Wimsey noted that he took pains to point out that he hadn't been spying on her. She admitted, "Yes, I bought some of Madelyn's furnishings. I thought they were valuable, but almost all of them turned out to be reproductions."

"Ouch. Really?" he said, white eyebrows arching. "In a way, I guess that's not surprising. She was kind of cheap. She'd walk out of the coffee shop without paying, and we always had to bill her through the office. I heard she did the same thing at the deli and the grocery store."

"Hmm," she said in vague concern.

"I also hear"—he lowered his voice, leaning toward her—"that the Llano County investigator thinks that the drowning was not an accident. You seem to talk to him a lot. What does he say?"

She allowed her face to settle in its naturally serious expression. "Not very much. You know how close-mouthed they are. Since I saw her and her son talking, the detective seems to think I should know more than I do."

Chas whispered, "You think the son did away with her? For her money?"

"No. I don't think so at all," she said in complete truthfulness.

"Huh." Did he look disappointed? "Well, I—" he

broke off at the approach of a customer while his helper was waiting on two others. "Excuse me."

"Talk to you later." She waved, taking her package underarm. As Cootie dragged her down the wide, grassy aisle between booths, Wimsey put one foot in front of the other without seeing anything, hearing anything. *Chas knows I'm talking to the detective, and suspects murder; Mrs. Rad knows, and Melinda knows—who else knows?*

She stopped to ostensibly look in a booth of framed cross-stitched mottos. *Does the murderer know that I've been helping on the case? Has he been watching me? Is that who's been trying to get in?*

She tried to calm her suddenly palpitating heart. *No —that makes no sense. Whoever broke into my house was looking for the computer disk.*

Then she realized, *So I assumed. He could have been looking for notes on Madelyn's murder—such as the file Lott gave me Friday.*

Wimsey continued to walk up and down aisles. Warm aromas from a hot-pretzel stand were drawing a crowd, so she stood in line to receive a soft, fresh pretzel. Since she had finished her coffee, she purchased a cup of hot cocoa from a neighboring stand to go with the pretzel. Cootie got a bite, of course, then Wimsey resumed her walk.

As she walked, the stands faded, the booths and tables melted away, and somehow she found herself on the north side of the pond. Again she was struck by how —*isolated* this spot was. Had she not just walked through hundreds of people to get here, she would never have guessed that they were anywhere near. While Cootie nosed around the water's edge, Wimsey stood at the scene of Madelyn's murder and looked at the murky green water.

What am I missing? There was something right in front of her . . . something so obvious that only blind stupidity could overlook it. What was she not seeing?

She looked up. The fountain in the middle of the pond blocked sight of whatever was directly across from her, but just to the left of it, partly obscured by the descending spray, she saw a man standing on the south edge of the pond. He wore a blue windbreaker with a ball cap and sunglasses, and he was watching her. The smoke from his cigarette wafted over his head before blowing away.

Wimsey returned his gaze, then slowly began retracing her steps down Whitehaven Path around the pond. He dropped the cigarette, crushing it in the grass before turning leisurely toward the field of booths. She picked up her stride, and he did, too. Walking quickly without running, he entered the crowds thronging the nearest aisle. And Wimsey lost him.

With Cootie straining to lead, Wimsey ran the rest of the way back from the pond to thread through the aisle in which he had disappeared. She looked right and left, seeing a lot of people in jackets, for the morning was cool.

A fair number of men wore ball caps that were obviously habitual attire. Only a few men wore sunglasses, as the sun was not bright yet. But no one was dressed in the combination she required.

She passed Melinda leading Tina-Marie by the hand and waved; she saw Chas attending a sizeable crowd at his tables; she saw Cliff in jeans and t-shirt blocking another aisle to load up purchases in his pickup for a customer. She saw an empty space where Norbert's booth had been yesterday. She covered every aisle and every corner of the field, but did not see the man in the windbreaker.

It is an easy thing to remove, she reflected, pausing to rest while Cootie panted. *Cliff could have thrown it and the cap into his truck before starting to load it up. Chas could have put it on to follow me out to the pond.* She looked back to the bustling sale, acknowledging the remoteness of both possibilities. As far as she could tell, neither man smoked.

Then again, there was the distinct, unflattering possibility that he had not been looking at her at all, but enjoying the lake view, as a lot of people came out here to do. Wimsey colored slightly, visualizing what would have happened had she caught him to ask why he was watching her. *"Watching you? Where were you? Why would I be watching you, old woman?"*

She took her majolica frog pitcher and went home.

A week passed, and nothing happened. Wimsey's back doors stayed closed and locked when she was not going in or out through them, and no mysterious cigarette odors materialized. Detective Lott called once, just to see if she had any new thoughts. Although she had gone through Madelyn's folder forward and backward, she had to confess she had nothing further to offer. When he didn't call again, she knew that the murder had taken a backseat to new cases that stood a greater chance of resolution.

During that week, Wimsey and Cootie spent a lot of time exploring along the lakeshore. Since this was the height of migratory season for a number of birds, Wimsey enjoyed some rare and wonderful sights. With the tents, tables, and people cleared off the Yorkshire Fields, and the turf inadvertently torn up to expose worms and insects, a flock of several hundred robins suddenly descended on the field while Wimsey watched from her back deck. To get a closer look, she strolled down the boardwalk, then the pebbled path, and the birds were not disturbed in the slightest.

Then a day later, as she and Cootie were standing quietly at the water's edge behind Mrs. Rad's house, Wimsey glanced up at the birdfeeder on her deck to see a Painted Bunting helping himself. She gazed in delight at the party-colored red, yellow and blue bird, knowing how rare they were, and wishing she could call Mrs. Rad out to see her illustrious guest. But he flew off.

So when she stopped by Mrs. Rad's house the next day, as she was in the habit of doing, she told her what she had seen. And Mrs. Rad informed her that the Painted Buntings made special trips to her birdfeeder for the high-end seed she offered them—not the cheap millet.

On one of Wimsey's visits to the coffee shop, Chas coaxed her into giving him her phone number. Ten minutes later he called to invite her to join him for bingo at six o'clock that evening. Wimsey agreed to meet him there reluctantly because that was when she usually liked to have dinner. But he assured her that they served a great buffet of hors d'oeuvres. So she went, but just walking to the bingo hall without Cootie made her regret it; she'd really rather spend the evening with her dog and a book than playing bingo.

The price of admission, which she insisted on paying for herself, was a $10 pack of ten bingo cards. Wimsey handed over the cash, received her pack and a fat pen, then surveyed the noisy, crowded hall. When she looked toward the buffet along the opposite wall, Chas asked in her ear, "Want something to eat before game time? We got about fifteen minutes."

"Yes, I do. Go ahead and get us seats; I'll be right over," she said. He nodded, taking her cards, and Wimsey went to get a small paper plate of stuffed mushrooms, cheese on crackers, and sardines, with a plastic cup of tea.

She turned to look for Chas, who stood and waved. She made her way to his table and sat to see that he had already laid out two cards for her. "You've played before, haven't you?" he asked.

"Umm," she said noncommittally, a sardine in her mouth.

"Good. How many cards can you play at once?" he asked.

"Hmm?"

"Why, hello, Wimsey." At the greeting, she looked up at Melinda taking her seat across the table.

"Hello, Melinda. Where is Tina-Marie?" Wimsey asked.

"Oh, she doesn't come to bingo. It makes her nervous," Melinda said, spreading her cards with a professional flourish.

"Eyes down!" a man at front called.

There promptly followed a rustling and hush all over the hall. "Get ready. Get your dauber," Chas whispered, uncapping the thick pen and putting it in her hand. "He'll call pretty fast."

"Um hmm," she said, popping a mushroom into her mouth.

"G fifty. Bull's-eye," the caller announced. Wimsey watched Melinda and Chas quickly mark the number on their various cards. While Wimsey was leisurely looking over her two, the caller said, "B ten, cock and hen."

Chas marked his cards, glancing at her. "Better hurry. You got it there," he said, pointing.

Wimsey delicately daubed the number with a spot of blue ink and reached for her tea. "I twenty-five, duck and dive," the announcer called. As she was looking at her cards, he continued, "I twenty, getting plenty." A titter rose in the hall, causing Wimsey to look around curiously.

Melinda glanced at her and hissed, "Pay attention! Once you start a card, it's not good for any other game!" She herself was daubing her array of cards with finesse.

Chas, playing fewer cards, managed to mark them in time as the caller said, "O sixty-six, clickety-click." Not even checking her cards, Wimsey studied the scene at the front of the hall. The bingo balls were tossed about in a blower before being ejected one at a time into the hand of the caller.

Next to him was a table of decorated baskets. Were those the prizes? Wimsey was unimpressed. Discounting whatever was in them, she could turn out a more elaborately decorated basket for less than ten bucks.

"I seventeen, dancing queen."

"Bingo!" a lady screamed.

Wimsey sat up to watch her wave her arms in exultation. There were scattered groans and applause as a hall employee took her card to verify it, which he did. She was then presented a basket from the front, and the announcer said, "Lovely Linda Peters has won the twenty-five-dollar gift basket from Coffee Au Lait!" Oohs of admiration followed, and Wimsey bet that most of the players here tonight would spend far more than that on cards.

"Eyes down!" the caller warned.

In a flurry all across the hall, the players swept away their old cards for new. Wimsey shoved the remainder of her cards toward Chas. "You can have these. I'm going to raid the tables." He nodded a little reluctantly.

As she got up, the caller said, "N thirty-two, buckle my shoe!" and daubers all across the hall danced.

She ate her fill from the buffet, then slipped out to go home.

That Saturday, October 19th, she went on the Llano River geology field trip that, coincidentally, had been canceled the previous Saturday due to rain. It was a wonderfully informative trip which she enjoyed very much—or would have, normally.

But occupying the bus seat in front of her was a middle-aged couple who were less interested in rocks than in themselves. They were discreet enough in their whispering, giggling and petting, but being trapped behind them for a half-hour's ride sent Wimsey into a mild fit of depression.

She used to be in love; she used to have someone who loved her, she thought; but once she began to show her age, he left for greener fields. Sometimes it was hard not to dwell on what might have been. So she kept her eyes on the window beside her and found a seat well away from the lovebirds for the return trip.

Still, it felt good to get out of the village; the excursion was a respite from her fruitless efforts at detection. But it wasn't enough to give her a fresh perspective on Madelyn's murder, and Cootie sulked for hours after Wimsey returned.

Monday, October 21, was the day that news rained down in buckets on Wimsey's head. First, she heard from Detective Lott: "Good morning, Ms. Reade. How have you been?"

"Fine, Detective," she said, then waited.

"Nothing new for me?"

"No, I'm sorry. I've been over the file, the photos,

the pond—I can't make anything of it," she confessed.

He grunted, "Well, the heat's on. Baby Boy Norbert has challenged his mama's will, claiming mental duress and senility, or what have you. As long as the ME says it's murder—based on the dog—then the presiding judge won't allow a verdict on the will till we at least make an arrest. That means nobody can spend the money, so the dog association is howling and Baby Boy's lawyers have spewed out a flurry of letters promising intense scrutiny till we announce that Norbert's in the clear."

"Can't you do that?" she asked.

"Not a chance. Since you feel so strongly that he's not guilty, he's probably not, but if the county issues a public statement to that effect, we're going to find out that he did it after all. My mom loves the furniture, by the way."

"Wonderful," she said, piqued at his bringing up the fake furniture to possibly question her judgment about Norbert—if that was his intent.

"Well, would you—keep your ears open down there? Go to bingo, go to events, and listen to the talk?" he asked.

"I'll try to mingle," was all she would promise.

"Okay, thanks." And he clicked off.

A little while later, Daphne Zurita called. "Hello, Ms. Reade? Your wonderful rug is in the catalog for our New York auction November second. Would you like to come? I will have a seat reserved for you."

Wimsey hesitated. "Oh, my. I would love to, but I know I can't. I'd be too tempted to blow whatever I made on the rug buying something else. Thank you. I hope it meets your expectations."

"Wonderful, darling." And she was gone.

Wimsey and Cootie went walking that afternoon, as usual. In their daily walks, she was beginning to recognize the same faces everyday, so she began making a point to stop and introduce herself to other walkers.

The first couple she met along Whitehaven Path today were the two that she had seen consistently before. So Wimsey stopped them with a smile. "I see you walking almost every day, and haven't introduced myself! I am Wimsey Reade."

The man reached out to pump her hand. "Doug Liebert. And this lovely lady is Amelie." Wimsey smiled broadly. These names she remembered immediately from Madelyn's file: they were the walkers who had found her body.

Ten

Wimsey did not pounce on her knowledge about the Lieberts at once, choosing to ease into casual conversation. "I hope I won't offend you by asking whether you're married?" Melinda had already warned her that family members with the same last names were common at the village.

"Yes, we are. No offense at all," Amelie blushed. She was a very pretty lady in her early sixties.

Her husband, the brash, ex-military type, squeezed her arm. "Yep. Six months now. Still honeymooners."

"Oh, congratulations, then! Married couples seem a little rare here," Wimsey observed. She ruthlessly smothered the stirrings of self-pity.

"Yes, and a lot of the women are after my Dougie," Amelie pouted, cuddling him.

"There, Amelie, no one can hold a candle to you." He reached down to pinch her rear and she squealed.

Wimsey kept a determined smile on her face. "I couldn't help but notice—one day I passed you walking and overheard you complaining about the orange barricades around the pond. They came down immediately, it seemed."

His military face darkened. "Dam' straight they did. They made the place look like a brig."

"Well, I can understand the village wanting to take precautions. It was a terrible thing, what happened to Madelyn," Wimsey said.

Amelie leaned forward to whisper, "We found her body."

"No!" Wimsey exclaimed. "What did you see?"

"Eh, not much," Doug said. "It was dark, so at first it just looked like a lump in the mud. But Amelie saw a shoe, so we went over to look. The woman was crumpled up, half in the water. Hard to see how she drowned in so little water. I suppose she passed out. The pharmacy hands out Valium to anybody with enough cash, you know, so I suppose that'd do it."

"I heard she was murdered," Amelie whispered with a shiver.

"Now, I wish you'd quit listening to that bingo-hall talk. If you keep bringing back these moronic stories, I'm going to yank your bingo allowance. She was an old bird, and it was just her time to clock out," he said firmly.

"Where was the shoe you saw?" Wimsey asked lightly. This detail was not in the report she read, and she kicked herself for not seeking out these people to talk to them earlier.

Amelie answered, "Why, it was three feet from where she was lying. Wouldn't you say, Dougie?"

"At least three feet," he said firmly.

"To the side . . . ? Toward the path . . . ?" Wimsey hinted.

"Ah, in the grass, as if it came off when she fell in the water," Doug replied.

"What kind of a shoe?" Wimsey asked. "A walking shoe?" She was irritated with herself for being unable to remember what kind of shoes Madelyn was wearing that day, nor did the report specify.

Amelie tittered, "Oh, can you imagine Madelyn in walking shoes? Oh, no, she was wearing her Via Spiga gold slingbacks."

"Easy to lose off your feet," Wimsey said, nodding in disappointment. So the fact of an errant shoe proved nothing.

"Easy to fall over in," Doug snorted. "The last thing you can do is walk in 'em."

"Oh, but they're so lovely," Amelie protested.

"Bet they were knockoffs, like the rest of her stuff," Doug said. "I heard that her son found some moron to cough up a thousand bucks for her worthless furniture."

"Imagine that," Wimsey murmured.

"The shoes were nice," Amelie insisted.

"You're not spending two hundred dollars on a pair of shoes," he said, irritated.

"Well, it's been lovely talking to you. Cootie's getting restless, so I think we'd best be moving on," Wimsey said.

"So nice to meet you." Amelie offered a wave, which Wimsey returned. Turning to take up the slack on

Cootie's leash, she started at the firm pinch on her posterior. With a gasp, Wimsey looked back. Doug winked at her over his shoulder and walked away, his hand at his wife's back.

Resuming her walk, Wimsey murmured, "I'd rather be single." From that point on, she was no longer troubled by brooding regrets.

When she returned home, she found, first, that she had forgotten to take her phone, and second, that Tara had called, leaving this message: "Mom! Have you checked the headlines? It's the most wonderful news! Call me right away."

So Wimsey called her right back. "Tara! Hello. What's so exciting?"

"Oh, Mom. I'm starting to think there's hope for Daddy after all."

"Why is that?" Wimsey asked.

"He's done a complete reversal. One eighty degrees. He came out from behind his lawyers and said he'll plead guilty and just throw himself on the mercy of the court. He's going to pay restitution and everything. They had this big press conference this morning, and his lawyers said they urged him not to take the rap, but he said he was responsible for anything that happened on his watch whether he knew about it or not. Bill Dwiggins has got to be off the hook, after this," Tara said.

"That's wonderful news," Wimsey said carefully. "Do they know . . . why he changed his mind so suddenly?"

"He said he just couldn't forget about all the small investors that put their trust in the company," Tara said warmly. "Now, there was one snarky reporter that claimed the D.A.'s office got hold of some damning new evidence, but I don't believe it. As much investigating as they did, there's no way something new just 'came to light,'" she scoffed. "I think they're trying to take credit for Daddy's change of heart."

There was a brief silence on the line. "Mom?"

Wimsey stirred. "I hope that's what it was, Tara. I think your dad never completely lost his moral compass."

Now Tara was silent. Then she asked, "Mom, do you know anything about some 'new evidence'?"

"Tara, you know that I didn't know anything about company business while I was married. I know even less now," Wimsey pointed out.

"If you say so," Tara said, unconvinced. "You haven't had anything happen out there, have you? Strangers following you, or anything?"

"That's ridiculous!" Wimsey laughed.

"Maybe, maybe not," Tara said, slightly offended. "Well, however it happened, I'm glad Daddy's owning up to it."

"Me, too, honey. Thanks for telling me about it," Wimsey said.

"Okay, talk to you later."

After putting up her phone, Wimsey went to her computer to check the Dallas news. She read several articles that confirmed the gist of what Tara said. Of special interest to Wimsey was the column by the "snarky" reporter who claimed that Corrister found his conscience after the D.A. presented his lawyers and the presiding judge with their new evidence. Citing an unnamed courtroom source, the reporter said that an anonymous informant had sent the "smoking gun" to the district attorney's office only days previously.

Wimsey closed the browser and logged off the computer. This was good, right? This was good news. Then why was her heart pounding and her throat dry?

Greg would know, or at least guess, where the new information had come from. Once he saw the spreadsheets, he would know that they were the ones on the disk he had hidden in a book that disappeared from his library. He would know that she was behind it.

She sat there for a few minutes, listening to the beating of her heart. Then she was badly startled by the doorbell ringing, and Cootie's barking in response.

Coolly, Wimsey left the room to go to the door. Looking out the peephole, she saw a strange man in a suede jacket. She deliberated a moment, then said, "Down, Cootie," and opened the door.

Regarding the fortyish man on her doorstep, she detected the lingering cigarette haze at once. "Ms. Reade?" he asked, smiling.

"Who are you?" she returned, unsmiling. Cootie sniffed his leg.

"I'm Guy Krenkel's nephew Jay. He said you bought Madelyn Treschler's furniture last Saturday, and he was wondering if you're ready to unload any of it.

He's got a buyer that specializes in junk." He inched forward as he talked.

"I'm sorry; I already did," she said, thrusting Cootie back inside with her foot. "Oh, hello, Mrs. Rad!" she called loudly, waving at an imaginary person across the street behind him. He glanced over his shoulder. "Please excuse me; I am rather tied up at the moment. Tell Guy hello for me." She shut the door in his face and locked it.

She sat on the couch and picked up her phone. Scrolling through the numbers, she found the one for Guy and dialed. When he answered, she said, "Guy, this is Wimsey Reade. How are you? Wonderful. Listen, your nephew Jay was just here asking about Madelyn's furniture, and I'm afraid I—"

She broke off to listen, then said, "I understand. If Jay's in San Antonio, then it couldn't have been him. I must have misunderstood. I'm sorry to have bothered you—excuse me? Oh, no thank you, I don't think I need any more furniture right now—yes, I bought some of Madelyn's things. Thanks anyway. Bye."

She sat a moment looking at the display screen of her phone, then reluctantly scrolled to the detective's number. Even more reluctantly, she pressed "talk."

"Hello, Ms. Reade. What did you just now remember that will break the case?" he answered.

"Nothing, Detective. I'm afraid this has nothing to do with the case, but it's time I told you." So she briefly apprised him of the CD that she had mailed, the break-in, Greg's sudden change of heart, and her bogus visitor today.

He listened without interruption, then said, "Okay, I'm sending someone right out. You stay put until he gets there."

"Thank you," she murmured. She put her phone away, feeling a great weight lifted off her shoulders. She should have said something to him long before now, but —she finally did, and she was glad.

About forty-five minutes later her doorbell rang. Attended by Cootie, she opened it to a uniformed Llano County sheriff standing on her porch. "Wimsey Reade?" he asked.

"Yes. Please come in. Down, Cootie." She gestured him inside and closed the door, glancing down the street.

He stood in the living room, glancing around as he withdrew a notepad from his breast pocket. "You called Detective Lott about a break-in, ma'am?"

"Yes. What happened was, I—"

"Okay, when was it?" he asked.

She paused. "My second bedroom was ransacked— let's see, it was Friday. Not last Friday, but a week ago Friday—I don't remember the date—"

"What all was taken, ma'am?" he asked, expressionless.

"Nothing. But I believe they were looking for a CD I had mailed to a friend—"

"Okay. And there was a stalker?" he went on.

She paused. "Well, I don't know. A man came to my door this morning claiming to be Guy Krenkel's nephew Jay. But I called Guy, and he said his nephew is in San Antonio."

"Okay. Do you know Mr. Krenkel's address?" he asked.

"No, but I can find out," she said, reaching for her phone.

"I'll do that, ma'am. I'll check it out and get back with you," he said.

"All right. I appreciate it," she said. Disconcerted, she watched him exit to his black-and-white car sitting at the curb. He sat in the car for a few minutes talking on his phone, then pulled away.

She closed the door and sat back on the couch. Cootie snuggled next to her, and Wimsey gathered her up for a hug. Then all she could do was wait. Her stomach knotted when she realized that she had been too distracted to even note the sheriff's name or badge number. *I can't get rattled*, she thought. *There is no reason to lose control now.*

About thirty minutes later her doorbell rang again, and she fairly jumped to answer. It was the sheriff again, who nodded. "Okay, ma'am, I just stopped by Mr. Krenkel's condo. His nephew was there with him. Mr. Krenkel had forgotten that he was coming in today."

Her mouth hung open slightly. "I see. Did he ask his nephew to check with me about Madelyn Treschler's furniture?"

"I don't know about that, ma'am," he said, his patience clearly strained. "But he is in the village."

"What does he look like?" she asked suddenly.

"Ah, medium build, brown hair, jeans, blue shirt," he said. "Would you like to go talk to him?"

It was a good suggestion, but his tone was just peeved enough to get her attention. In a flash she saw his resentment at being dispatched to the old folks' village to take this batty old broad's complaint.

She glanced at his name tag, and he stiffened slightly at the implied threat of her calling in a complaint on him. "No, thank you, Deputy Remick; that answers my concerns well enough. I appreciate your taking the time to come out here."

He relaxed. "You're welcome, ma'am. Be sure to call if you have any other trouble."

"I will. Thank you." She held the door open for him, watching as he returned to his cruiser.

Then she shut the door and sat deliberately on the couch to pick up her phone. Scrolling through the numbers, she selected one and pressed "talk." She waited a moment, then said, "Guy? Hello, this is Wimsey again. You know, I believe I've changed my mind: I would like to see some of your furniture. . . . In the storage units behind the condos? All right, I believe I can find that.

"Listen, Guy, is your nephew still here? Does he have a truck? Wonderful. Yes, if you're free, I'd appreciate seeing it now. I'll bike on over to the storage units—yours is number 25? Great. Excuse me? Oh, no, no more golf carts for me," she laughed. "See you in a minute."

She apologized to Cootie for having to leave her behind. Slinging her purse over her shoulder, she walked her bike out of the second bedroom and took it out the back doors. She made sure they were locked before walking the bike off the back deck and down the steps to the boardwalk.

Here she hopped onto the seat to ride east down the boardwalk past the last house, 128, which was apparently vacant. Then she went south down the alley, which intersected St. Mary Mead Lane right before it curved between the apartments, condominiums, and storage buildings. Going the back way was longer, but she hadn't taken this route before and wanted to see it.

Cruising down the storage facility parking lot, she saw Guy waiting in front of one unit with another man. Wimsey pulled up to them and dismounted. "Hello, Guy. So nice to see you again." She extended her hand.

He shook it firmly, eyeing her. "What was all that, calling me asking about Jay, and then the cop showing up asking about Jay?" Guy was short and shriveled with an equally short and shriveled manner.

"Oh, that was a stupid mix-up on my part!" she laughed. "Did you know that I had bought some of Madelyn's furniture?"

"Not till you told me," he said, clearly offended. "You said you were going to come by my booth and you didn't." He was the one who had been passing off the department-store seconds as his dear departed wife's possessions.

"Oh, but I did!" she protested, smiling. "You had too big a crowd for me to get through! But I really wanted to see what you had, which is why I called today."

This was sufficient appeasement. He jerked his

thumb at the man beside him. "Well, *this* is my nephew, Jay."

Turning to him, Wimsey shook his hand. "How do you do." He was a fifty-year-old with glasses and brushy mustache: assuredly not the man who had been on her doorstep today. However, he was wearing a blue shirt and jeans as the deputy said.

"How do you do," Jay replied. "My truck is right here."

Wimsey glanced at the battered blue Ford. "Fine. Well, let's see what you have," she said to the uncle.

He opened his storage shed and she began looking though it for the smallest, cheapest piece that she could find to make it worthwhile for him to come down here. Nephew Jay rather endeared himself to her at this point; when she indicated an interest in seeing any particular piece, he cleared all clutter off it and brought it out into the light for her inspection.

While she was looking, Guy wondered aloud, "What did you tell that cop about Jay, anyway?"

She glanced at him blankly. "Cop?"

"Yeah, right after you called about Jay, this cop came to my apartment, asked if I'd heard from him, and I said, 'Well, here he is right here,'" Guy said.

Wimsey ran her hand over a settee. "What did he want to talk to you about?" she asked, eyes on the furniture.

Jay replied, "Nothing. He just looked at me and said, 'Well, that settles it,' or something."

"Hmph. Well, I didn't accuse you of a thing. It

would have been courteous for him to tell you why he was asking for you," Wimsey sniffed, scrutinizing a large armoire.

"Yeah, that's what I said," Jay agreed. The customer was always right, after all.

Having sidestepped Guy's question by finding fault with the deputy, Wimsey was meanwhile thinking, *Had the deputy told Jay why he was there, or asked any questions at all, he would have discovered that Jay wasn't the man who came to my door. But he didn't take me seriously enough to do that. I knew there was a reason I didn't want to call anyone for help.* She disguised her irritation by giving thoughtful consideration to piece after shoddy piece. Suddenly she empathized with Daphne Zurita in wanting to dismiss the lot with a condescending wave of her hand.

After an hour's inspection of junk, she finally said, "Well, these are all most interesting pieces—"

She was about to indicate her enthusiasm for a Hepplewhite-style coffee table when Jay noted, "There's a chair you haven't seen."

"Where?" she asked tiredly.

"Here." He lifted a moth-eaten rug, and Wimsey stared down at a fine reproduction of a Victorian gentleman's oak chair with leather seat and back.

"That is lovely," Wimsey admitted. "I doubt it's antique, however."

Guy began a studied discourse on why it most certainly was, but Jay said, "Probably not. Still, it's a nice chair."

Wimsey looked at him. "I agree. How much do you want for it?" she asked Uncle Guy.

"Eh." He glanced at his loose-lipped nephew from under his bushy white brows. "Hundred bucks."

"Taken," Wimsey said. "But I don't have that much cash. I'll have to give you a check."

"That's fine," he said stiffly.

Wimsey wrote out the check and handed it over, then Jay loaded up the chair and her bike in the back of his truck. She shook Uncle Guy's hand. "Thank you so much. I'm glad I came to look at what you had."

"Me, too. Now, you tell anybody you know who needs furniture to come to me," he instructed, pocketing the check.

"I will." Waving, she climbed into the passenger seat beside Jay.

Under her direction, he drove down St. Mary Mead Lane toward her house. Passing the vacant house at 128, Wimsey saw a sign in the front yard that proudly proclaimed, "New Tenant Coming Nov. 15!" The village was keen to let residents and visitors know that vacancies were rare and short-lived.

Jay pulled up to the curb in front of her house. Wimsey unlocked the front door, glancing inside, and Cootie came out to greet her. Jay carried in the chair; she followed with her bike, but when she tried to tip him, he waved in mild horror. "Oh, no. I'm just glad to help Uncle. He's leaving me a bundle in his will."

She stifled a laugh at his bald honesty. "Well, thank you, Jay. Have a good day."

He lifted a hand on the way to his truck and she glanced at Melinda's face in the window next door. "Great," Wimsey sighed, shutting the door. "What are the neighbors going to think of me buying still more furniture?"

First thing, she checked the back doors, which were still locked. She made a brisk inspection of the small house, finding nothing out of order. So she set the chair beside the deck doors on the inside, making for a nice place to sit and take off dirty shoes. Then she pulled out her sketch pad and pencils to draw the best likeness she could remember of the man who came to her door.

She concentrated hard on the light pencil lines that began sweeping across the paper. *Nondescript* was the perfect word for him: brown hair, round face, cleanshaven, about five foot ten, medium build.

When she had something of a portrait, she scrutinized it, dissatisfied. It looked like every other middle-aged man one might meet on the street. It suddenly dawned on her, however, that it fit the deputy's description of Jay better than the real Jay.

She looked up at the wall in concentration. If she were asked to describe the Jay she had just met, she would say, *"Fifty years old, with a mustache and glasses."* But the deputy had said, *"Brown hair, medium build"* with the added illumination that he was wearing a blue shirt and jeans. Jay's hair *was* brown—a weary, graying brown—but it wasn't his most distinguishing feature.

What did this mean? She did not know. She could

not bring herself to suspect either that the deputy was part of some dark conspiracy or that Guy was switching nephews back and forth. So she concluded that the deputy really hadn't paid that much attention to what Jay looked like.

Sighing, she regarded her sketch again. Was this man also the one in the windbreaker and ball cap, who had been watching her from across the pond? She could not say for sure. The only thing she did know was that the imposter knew something of the village and its residents. He knew Guy, that Guy bought and sold furniture, that his nephew Jay was coming to the village today, and—that she had bought Madelyn's furniture.

He's watching all of us, she thought. *He's certainly watching me. And he's getting bolder—he's let himself be seen face-to-face, using a name I'm sure to find out is not his.*

Then it dawned on her: *He never intended I should have time to find that out. Whatever he intended to do, he meant to do it today.*

She looked aside to the back doors. *Which means he's running out of time, and must know it.*

Eleven

Over the next few days, Wimsey did not alter her daily routine. She still checked on Mrs. Rad, still walked Cootie, still stopped by the coffee shop for a latte from Chas or Lauren. Often she walked up Shrewsbury Circle just to see what was going on—the bingo hall in particular seemed to draw the most action.

Once Wimsey observed a catfight between two woman out front of the hall. She deduced that it was precipitated by (a) a man or (b) one of the women's bingo winnings—a gift basket from the pharmacy, perhaps? Occasionally, Wimsey stopped in the chapel, although it was much less interesting because no one ever seemed to be there.

She inspected the gift shop and hardware store thoroughly. Being rather proud of her handyman skills, she found more to interest her in the latter store. She checked out the library, but due to the residents' demand, their stock consisted overwhelmingly of torrid romance novels. These did not appeal to Wimsey.

Once, just for a change, she walked down St. Mary Mead Lane around the apartments and condos. However, the traffic here, both of golf carts and cars, was so bad that she was constantly skittering out of somebody's way. One elderly driver actually ran up on the sidewalk barely fifteen feet in front of her, taking out a No Parking sign.

After that experience, she stayed closer to the lakeshore for her walks with Cootie. She also stayed away from the golf course, choosing not to brave the likely hail of golf balls propelled from uncontrolled drivers. And she continued to walk Whitehaven Path around the pond.

The only change in her routine was that wherever she went, she maintained constant surveillance of who was around her, especially behind her. She never walked all the way to the north side of the pond unless she was sure that no one else was in view, or that a number of people were in view. And, she religiously carried her phone.

So that took care of her forays out of doors. But inside her own home, she still felt vulnerable. Whether it was one man or more than one, a stalker had already been in her house without her permission, and convinced her to open her door to him. So morning and evening she checked locks, and began leaving her deck lights on all night. Cootie was something of a comfort, being a good alarm system. But an alarm was just that; it was not a defense. The stalker still knew she lived alone with a dog that did not bite.

Thursday, October 24th, she was out walking Cootie after two days of cold rain. The grass was still wet, compelling Cootie to drop her pile on the path, much to her owner's displeasure. Today was chilly as well, with rain clouds lingering on the horizon, so other walkers were few. Wimsey passed the Lieberts with a greeting and a smile, but veered off into the wet grass to avoid Doug's outstretched fingers.

She walked to the north side of the pond, and from there to the shore to look over the lake. The water was choppy today, tossed up by the wind, shrouded with a rainy haze in the distance. It looked rather ominous. Wimsey glanced down at Cootie, who had her nose uplifted and eyes half-closed in concentrating on the mingled scents of rain and lake life.

Wimsey stood at the shore until the sense of foreboding made her return to Whitehaven Path. She glanced both ways down the path and saw no one. So she walked back to the coffee shop to order her standard latte.

Just before Chas came to the window, she noticed the muddy boots sitting against the wall outside the door. "Oh, dear! Are those yours?" Wimsey asked, pointing.

He stuck his head out the window to regard them disgustedly. "Yes. I wear them to walk the shortcut back and forth to the shop from my apartment, but with all the darn rain I stepped right into the biggest mud pit you ever saw. Latte as usual?"

"Yes, please," she said. "I hope you haven't ruined them for work."

He glanced back at the window. "Oh, I don't wear them to work; I have to wear special orthopedic shoes for all the standing. It's murder on your feet."

"I guess so," she said, then paused, staring at the

boots. She was remembering a little trick employed by a single friend from years ago—a gorgeous girl who didn't want to advertise the fact that she lived alone.

Wimsey suddenly pulled all the cash she had out of her pocket. "Chas, I want to buy those off you."

He looked up from the coffee machine. "Buy what?"

"The boots. How much do you want for them?" she asked.

He paused with the cream dispenser in hand. "The boots? Oh, geez, they're ten years old. At least let me clean them up."

"No, no—they're perfect as is. I understand you'd need to buy a replacement pair. Sixty bucks?" she offered, trying to count her cash.

He looked shocked. "Not on your life. Take 'em."

He handed her the coffee and she gave him a five. "No, I insist on paying you for them."

"If you insist on paying for them, you can't have them," he said, counting out her change. "They're not even worth giving to charity. Take 'em. What do you want them for?" he asked curiously.

She smiled. "I'm thinking about using them for a Halloween display."

He laughed, "Well, that's a perfect fit. Take 'em."

"Thanks, Chas." She looped Cootie's leash on her wrist and picked up the boots, then raised her cup to him in acknowledgment. He waved her away, looking satisfied.

But Wimsey lingered at the corner of the shop, out of sight, until she glimpsed him going into the back room. Then she dropped the boots and hurried Cootie inside to stuff a twenty-dollar bill into the tip jar. On the way out, she retrieved the boots, and an incoming customer stared at her. She smiled.

Arriving home, she led Cootie up the slippery cedar steps to the back deck. She dropped the big, muddy boots beside the door, unlocked it, and went on in. That was the simple trick she had learned from her friend: a man's shoes outside a door implied a man within.

Shortly after she came home, the rain swept in from the lake, engulfing the village in a torrent. Wimsey was content to sit in bed and read with Cootie curled up on one side and a cup of hot cocoa on the other. After two chapters, she dozed off, then awakened again in late afternoon. Lazily, she watched the rain splatter on the large picture window, blurring the lake in the background.

Stretching, she climbed out of bed, and Cootie did likewise. Now chilled, Wimsey pulled on a bulky sweater, placing her phone in the pocket. On her way to the kitchen, she paused by the second bedroom, then decided to go ahead and check headlines on the computer.

Scrolling through the Dallas newspaper's home-page links, she found there was not much new in Greg's case, except for the additional information (again from the anonymous court source) that the new evidence had been mailed from downtown Chicago.

Wimsey exhaled in satisfaction, closing the browser window. Artie lived in Des Plaines; Greg did not know this, or Artie; the source was then untraceable. Whatever Greg's suspicions, Chicago was a long way from Lake

LBJ. And she had men's boots by her door to give an intruder second thoughts. So Wimsey began to feel a little too secure in her simple machinations.

With the rain bringing twilight an hour earlier than usual, she poured Cootie her dog food and put soup in the microwave. Waiting for it to heat, she folded her arms and regarded the faux Messel tables in the living area with a little laugh. She really liked them.

Cootie suddenly perked her ears and looked toward the back door, issuing a low growl. Tail rotating rapidly, she charged a few feet toward the door, stopping a safe distance away to bark in excitement.

Wimsey glanced at the door. Seeing nothing, she scolded, "Hush! If one of the neighbors' dogs is looking for a dry place on our deck, we're going to let it stay." As she went to the doors to make sure they were locked, it suddenly dawned on her that she hadn't seen any dogs in the village other than Cootie and Madelyn's two Reggies. She saw a cat or two, but no other dogs.

Thinking about this, she put her hand on the door handle and discovered, to her great irritation, that it was unlocked. Then she looked up at a man's face.

She froze with her hand on the handle of the unlatched door. It was the counterfeit Jay, standing on the other side of the door not eighteen inches away. Soaking wet, with water dripping down his head onto his blue windbreaker, he was regarding her slack face in satisfaction.

Then he said through the door, "I have a message for you." He smiled as he reached for the door's outside handle.

Wimsey's hand tightened on the inside handle. She set her feet and thrust the door open with both hands as hard as she could. Since he was coming forward at the time, the door hit him solidly in the face, and she glimpsed blood smear on a glass panel when it cracked.

He staggered back, giving her precious seconds to slam the door and lock it. "Cootie!" she cried, rushing to the hall. With a last bark at the intruder, Cootie followed her mistress into the master bedroom. Wimsey slammed the door and threw herself to sit on the bed. With shaking hands, she pulled out her phone to dial 911.

"Please give me your name, your location, and the nature of your emergency," a woman's voice said.

Wimsey swallowed. "My name is Wimsey Reade; I live at one-twenty St. Mary Mead Lane in the Old England Retirement Village. There is a man at my back door who attempted to force his way inside."

"Where are you right now, ma'am?"

"I am in the master bedroom of my house. He is at my back door," Wimsey stressed.

"I am sending someone right out. Please stay right where you are. Please do not leave your room until an officer comes to give you an all-clear," the operator said.

Wimsey looked toward the closed bedroom door which had no lock. "If he gets here in time." She heard the operator's voice in the background relaying the emergency call.

The operator came back on the line. "All right; we have a sheriff's unit en route. Is there anyone with you?"

"My dog," Wimsey said, gathering Cootie under-arm. The dog was periodically shivering and barking.

"Is there anyone else in the house?" the operator asked.

"The intruder, when he gets in," Wimsey said. She looked up sharply at the faint, tinkling sound of glass breaking.

"Help is on the way. Are you armed?"

"No," Wimsey said. She momentarily lowered the phone to listen. Was that the back door banging? She glanced around the darkened bedroom for something, anything to defend herself with. The she looked out the uncovered picture window. The rain had not abated; between it and the darkness, she could not see anything outside but blurred, far-off lights across the lake.

"Okay, just stay right there. We have three units on the way."

"I'm going to put you down so that I can block the door," Wimsey replied. As stated, she put the phone on the bed and pulled the nightstand across the door. Then she regarded the little piece of furniture in mild disbelief. Why did she think that would stop him? He'd just push it away opening the door. And why didn't she run into the second bedroom, where she had the sideboard that might slow him down?

She leaned against the door to listen—yes, that was definitely the back door banging. She thought she had locked it, which obviously meant nothing.

Footsteps? She listened harder. Suddenly she thought of the Goodspeed on the coffee table and wished she had it with her, even though she had not picked it up for days. Strangely, she felt an irrational compulsion to run out and get it.

"Ma'am? Ms. Reade? Are you still there?" She could hear the operator's voice.

Wimsey returned to the bed to pick up the phone. "I can hear the back door banging," she reported calmly.

"You just wait right there. Sit tight," the operator instructed.

Wimsey lowered the phone again, then replaced it at her ear. "I hear sirens."

"Good. They know just where you are," the operator said.

Because they were called out here when Madelyn died, Wimsey thought. She lowered the phone to listen. Madelyn was the only other resident with a dog.

There was something significant in this, but Wimsey was unable to process anything but the simple externals: Sirens that grew louder. Faint reflections of red and blue flashing lights through the rain.

Minutes of eerie quiet, then footsteps in the house. Footsteps coming down the hall. She looked at the door. Cootie exploded in barks.

"Ms. Reade? Sheriff's department. Are you okay?" a male voice called at her door.

"Yes," she said, bounding off the bed. "Hush, Cootie. It's okay." She stroked the dog to calm her, then went to the door to move the nightstand—and stopped.

"Ms. Reade?" he said again.

"Shove your ID under the door," she instructed.

She heard a rustle, then looked down at the corner of a slim leather wallet protruding under the door. "It won't fit," he complained from close to the door on the other side.

So she opened the door, freeing his ID. The officer stood, replacing the wallet in his pocket. He wore a dripping plastic cover on his hat and a wet black slicker with "SHERIFF" stenciled on the back in large reflective lettering. "Okay, uh, ma'am, you're all clear. Will you come—"

They heard a shout from outside. Sprinting down the hall, he turned with a raised hand. "Wait there, please."

Not on your life. She paused long enough to shut Cootie safely in the bedroom, then sidled down the hall to take a peek.

No one was in the house. There were muddy footprints leading in and out, and the back door was banging open and shut in the wind over pieces of broken glass. Wimsey went to the door to look out.

Flashing lights from vehicles on the west side of her house colored the falling rain red and blue. Figures in raincoats were going up and down the deck with flashlights. There were a lot of lights and activity around her boat slip.

One figure looked up toward her in the doorway, then began ascending the wet cedar steps at a trot. He slipped, grasping the handrail to catch himself before proceeding more cautiously.

She watched the sheriff—the one who had found her in the bedroom—enter and gently close the door. He gestured to the small bistro table in the kitchen, saying, "Let's you and I sit down together and you tell me what happened."

Wimsey sat while he removed his wet hat and slicker, leaving them by the door. She looked toward the

Goodspeed on the coffee table just to see that it was still there.

Then he sat and pulled out a notepad. "Okay, ma'am. I'm listening." And he took notes while she described succinctly everything that happened. As she talked, she watched over his shoulder while a crime-scene technician (not Boltrain) took photos of her back door and samples of the blood.

"I have seen him twice before," she told the sheriff, who glanced up from his pad. "Once was Sunday, October thirteenth, at the village garage sale. He was wearing the same blue windbreaker as he had on tonight, and he was watching me across the pond."

She swallowed and continued, "The second time was when he came to my door this past Monday, the twenty-first. He introduced himself as Guy Krenkel's nephew Jay, but I wouldn't let him in. When I discovered that he was not Jay, I called Detective Lott because my home had been broken into previously. I also sketched him at that time."

He stopped writing. "You have the sketch?"

"Yes." She went to the spare bedroom to retrieve her sketch pad and bring it to him.

He was studying the sketch when someone at the back door called, "Sheriff Jahns?"

"Excuse me for a moment." He got up, taking the sketch. At the back door, he conferred in whispers for what seemed like half an hour with two others in dripping slickers. Wimsey watched the runoff water puddle on the tile by the door, and listened to Cootie whine and scratch at the bedroom door.

The sheriff turned to ask her, "Ma'am, whose boots are these by the door here?"

"They belonged to a friend of mine who works at the coffee shop. His name is Chas. I bought them to make a Halloween display," she said vaguely.

At the approach of yet more sirens and lights, Wimsey suddenly stood. Three figures turned to block her exit, but not before she saw the ambulance backing toward the lake. The vehicle stopped, and other figures began lugging something toward it. "What happened?" she asked, alarmed. "Who else did he get to?"

"Please sit down, Ms. Reade," the sheriff instructed.

She backed up only a few feet. "I want you to tell me who that is you're dragging from the lake," she demanded, angry and fearful. *Melinda? Mrs. Rad? Oh, dear God, no.*

"Your visitor," he said. "As near as we can figure, when you hit him with the door, it either knocked him out or made him lose his balance. He fell down the steps and drowned in your boat slip," Jahns replied.

"What?" she gasped.

"Ma'am, is there any place you can go for the evening?" he asked.

She stood at the door, shivering in the cool gusts. Then something hardened inside her: the will not to be bullied. She looked at the sheriff. "Thank you for your concern, but I like this house and I'm going to stay here."

"Uh, your door's broken," he pointed out.

"It wasn't any good before," she countered.

"There may be people out here for a while yet."

She replied, "They won't bother me. I left my dinner in the microwave. Excuse me—do you mind if I shut this door? I need to keep my dog inside."

He nodded, rolling up the sketch to stow it under his slicker. Replacing his hat, he turned to gingerly tread down the slick steps while Wimsey shut the door and went to the bedroom to release Cootie.

The dog took interest in the activity out back, but ceased to bark, and eventually came to the kitchen to see what her mistress was eating. Wimsey ate her reheated soup, watching as more law-enforcement personnel arrived with bright lights and crime-scene equipment.

Wimsey brushed her teeth, but did not undress. She closed the bedroom blinds, shut the door, and gathered Cootie under the covers with her. She lay awake for a long time watching flickers of light through the blinds, then fell into a restless sleep.

In the morning, she was awakened by her cell phone bleating. It took her a few moments to dig it out from the pocket of her sweater on the bed. She looked at the display and murmured, "Good morning, Detective."

"Good morning, Ms. Reade. I hear you had an interesting evening."

"Yes, I did," she sighed, glancing at the bedside clock. It said 8:32.

"Where are you?" he asked.

"In bed," she said, slightly irritated. "At the house," she corrected herself.

"All right, then, I'll be there in about a half hour," he warned her.

"Um hmm." She closed the phone and dozed off

again for a minute, but Cootie was now breathing in her face. So Wimsey got up and opened her blinds to look out.

The morning was clean and fresh, the rain gone, though the ground was still wet. There was crime-scene tape all around her property, clear down to the lake. But no one was there, so Wimsey changed clothes and went to the back doors. She paused to regard the blood smears and broken glass, then let Cootie out.

The dog hopped down the deck to do her business in the buffalo grass while Wimsey descended the steps (carefully) to look over the boat slip. She saw the tire tracks of the emergency vehicles and a jumble of muddy footprints.

With the doors standing open, she heard the front doorbell ring. Leaving the back door open for Cootie, Wimsey reentered the house. As she passed through the living area, she reached down for the Goodspeed, placing it in her sweater pocket. She peered though the peephole, then opened the door. "Good morning, Sandy. Please come in."

"Thank you, Ms. Reade. Are you all right?" The village day manager was a perky young woman, professional and adroit at staying out of reach of the male residents. She entered around Wimsey and looked toward the back deck.

"Yes, I'm fine," Wimsey said. Noticing Sandy's glance, she added, "Would you like to see the—damage?"

"Yes, I need to, if you don't mind." Sandy looked determined to smile even as she spilled out, "Oh, Ms.

Reade, I'm so sorry for what happened. I have to tell you that when the sheriff's people came to see me this morning, I just about lost my breakfast. I am so grateful that you weren't hurt. How you kept your head, I'll never know.

"And I hate to say it, but I'm not sorry that man is dead. I never trusted him. But since he didn't have a record, we didn't have any reason not to hire him. Oh! I shudder to think. At least they know who killed Mrs. Treschler, God rest her soul."

Twelve

While Sandy looked toward the back doors, Wimsey was trying to make sense of what she had just said. "You . . . know the man who tried to break in last night?" Wimsey asked.

Sandy turned to her. "Yes, I identified him from a picture they showed me this morning. He wasn't a regular village employee, just a freelance handyman, like Cliff. I think Cliff used him occasionally when he needed help with something. Like I said, he had no prior record, not even a parking ticket, and his drug test came back clean. The sheriff said he's the one who drowned Madelyn, but, I can't imagine why! He had only been working here about a week before she died. The village is disavowing any responsibility in that, by the way. But between you and me, our insurance company is quietly paying a settlement to her son, as they should, which is why I needed to come talk to you."

When Sandy took a breath, Wimsey asked, "What is his name?"

"Norbert Treschler," Sandy replied.

"No—the man who attempted to break into my home," Wimsey clarified.

"Uh, Wayne Theis," Sandy said with noticeable discomfort.

"Where does he live?" Wimsey asked.

"Marble Falls. Listen, Ms. Reade, I've been told to ask you to not to talk to anyone about this, except the police—not neighbors, or reporters, or anyone. After the suicide here, and now this—we are very concerned to keep this out of the news. If you will not tell anyone about this, we're prepared to offer you free lease on this home for the next year."

"For the next five years," Wimsey countered.

Sandy hardly hesitated. "For the next five years," she agreed. "But only if you say nothing, including to your family."

"What about the neighbors? They're going to wonder about the crime-scene tape." Wimsey nodded toward the deck.

"Yes. We're posting a notice to the residents that Wayne fell off the boardwalk and drowned last night, presumably drunk. It just happened to be in your slip," Sandy said.

Wimsey nodded, thinking, *It won't fool Mrs. Rad. She already saw him at the back door.* "All right. I believe Detective Lott is stopping by this morning. Obviously, I need to talk to him, but I won't discuss it with anyone else." This plan is what Wimsey would have preferred in the first place. She was rather surprised to have it urged on her, along with a bonus.

"Thank you so much." Sandy squeezed her hand in gratitude, and Wimsey smiled slightly. Sandy glanced back at the door. "I'm sending someone out right away to fix your door—"

"Please have him fix the lock, while he's at it. The doors have never locked properly," Wimsey said.

"Certainly. We will also be installing anti-slip strips on the deck steps of all the lakefront houses," Sandy added.

"That's a wise precaution," Wimsey agreed.

"Okay, then. Call me if you need anything," Sandy said.

"Sure." Watching her retreat quickly down the front walk, Wimsey felt almost sorry for her. What does the manager say to a resident who was almost the village's second murder victim?

While standing at the door, Wimsey saw the detective's car pull up to the curb, so she waited for him to amble up the walk on gimpy knees. Recognizing him, Cootie slipped out to greet him with wagging tail and escort him to the door. "Good morning, Ms. Reade," he said, eyeing her as he reached into his breast pocket for his notepad.

"Good morning, Detective. Come in." He did, heading right for the back door. Wimsey followed him as far as the kitchen, where she stopped beside the sink. "Would you like some coffee?"

He glanced back at her. "Yeah, actually. Black. Thanks."

She nodded, filling the carafe with tap water. As she

located the coffee and spooned it into the filter basket, she glanced at his regarding the broken door pane with his hands on his hips.

She brought two filled cups to the coffee table and sat on the couch. "It's not as good as the coffee shop's, but I'm spending too much money there, anyway."

Cootie waited until Lott seated himself before jumping up on the couch between them. Neither tried to move her. "Okay, tell me what happened," he said, leaning back.

She covered the relevant events of last night in about five minutes. When finished, she took a sip of coffee, waiting. He finally said, "Okay, now tell me what happened after you called me about Guy Krenkel's nephew."

Wimsey set down her cup to relay the facts of the deputy's cursory investigation followed by her calling Guy to set up a meeting with him and the real Jay at his storage unit. "I bought the nice reproduction Victorian gentleman's chair from him," she said, nodding toward the chair still beside the back doors. "And I sketched the man who came to my home posing as Jay—the same man who tried to break in last night."

"Let me see it," Lott requested.

"I gave it to Sheriff Jahns last night. It's a rather good likeness, if I say so myself."

He nodded unhappily. Wimsey could have been offended that he didn't even express relief at her unmurdered state, but she guessed that he was most disturbed by the department's failures which had put her at risk to begin with. He confirmed this by asking, "So who was the idiot deputy that came out to talk to you?"

Deputy Remick. "I don't remember," she said. He looked disbelieving, but she had other matters on her mind: "Why does the department assume that Theis murdered Madelyn? You haven't touched your coffee."

He took a gulp. "The similarity of victims, her and you."

Now she was offended. "That's pretty slim evidence," she observed, and he groaned slightly. "What physical evidence do you have linking him to her murder?" she pressed.

"None, yet. We're searching his apartment," Lott said.

"Did he leave behind a family?" she asked.

"Ah, elderly mother in a nursing home, ex-wife, no kids," he said.

"Well, he may very well have been the hit man. But he wasn't the one behind it. He told me plainly, 'I have a message for you,'" she pointed out.

"Is there any chance that—that he really did? That he just came to deliver a message?" Lott blurted.

Wimsey stared at him. "You would have gotten the definitive answer to that had he gotten in. Anything he wanted to tell me, he could have told me through the door. He tried to force his way in, Detective—after attempting to get in by false pretenses days before." She tried to keep her rising anger in check.

"I realize that," he said quickly. "I . . . wouldn't have been able to live with myself had you been hurt."

"Thank you," she said a little caustically.

"It's just that it complicates everything all over again," he muttered. "Now we have to find who would want to murder you *and* Madelyn Treschler."

"Are they related?" she asked, studying him.

"C'mon, Ms. Reade, doesn't it strain credulity that there would be two unrelated murders back-to-back in a retirement village? What is this, Eighteenth Street?" he pleaded, referring to notorious gang territory in Los Angeles.

"You're right," she murmured, and it struck her again that she and Madelyn were the only dog owners in the village. But since that seemed to be an unrelated coincidence, she offered, "It must have to do with the fact that I talked to her the day of her death. The murderer must have observed that, and was afraid that she had told me something which might incriminate him."

"Then that would mean it's Theis, period," he observed. "You talked to her at the pond and a couple of hours later she was dead in the pond. He wouldn't have had time to leave the village to consult with anyone."

"No. But he could have called someone to report what he had seen. Someone was afraid of what Madelyn might have said to me—or what I might have overheard between her and Norbert," she mused.

Lott brightened. "Are we back to Norbert as a suspect? That would really make my day."

She thought about that, then shook her head. "It still makes no sense. Is he going to have me killed for hearing him complain that she changed her will? How many people knew he was unhappy about that? Didn't Norbert talk to her lawyer?"

"Yeah, and I understand Norbert promised him a lawsuit, which he delivered on," Lott admitted. "Okay, temporarily ruling out baby boy Norbert again, we have to remember that we know what you said and heard; Theis didn't. He could only report to his client that he saw you talk to Madelyn. So we have to find out what this client *thought* might have been said. It could have been about the faked furniture, the dog shows, a boyfriend in the village—"

"A boyfriend," she mused. "Someone who didn't like what was being said about him."

He watched her, and she murmured, "I think I need to go talk to Melinda again."

So Detective Lott rose to leave. But before departing, he reached into his pocket to hand her something. "I want you to start carrying this."

Wimsey regarded the can of mace. Deadpan, she asked, "Don't you trust me with a gun?" He shook his head and went out to his car.

She stowed the mace in her bedroom, then gave Cootie a recently purchased chew toy to placate her over being left behind again.

Putting her phone in her jacket pocket, Wimsey touched the Goodspeed still residing there—but she did not look at it yet; she went next door. Barely five seconds after she had rung the doorbell, the door was opened by Melinda, brimming with curiosity. "Well!

Wimsey. Did you have an exciting evening? Come in."

"Thank you." Wimsey smiled briefly, entering the living area to see Melinda's roommate painting her fingernails over a silver tray on the coffee table. "Hello, Tina-Marie! How are you? My, that's a lovely color," Wimsey said, regarding the bright pink fingernail polish. And it was—for a twenty-year-old. On bony, wrinkled hands, it looked like a sick joke.

Tina-Marie did not reply, of course. Melinda waved Wimsey to the couch and leaned over her silent roommate to tell her, "This lady wants your silver."

Wimsey's lips parted in mild shock, but Tina-Marie simply closed the bottle and set it on the tray before taking it all out of the room. Wimsey looked at Melinda, who said, "I'm sorry. I didn't want to disturb her with our conversation and that was just the easiest way to get her to leave. She won't hold any hard feelings toward you. She won't remember. Have a seat. Would you like something to drink?"

"No, thank you." Wimsey glanced around the white and chrome furniture—everything was white and chrome, and was obviously Tina-Marie's. As Melinda sat beside her, Wimsey asked, "Does she have Alzheimer's?"

Melinda shrugged. "It's dementia of some sort, but not quite like Alzheimer's. She doesn't wander off or go into rages. She's gentle as a lamb, just—not in the same universe. She's not been the same since her only son died. He committed suicide."

"Oh! I'm so sorry," Wimsey said.

"Yes. It's sad." Melinda settled on the couch and adjusted her glasses. "So who died on your deck? Was it another murder?"

"Oh, no, nothing like that." Wimsey laughed uneasily. "Do you know Wayne Theis, the handyman?"

"Sometimes works with Cliff?" Melinda asked, frowning.

"So I understand. I had never met him before. But apparently, he got drunk last night and went staggering around on the boardwalk. I saw someone outside and got frightened, so I called the police. The sheriff's department came out and found that he had fallen off the deck and drowned. Very tragic."

"How awful for you!" Melinda said, watching her.

"Not as awful as for him," Wimsey said. "Of course, I had no idea who it was they found out there, so Sandy came by this morning to tell me. I wanted to let you know, too, since I'm sure all the lights and sirens would have kept you up half the night."

"I appreciate it. Why were they all clustered around your back door?" Melinda asked.

"I broke it, slamming it!" Wimsey exclaimed, wondering how much she had seen.

"Oh, my," Melinda said. There was a moment of silence while Wimsey pondered how to redirect the conversation toward Madelyn's boyfriends. Then Melinda added, "It reminded me of the night they found Madelyn's body."

"Oh, yes, me too." Wimsey shuddered. "Which made me think . . . I've been by the chapel a few times, and I was wondering if they would have a memorial service for her."

"Her son's taking care of that. But it won't be here," Melinda pointed out.

"Yes, I'm sure he is, but . . . I was wondering about a village service for her, since she had been a resident for so long. Surely there are people here who are grieving for her."

Melinda raised an unplucked eyebrow in amusement. "Not really."

"No—love interests?" Wimsey asked delicately.

"Please," Melinda snorted. "The way she used men? Like she was thirty all over again, shopping for the next rich husband. Once they found out she was just interested in what they would do for her, they went on to someone else. Plenty of other women to choose from. Besides, the men are mostly after the younger women— Sandy and the girl who works at the coffee shop."

"Lauren?" Wimsey asked.

"Is that her name? Anyway, they could have the pick of any man in the village, if they wanted. No one got really worked up over Madelyn, except maybe your boyfriend."

Wimsey stared at her. "Excuse me?"

Melinda laughed, "You looked so shocked!"

"I have no idea who you're talking about," Wimsey assured her. She had almost said, *"I didn't know that Detective Lott had ever talked to her."*

"Why, your coffee-shop boyfriend, Chas," Melinda said teasingly. Wimsey's mouth hung open. "Why are you so surprised? You and Madelyn are two of a type, and that's Chas' type."

Wimsey was so flustered she could hardly form a sentence. "Madelyn and I are not at all alike." *She was at least ten years older than I am!*

"Oh, I've offended you. I'm sorry. I don't mean you're money-grubbing or fake. I mean you and she are both—oh, society ladies. There's this aura that rich people have—people who are used to the best hotels and restaurants and first-class travel. People who wear tailored clothes and have their hair done and get plastic surgery," Melinda said.

Wimsey closed her hands. "I have never had plastic surgery. If I had, I would look a lot better than this." That was the only attribute on Melinda's list that Wimsey could flat-out deny.

Melinda patted her visitor's stiff hands. "Oh, I know that! Once I got to talking to you, I knew you weren't really like that. But on first glance, you look to be the same type of person."

"But, the village is full of money. Who else but 'rich people' could afford to live here?" Wimsey argued. Even as she said it, she noted Melinda's bargain-store pants set. *Some* people here were wealthy, and some lived off others who were wealthy.

Melinda settled back on the couch, looking amused. "Oh, sure, most of the folks here have money; it's just that they *wear* it differently. After you're here a while, you'll see what I mean. A lot of 'em like to act like they're poor as church mice—like Guy Krenkel. He's worth millions, but you'd never know it because he's hawking that cheap furniture all the time, like the chair you bought from him. Well, Chas likes people who wear their money well—not showy, but not pretending to be poor. I guess they remind him of his glory days, or something. He was just gaga over Madelyn, but she treated him like the yard boy. So, after she died, he started going after you the same way."

Chas? Wimsey tried to evaluate this, but the only thing she could think was, *Since he gave me the boots, he knew that there was no corresponding man living with me. They sure didn't deter Wayne any.* "I see."

"I hope I haven't upset you," Melinda said, but to Wimsey it appeared that she was enjoying her guest's discomfort.

"Not at all. Well," Wimsey said, standing. "I'll let you know what else I hear about Mr. Theis, but it appears pretty clear what happened to him. Talk to you later."

She was only vaguely aware of Melinda's opening the front door for her to stagger down the sidewalk. Chas murdering Madelyn in a jealous rage? He could see the pond from the coffee-shop window; he could see when Madelyn's son left her alone at the pond. Then he would have called Theis and said—

Her phone bleated from her pocket. Glancing around the otherwise unoccupied sidewalk, she pulled it out to look at the Caller ID display. "Hello, Detective."

"Hello, Ms. Reade. The boys just searched Theis' apartment and found over ten thousand dollars in small bills hidden in the freezer. It was wrapped in butcher's paper, marked, 'deer meat.'"

"Hit money," she said.

"Sure looks like it," he admitted.

"Does it. . . . Is there any way to tell if it was all one payment, or two?" she asked.

"For two hits? I dunno. They're tracing the serial numbers now," he said. "Did you find out anything interesting from your neighbor?"

"Not really, no," she hedged. She was having too much difficulty imagining Chas a murderer. And what message would he have Theis delivering to her last night? *"Be nice to me, or else"*? "I'm . . . going to take Cootie for a walk, Detective."

"Fine. Ah, I'm thinking we should put a bodyguard on you."

Wimsey recoiled at the thought. "I'll let you know when I think it's necessary," she said, and closed the phone with finality.

"Ms. Reade?"

She jumped. "Oh! Cliff. I didn't see you." He was leaning out the cab window of his pickup, which he had pulled over to the curb.

"I'm sorry. I just wanted to let you know—the cops asked me about Theis this morning, and I was so—I couldn't believe the—that he—the—" He was apparently finding it impossible to express himself on this issue without profanity.

"That's all right, Cliff," she exhaled.

"Whatever I can do for you, let me know; there'll be

no charge. And if you're uncomfortable with me alone, I'll get Ms. Schirm or the maintenance supervisor to come, too," he said.

"No problem, Cliff. Excuse me." She turned up the walk to her front porch and unlocked the door.

As soon as she opened the door, she heard Cootie barking. And when she glanced up and saw the male figure at the back door, her heart constricted. But then she saw the utility coveralls he wore, and that he was in the process of removing the doors. So she hastened back to corral Cootie.

The stranger nodded to her through the gaping doorway. "Ms. Reade, I'm Hy Eckwert, the village's maintenance supervisor. We're going to get you a new set of doors up here right away."

She looked out to see the maintenance truck parked on the grass by the deck, and an assistant angling one door out of the bed. "Oh! Thank you."

"We'll be done in about thirty minutes, then we'll key your front door the same. How's that?" he asked, glancing back at his helper walking the door up the deck steps.

"That would be great. Let me get Cootie out of your way, and I'll be right back," she said.

"Yes, ma'am," he said, preoccupied with his assistant's progress.

Wimsey leashed Cootie to take her down the street toward the coffee shop on the far intersection of Shrewsbury Circle. A bodyguard? Was she still in danger? She tried to calm down and think.

Yes, it seemed likely. Until they could find out who solicited Theis, and why, she had to assume his death changed nothing.

Greg? The thought made her stop in her tracks. Cootie stopped to wait, and gradually Wimsey began to breathe and walk again.

No, she didn't see how it could be. If there was *any* connection between Madelyn and herself, then Greg was not involved. Neither Madelyn nor her late husband had anything to do with ShaftCom. Yes, she could see Greg out for revenge, if he guessed she was behind the new evidence. But in that case, someone else murdered Madelyn for an unrelated reason.

Then there was the lack of connection with either of them to Theis: aside from the fact that both Theis and the person who had ransacked her second bedroom smoked, there was no indication that person was, in fact, Theis.

At that point, Wimsey realized with some irritation that she was fingering the Goodspeed in her pocket. "It's not a talisman," she chided herself, removing her hand. And she went on to the coffee-shop window.

Chas wasn't working now; Lauren was. As usual, she had a cluster of male customers and no one to help her. Unwilling to burden her further, Wimsey started to turn away without ordering. But Lauren saw her and exclaimed, "Latte as usual, ma'am?"

Wimsey hesitated. "If you're not too busy."

"Nah. These gentlemen don't mind if I serve you first. Ladies first, right?" Lauren said cheerfully to her waiting crowd. They chivalrously waved and nodded consent while Lauren began mixing Wimsey's coffee with labored inefficiency and numerous extra steps.

She placed it on the counter and Wimsey paused again. "Something wrong?" Lauren asked expectantly. When Wimsey met her eyes, Lauren mouthed, *Three more minutes.*

Wimsey's mouth hung open, then she shut it and said, "I'm sorry; this coffee won't do at all. You forgot the whipped cream."

"Oh, I did!" Lauren exclaimed in feigned surprise. "I'm so sorry! Let me make that over for you." With that, she dumped the unsatisfactory coffee and began a new one with great care.

By the time she handed it to Wimsey, a male teenager in coffee-shop apron ambled out to begin taking orders from disappointed men. Lauren looked at the clock and said, "Shift's up! See you all later."

"Wait—" Wimsey began, holding out a bill.

Lauren glanced at her on her way to the back room. "It's on the house." When the young woman left, so did three quarters of the men.

Shaking her head, Wimsey repocketed the bill and started across the street with Cootie toward the pond. Then she heard, "Ma'am!" and turned.

Lauren had emerged from the back door of the coffee shop to catch up with her. "Thanks for playing along with me. I just had all of those old men I could stomach for the day."

"Why do you put up with them?" Wimsey asked.

"Oh, it's not that bad, and it will only be for another semester. With tips, I make enough to pay my way through community college," Lauren said.

"Very smart," Wimsey said, sipping her latte. "Then again, you could always have a boyfriend come pick you up from work. That should discourage some of the more obnoxious men."

"And cut into tips?" Lauren said dubiously. "I don't think so. Besides, I really don't want to date anyone right now. I've gone out with Cliff a couple times, but. . . ."

Lauren trailed off and Wimsey watched her. "What's wrong with Cliff?"

"Nothing, really." Lauren shrugged, looking around as if watching for someone. "He's nice and all, but, not smart with money. He gambles, and I don't want to get involved with somebody who's always asking me for money. I work too hard for what I earn." Wimsey opened her mouth but Lauren said, "There's my ride. Thanks again."

Wimsey watched her get into a car that had pulled up to the curb, driven by an older woman. When they drove off, she and Cootie resumed their walk to Whitehaven Path. "Cliff gambles," she murmured. "And Chas—"

Out of the blue, she remembered that Chas had owned a business in Dallas for many years. Before Greg had become CEO of ShaftCom, he was president of a company that brokered insurance for many manu-facturers in Dallas. Did he know Chas?

Since she couldn't cross-examine either Cliff or Chas right now, she still wanted to walk and clear her head. The day was overcast enough to discourage most walkers with the threat of another storm like last night's, so she and Cootie had the pond all to themselves today.

They walked clear to the desolate north side; Wimsey's eyes swept the gray lake, then she turned to sit on the bench facing the pond. She pulled the Goodspeed from her pocket and opened it at random to read: "Listen to this, and grasp it! It is not what goes into a man's mouth that pollutes him; it is what comes out of his mouth that pollutes a man. . . . Out of the heart come wicked designs, murder, adultery, immorality, stealing, false witness, impious speech. It is these things that pollute a man, but not eating with unwashed hands."

She thought about this, then skipped a few pages to read, "If your own hand or your own foot makes you fall, cut it off and throw it away. You might better enter upon life maimed or crippled than keep both hands and feet but be thrown into the everlasting fire. And if your own eye makes you fall, dig it out and throw it away. You might better enter upon life with only one eye than be thrown with both eyes into the fiery pit"—

"Has my Wimsey taken a fancy to being alone?"

She quickly looked up at Chas, smiling down at her from behind the bench.

Thirteen

Wimsey looked back at Chas curiously. "Have you ever read the Bible?"

"Sure, growing up," he said, easing to the bench beside her. "Not as much as I should lately, I'm sorry to say. Why?"

"I'm reading this passage that says if your hand or foot makes you fall, you should cut it off. Rather barbaric, isn't it?" she observed.

"Oh, an old Baptist preacher I once knew said that's a parable—something you don't take literally. It means that if there's something in your life that is dragging you down, you should get rid of it, no matter how necessary it seems to you," Chas said, looking over the pond.

"Ah," she said, enlightened.

"Money," he sighed.

"Pardon?" she asked.

"For most people, that's money. 'A root of all kinds of evil.' Most people think it's the most necessary thing in the world, so they do anything for it. Lie, steal, and kill." He looked sad.

"I see," she murmured, and waited.

Large drops began making rings in the pond. "Look, it's raining. Let me walk you home," he said, standing.

"I usually just cut through the field." She stood as well, taking up the slack in Cootie's leash.

"Fine. Let's hustle." Chas took her arm firmly to lead her somewhat against her wishes. "Oh, the field's all muddy," he said, so steered her toward the pebbled path along the shore.

"I can walk," she said, attempting to ease her arm out of his grasp. He was rather strong.

"I know you can," he chuckled without letting go.

They trotted toward her house a quarter-mile away. Wimsey was on his left, between him and the water. She glanced over the restless, wind-driven waves. No one else was in view. The rain began coming down harder. Cootie, disliking to get wet, strained at the leash.

Wimsey tossed it ahead of her. "Go, Cootie! Go on home!" The dog began running.

Chas glanced at her, blinking water out of his faded blue eyes. "What did you do that for?"

"She'll get home quicker, and I don't want her to get wet. She catches cold easily," Wimsey said with a slight heartache. She didn't want anything to happen to Cootie.

Chas' foot caught her heel, and Wimsey stumbled out of one shoe into the mud along the shore. A floating piece of hydrilla wrapped itself around her ankle. As she bent to remove it, she saw the shoe behind her and the water inches from her face. She smelled the odors of churned lake dredge strongly—could almost taste it.

"Oh, gosh, I'm sorry. Clumsy me," Chas said. He released her arm to retrieve her shoe and hand it to her.

Wimsey took it, removing the other shoe to carry them. "They're leather," she explained.

He grasped her arm again. "Well, hurry now, it's really starting to pour."

They started to run through the rain, and Wimsey saw Cliff's pickup sitting on St. Mary Mead Lane. He was watching them through the open driver's side window. Had Chas seen him watching? "Your dog's right by the back door," he noted.

"She does *not* like getting wet," Wimsey reiterated.

By this time they had made it to the boardwalk, and were shortly clambering up the steps to her back door, catching up to Cootie. The crime-scene tape was gone, but they were slowed by the need for care on the slippery steps.

Dripping, Chas and Wimsey stopped for breath under the shelter of the eaves while she looked at her new doors. She reached out tentatively to open them. Cootie darted inside to shake herself over the tile floor.

"Oh, gosh, Wimsey, lock your doors," Chas chided.

"I will from now on," she said. "Thank you for running me home. Don't get too wet."

"Too late," he grunted, hopping off the deck to run toward the street. The rain was now coming down in sheets.

Wimsey tiptoed inside, trying not to drip too much. She turned to lock the doors, and listened in satisfaction to the movement of the deadbolt—there was no doubt about *these* doors being locked. Then she stripped off her sodden socks and grabbed a towel from atop the dryer to wrap around herself.

Entering the living area, she spotted the pair of identical keys on her glass table. Taking them to the front door (which was also unlocked) she tried both keys to make sure they worked. She repeated this exercise at the back doors, then unleashed Cootie and performed her standard house check. Everything looked fine.

So Wimsey changed clothes, happy to find that her Goodspeed and phone had been protected enough in the pocket to not get wet. She poured dinner in Cootie's bowl and put stew in the microwave for herself. While it heated, she fetched her sketch book and sat at the little tea table next to the French doors. With the rain pelting the deck outside, she sharpened a pencil and set it to the page. But she wasn't drawing as much as diagramming.

She titled it, "Connections." Then she wrote in the center, "Madelyn." Close by she wrote, "Theis," and drew a line between them. On the line she wrote the most obvious connection between them: "village." Below the line, in parentheses, she noted the less obvious connection: "murder?" Without hard evidence, she was not convinced Theis murdered Madelyn.

She drew another line from "Madelyn" to "Chas." On the line she wrote, again, "village." Below it she wrote, "boyfriend?" She drew a third line from "Madelyn" to "me." On the line she wrote, "village"; below it she wrote, "dog owners." This trivial connection still bothered her; she did not know why.

Then she drew a long, arching line from "me" to "Theis," and over this line she wrote, "attempted murder." This was a certainty: he had been intent on doing her harm. She drew another line from "me" to "intruder." Above it she wrote "ShaftCom?" and below it wrote, "Madelyn?"—because she did not know for sure what he had been looking for in the second bedroom. Nor did she clutter her diagram linking the intruder to Theis—again, there was no evidence to do so.

Another line went from "me" to "Greg," and below that went, "marriage/ShaftCom." Off the diagram, she listed those in the village who had a tenuous connection with both her and Madelyn. Then she sat back and looked at the results in dissatisfaction:

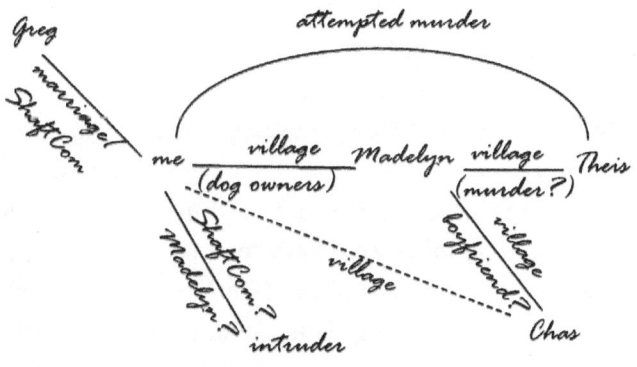

"There's a problem with my viewpoint. I've made this look more about me than Madelyn," she muttered. So she attempted to rectify this flaw by listing those outside the village who stood to gain something from Madelyn's death:

children: Trentham
Michelina
Norbert
Dandie Dinmont Assoc.
antiques dealers???

Tapping this list with her pencil, she mused, "If any of these people sent Theis after me, it would have to be because of my helping with the investigation. They would only risk coming after me if they believed I was about to expose them."

The microwave timer dinged, so Wimsey got up to remove her bowl of stew and bring it back to the table. She stirred it absently for a moment, studying her diagram, then stopped and said, "All that is absurd. No one in his right mind would assume I could do more, or knew more, than the police. If any of these people outside the village wanted the investigation stopped—and were clever enough to hide their tracks so far—they would pressure the department to drop it. So far, the detective tells me that the pressure has been entirely to get it solved." So she crossed out her list of non-villagers.

Frustrated, she pushed the diagram aside to eat her stew while Cootie sat at her feet, begging for a bite.

Hearing her phone bleat from the bedroom (and getting tired of that irritating bleat) Wimsey put the bowl on the floor for Cootie and hastened back to answer it. She barely looked at the display before putting the phone to her ear. "Yes, Detective?"

"How do you *know* these things?" he said in aggravation.

"Detective, I have Caller ID on my phone, just like you do," she said, equally aggravated.

"No, I mean, you answered as if you knew I was going to tell you something," he said.

"Why would you call me if you weren't going to tell me something?" she returned.

"No, you—never mind. Okay, do you remember Madelyn wearing a brooch when you talked to her?" he asked.

She closed her eyes momentarily to think, then said, "No, not specifically. But she could have been, as she was wearing a sweater."

"Right. Well, the boys found a brooch in Theis' apartment that Norbert identified as hers," Lott said.

"A—souvenir?" she asked.

"Yep. And it's plastic," he added with a snort.

"Did they find any other trinkets that might have come from other residents' homes?" she asked. In response to his groan, she said, "I agree that the brooch ties him to her murder *unless* you find more 'souvenirs.' He was a village handyman; he would have been in and out of many of their homes, and some of them would be very easy to steal from."

"I'll check," he conceded. "But they also located his vehicle, a pickup. And guessed what he had in the back?"

"Tools belonging to the village?" she said.

"Yep," he said almost in vindication.

"I bet if we check Cliff's truck, or that of the maintenance supervisor, we'll find the same," she observed.

"Well then, if we *don't* find property stolen from other residents in his apartment, would you concede that the weight of the evidence against him is significant?" Lott demanded.

"Yes," she said.

"Good," he grunted, and clicked off.

With this new information, Wimsey returned to her chart to circle "murder" on the line between "Madelyn" and "Theis." But she added a question mark above Theis' name: Who was behind him?

Wimsey mulled over the faceless shadow all evening; when she went to bed, she woke frequently from troubled dreams in which showers of cheap costume jewelry were raining down upon her. She held out her hands to sift the flow, because every now and then a genuine diamond or gold piece appeared among the fakes. But they always slipped through her fingers with the rest.

The next day, Saturday, Wimsey leashed up Cootie for a late-morning walk. The rain had cleared, leaving gentle fall sunshine on golden leaves and green water. As usual, Wimsey turned toward Shrewsbury Circle, then paused. She really needed to talk to Mrs. Rad about Theis. So she changed course to head for her house instead. Arriving on the porch, Cootie sat to wait, knowing that she would not be allowed inside.

Wimsey rang the doorbell and waited. Minutes later, she heard the familiar shuffling, then the door cracked open. Wimsey smiled tentatively at the faded eyes behind the thick glasses. "Good morning, Mrs. Rad. I felt I should tell you what happened Thursday night."

"It's about time," the woman sniffed, backing up to open the door.

Looping the leash on the finial, Wimsey said, "I'm sorry. There was so much follow-up with the police, and all. . . ." She entered and sat on the couch, contemplating exactly what to say. She was not going to lie to Mrs. Rad, but she had made a firm deal with Sandy.

When Mrs. Rad lowered herself to the couch, Wimsey asked, "Do you know Wayne Theis?"

Mrs. Rad narrowed her eyes in disdain. "A bad one. I never let him in my house."

"He drowned off my slip Thursday night. The police believe he was drunk and fell into the water," Wimsey said.

Mrs. Rad shifted, eyeing her. "So he was the one I saw trying to get into your house."

Wimsey raised her shoulders. "Possibly. I don't know. But . . . they also believe he killed Madelyn."

"Ah ha," Mrs. Rad said in comprehension. "You look alike."

"Pardon?" Wimsey said, taken aback. *That's what*

Melinda said. That's what Detective Lott said.

"You and she look alike. The pervert. He went after Madelyn, and was going after you," Mrs. Rad said.

"I . . . don't think it was a sexual crime, Mrs. Rad," Wimsey said uncomfortably.

"No? Maybe not. Then he was working for somebody. A lot of people here hated Madelyn. You show up here, you look like her—a lot of people would get resentful toward you. The Schirm woman wanted to kill her."

"Sandy?" Wimsey said, incredulous. "Why on earth?"

"Madelyn complained about her to the owners, almost cost her her job, and she's got her sights set on somebody here with money. If *I* heard this, then surely Melinda told you about it, too."

"Mrs. Rad, I can't imagine—"

"How can you find out who killed Madelyn without any imagination?" Mrs. Rad said derisively. "You can't imagine anybody being jealous enough of her to pay this lowlife Theis to kill her? And this somebody being jealous enough of a young newcomer—you—to have him do it again? You can't imagine what people will do with their money when they don't want to give it away?"

Wimsey absorbed the bombshell while Mrs. Rad eyed her in superiority. *Why have I been assuming that Theis' client is a man?* Blinking rapidly, Wimsey looked around the room. "How are your birds?" she asked.

"I'm almost out of bread crumbs," Mrs. Rad observed.

Wimsey pursed her lips. "I was just heading out that way. Let me pick them up for you."

"All right," Mrs. Rad agreed.

Still dazed, Wimsey retrieved Cootie from the porch and began walking toward Shrewsbury Circle as she had originally planned. She hardly saw anything in front of her for thinking, *Jealousy is the oldest motivation for murder there is. Why did I rule out any women?*

"Ms. Reade? Hello?"

She started, looking at Cliff inching along the street beside her in his pickup. "Oh! Hello, Cliff. I'm sorry; I was in a cloud."

"Yeah. Are you okay?" He was peering at her across the seat through the open passenger window, remembering to glance at the street in front of him now and then.

"Yes, I'm fine. Are you keeping an eye on me?" she asked.

"I'm trying to," he admitted. "I just feel kinda responsible—"

"No, you shouldn't," she said quickly. "Cootie!" The dog had stopped so suddenly to nose in the grass that Wimsey almost stumbled over her.

Cliff chuckled, craning his neck to look down at her. "Cute dog. What kind is it?"

"Oh, she's just a mongrel," Wimsey said fondly.

"Yeah. The pound dogs are the best," he said.

"I think so," she said.

As they came upon the first intersection of St. Mary Mead Lane and Shrewsbury Circle, Cliff said, "Gotta stop by the ATM. You take care now, Ms. Reade."

"Sure." She waved as he turned his truck into the drive-through, but she wasn't watching. Her attention had been drawn to Doug and Amelie Liebert walking Whitehaven Path, as usual. Passing another walker, a woman, Doug reached out for a quick pinch, as usual. And Wimsey saw something significant:

The woman glanced back at Doug. Wimsey was not close enough to see her expression, but her body language did not suggest anger or surprise—Wimsey could almost envision her winking.

Moreover, Amelie saw. She saw the pinch and the woman's response, but turned her head in deliberate disregard. And the happy couple kept walking. Wimsey kept going toward the second intersection of Shrewsbury Circle, thinking hard. Was Amelie that spineless? Or did she exact revenge in a different way?

They were the ones to find Madelyn's body, Wimsey recalled. Had Madelyn met them walking around the pond? Had Doug pinched her, and . . . ?

Wimsey shook her head impatiently—there was still Reggie drowned with a wrench, and she had never seen either Liebert walking with heavy plumbing tools!

Doug's sudden movement thirty feet away caught her eye, and she watched with shattered incredulity as he bent to pick up a large pipe wrench from the grass beside the path. He resumed walking toward her, swinging it angrily. "What are you doing with that?" Wimsey shrieked.

He shook it at her. "This is the second tool I've

found just lying on the ground! They're a hazard and management is going to hear about it!"

She held her breath while he stormed down the street ahead of her. He bypassed the maintenance office, headed for the manager's office. Amelie followed without acknowledging her presence.

Numbly, Wimsey continued walking a safe distance behind them. All of her neat little diagrams and scenarios began falling apart in front of her face. She didn't know what to think anymore.

Sandy approached driving a golf cart; Doug waved her down to begin shaking the wrench at her. Guy Krenkel was in the cart with her, and watched curiously from the passenger seat.

Sandy took the wrench and tossed it in the back of the cart, then proceeded down St. Mary Mead Lane, waving to Wimsey as she passed. *Sandy? No.* Wimsey rejected Mrs. Rad's suggestion. But where was Sandy carting Guy? Was she trying to pacify a constant complainer like Madelyn, or did the fact of Guy's wealth have anything to do with such preferential treatment? And what would she do about a tenant as troublesome as Wimsey?

When Guy turned in the seat to stare back at Wimsey, she suddenly thought, *What if I was wrong, and the deputy had described "Jay" accurately?—that it had been Wayne Theis sitting with Guy in his apartment? What if Guy held a grudge against Madelyn, and I came around asking too many questions?* Mrs. Rad's observation came back to taunt her: *"You can't imagine what people will do with their money when they don't want to give it away?"*

She looked ahead at the coffee shop and Cootie led in that direction as if it was their destination. So Wimsey stopped at the window, and Chas came over. "Ah, there you are!" he said with a big smile. "I was wondering when you'd be by. Latte as usual?"

She blinked. "No. Today I think I'd like a Pumpkin Spice Frappuccino."

He stared at her, then laughed, "Getting into the spirit of the season! Except, it's a cold drink. Did you know that a frappuccino is blended with ice?"

"Yes. That's what I want," Wimsey said.

"Well, I haven't made too many of those, but I sure will try. You'll just have to be patient with me," he said, winking.

"All right." She waited attentively, watching him handle little paper cups with big hands, mulling over the recipe book, adding spices to the coffee mix that went with ice into the blender.

He grew a little self-conscious at being watched, but finally handed her the whipped-cream-topped coffee. "There you go. In celebration of your spirit of adventure, that one's on the house."

"Don't be absurd," she said, digging in her pocket.

"Wimsey," he said, and she glanced up, counting out change. "Could I see you more often?"

She produced two ones and a fistful of change, all of which she laid on the counter. "I don't know if I could afford it, Chas."

"You know what I mean," he said, ignoring the money. "I just would like to spend more time with you. There are other things to do here besides play bingo— they have live concerts in the bingo hall at least once a month. But, gosh, I even liked running you home in the rain. Can we step out an evening or two? Have a private moment?"

She opened her mouth but nothing came out. He interjected, "What kind of gossip have you been hearing about me?"

"Gossip?" she repeated.

"Some of those old hens are saying I'm a player, aren't they? Sometimes I'd just like to—" He caught himself at the vehemence. "I admit I like stepping out with the ladies, but I'm a gentleman, Wimsey."

She nodded toward another customer who had just entered the shop. "I know you are, Chas. I'll think about it. Thanks." She lifted the cup to him, leaving the bills flapping under the change on the window counter. He turned in disgruntlement to the newcomer.

She walked quickly across the street to the deli shop. With the frappuccino in one hand, she knocked on the glass door with the hand that held the leash. "Hello? Do you have bread crumbs for Mrs. Rad? I've got my dog and can't come in."

The counter worker waved, bringing out the large plastic bag of old bread. "You've got a handful already, don't you, dear?" She was a comfortable, cheerful fiftyish.

"Yes, but I'll make room. Thanks." Wimsey tucked

the bag underarm and began retreating down Shrewsbury Circle. Cootie indicated her desire to go down Whitehaven Path, but Wimsey redirected her back to the street. "We'll go ahead and take Mrs. Rad her bread crumbs, and then we'll walk some more."

She looked to her left, down the path to the pond, a serene, innocuous death trap. Tools lying around? "Don't pull so, Cootie." She looked back over the rest of the village, with its lamp posts and clean gutters. "Cootie! Stay with me." A player? She focused down the street toward Mrs. Rad's house. Murderous jealousy?

All the while Wimsey's mind was working, toiling, arranging and rearranging the bits and pieces of her mental diagram, everything she knew, everything that she had heard—

A comic *toot-toot* startled her, and she stumbled out of the way of another golf cart coming up behind her, this one manned by a little old lady hunched over the wheel. "Oh! Rude drivers!" Wimsey exclaimed.

But then she saw that, in her preoccupation, she had wandered down the wheelchair incline into the street, and Cootie had been pulling her back toward the sidewalk.

"Oh! Sweet ol' Cootie! You were watching out for me—" Wimsey's hands went limp, dropping the bag of bread crumbs and the frappuccino. With sightless eyes she watched the creamy orange drink spread over the sidewalk and drip into the gutter. All at once, she made the connection. She knew who killed Madelyn. She knew who was trying to kill her. And she knew why.

Fourteen

Still dazed, Wimsey watched the puddle of frappuccino spread, but when Cootie began licking it up, she came out of her haze. She picked up the empty cup and the bag of bread crumbs. Detouring cautiously across the street, she tossed the cup into a trash barrel before proceeding to Mrs. Rad's house. She delivered the bag of old bread with a smile, then returned home to sit and think.

The phone in her pocket bleated. The sound was beginning to grate on her so much that she contemplated finding out how to change it. Wimsey looked at the display, then answered, "Hello, Tara."

"Hi, Mom. I'm sorry I haven't called in a few days. Is everything okay?"

"Yes, Tara, everything's fine. Cootie and I have been greatly enjoying the lake and weather. I never knew fall could be so beautiful," Wimsey said.

"Yeah, it is. Except for Halloween. Oh, we're having such fights with Halle about Halloween—she's heard about the other kids' trick-or-treating, so she wants to go. And then she saw a commercial for a horror movie and it just gave her nightmares. I can hardly turn on the TV anymore," Tara vented.

"Halloween," Wimsey murmured. She looked to the back deck where Chas' boots still resided.

"I'm sorry; I'm rambling. Well—have you heard anything more about Daddy?"

Wimsey's attention snapped back to the conversation. "No, dear. I figured if there were any further developments worth knowing, you'd tell me. Tara, have you . . . talked to anyone here?"

"Talked to anyone there?" Tara asked blankly.

"Yes. Have you talked to anyone here in the village about me?" Wimsey asked.

"No!" Tara said in reproach. "I respect your privacy. Why do you ask?"

"It's nothing. Just a misunderstanding."

"Okay, well—" Wimsey heard the click of Tara's call waiting. "Oh, Mom, that's Randy. I'll call later."

"Okay, honey. Bye." Wimsey sat looking at her phone, then keyed in the village office number and asked to speak to the maintenance supervisor. The receptionist gave her his cell number, which Wimsey entered in her phone list and dialed.

He answered, "Eckwert."

"Mr. Eckwert, this is Wimsey Reade. I just got home and found beautiful new doors waiting for me! I wanted to thank you for getting them up so quickly."

"Oh, you're welcome, ma'am. I'm sorry for the inconvenience."

"No trouble at all. I did see something strange that I wanted to ask you about, however. Someone or other keeps finding village tools laying around, and—"

"Don't that beat all?" he exclaimed. "We did an inventory and found so many missing that we notified the techs to turn in what they had. But do they get turned in? No, they get tossed on the ground. I'm gonna fire whoever's doing that."

"Well, that's certainly understandable. Anyway, thank you again for my new doors. Have a good day."

"You, too, ma'am."

Wimsey put the phone on the glass table and sat back. Cootie jumped up to lay her chin on her mistress' leg. Scratching the dog's ear, Wimsey murmured, "That settles it. There's no question about it now, except . . . what to do."

Call the detective and tell him what she had deduced? Wimsey thought about this. She trusted Detective Lott. She even liked him, somewhat. But her knowledge did not constitute proof—that would have to come with the next attempt on her life, which was inevitable. With the murderer's original tool—Theis— put out of play, another was required to take his place, and Wimsey knew who that must be.

So if she told the detective, he would "put someone" on her, who may or may not protect her while possibly uncovering the link between the tool and the solicitor behind the scenes. Calling anyone to help her with this situation would effectively take it out of her control.

And that was her trump card right now: she was in

control. Almost certainly, neither the solicitor in the background nor the tool knew that she was on to them. She wished to retain that advantage, and play it at just the right time.

Once again, she looked out to the deck, and Chas' boots. "Halloween is five days away," she murmured. That was the perfect time for Theis' replacement to strike, and for her to play her trump. All she had to do was plan it. . . .

The first thing she had to do was insure that the tool did not make the next attempt on her life before she was ready. She considered going back to stay with Tara for a few days—then rejected the idea. The tool was in the village, and she must keep abreast of village life to plan an effective trap.

Wimsey took one new door key out of her pocket and weighed it in her hand, glancing at the back French doors. Almost anyone could have a copy of this key by now, even if the maintenance supervisor had not left them sitting out in an unlocked house. Maintenance had copies of all the residents' keys—probably on a pegboard in the break room. So the first thing Wimsey decided to do was secure her quarters.

Leaving Cootie with a chew toy, Wimsey took her bike to the hardware store on Shrewsbury Circle. She entered with the intention of buying door bolts, but then stopped and stared at their huge Halloween aisle.

"Good afternoon, ma'am. Going to decorate for Halloween?" a friendly clerk asked. He was a young man in a work apron whose name tag read, "Carlos."

"I might," she said. "I'm kind of surprised to see such a big Halloween display in a village shop. Do you sell much of it?"

"Oh, you wouldn't believe!" Carlos laughed. "The old folks love to play dress-up! [*I'm not an old folk?* she wondered.] We don't have much call for the 'gross old man' masks, but all the other costumes are big sellers. Our biggest sellers for the women are the French maid, the pussycat, and the sexy witch. For the men it's the pirate and the Phantom of the Opera."

"How adolescent!" she laughed, looking through the rack of costumes. Her eye landed on a row of life-sized mannequins made of unbleached cotton muslin and stuffed with pellets to give them approximately human shape. They were propped up in a sitting position on a low shelf, some with legs crossed jauntily, some with arms akimbo. The head, torso, arms and legs were realistically proportioned, though without fingers or facial features. Wimsey reached out to reposition one dummy's hand, supported by a simple wire skeleton. "Are these for dressing up?"

"Sure are. Look." He took out a Phantom of the Opera head mask, which he pulled down over one mannequin's head. Then he put white gloves on its stumpy hands, a cape over its shoulders, and repositioned the dummy to sit upright—suddenly there was the Phantom killing time in a hardware store, awaiting the next performance. "You just dress it in the costume of your choice and set it on your porch for all the little buggers who want to come steal your candy."

Wimsey stared at it, her mind working. "I like it."

"Oh, and look at this." Carlos went to another shelf for a small black device into which he inserted a battery, then placed out of sight under the dummy's hand.

"Back up and walk toward it," he instructed. When Wimsey did, the device emitted a loud, creepy chuckle. "Motion-detector sound effects."

"That will work. I want two mannequins—" She started to pick one up, then dropped it. "Oh, dear. It's too heavy for my bike. Can you deliver them?"

"I sure can, but it'll have to wait till we close at six. Is that all right?" he asked.

"Yes. I want two dummies and one sound device."

"Just one?" he asked.

She said, "Yes. But I also need two costumes. . . ."

After looking through the selections, she ruled out costumes for the mannequins—they did not cover enough of the muslin. Instead, she chose two head masks: a creepy smiling face and a funny troll's face with a big nose. The masks would cover a person's whole head and neck, down to the collarbones.

In addition to the mannequins, the masks, and the sound effects box, she selected a silver wig and a black widow costume: a lacy black dress with a red hourglass on the back. It had long sleeves and a dramatic collar that extended high up the neck in back and tapered down to a plunging front neckline. She made sure Carlos had her address, and he promised the delivery of the mannequins shortly after six o'clock.

Following that spending spree, she remembered to

buy two heavy-duty barrel bolts. She loaded everything on her bike except the dummies. Then, with her plan coalescing in her mind, she stopped at the gift shop to buy Halloween decorations and the requisite trick-or-treat placard.

As the details of her plan fell into place, she went to the deli to arrange catering for a party at her house on Halloween. Following that, she went to the grocery store to buy Halloween candy and all the alcoholic drinks her overstuffed bike basket could accommodate.

Finally she pulled up to the window of the coffee shop. Chas looked over. "Wimsey! What'll you have?"

"Nothing," she said. "I wanted to invite you to my Halloween party at six Thursday night. Bring anybody at all—the more the merrier—and come in costume."

"Okay," he said, looking at her alcohol-laden basket dubiously. "Sounds fun."

"Good! See you then." She pushed off on her wobbling bike and laughed all the way home.

Once inside, she took the time only to put the alcohol in the refrigerator before grabbing her wallet to go next door. She rang the doorbell and impatiently waited till Melinda opened it curiously. "Hello."

"Hi, Melinda! Do you still have any of the men's clothes you were selling at the garage sale? I need to outfit two dummies," Wimsey said.

"What? Yes, come in. You need to what?" Melinda asked, stepping back from the door.

"Thank you. Oh, I'm having a little Halloween party Thursday night at six, with drinks and hors d'oeuvres. I want you and Tina-Marie to come," Wimsey said.

"All right. Did you get permission from the office? Parties with alcohol require notice," Melinda said.

"Well, we'll just be real quiet and not disturb anybody." Wimsey put a finger to her lips with a conspiratorial wink. "I got some fun ideas at the hardware store. I bought two dummies, but none of the costumes fit, so I just bought masks. I still need men's clothes to dress them, though. Can I see what you have?"

"Sure. I'll bring them out," Melinda said, sounding a little disoriented. She disappeared down the hall and returned a few minutes later dragging two large garbage bags. "I was going to throw them out."

"Good thing you didn't!" Wimsey said, opening one bag. "Where is Tina-Marie?"

"Sleeping," Melinda replied. "She sleeps a lot."

"I see." Wimsey paused, then began hauling out articles of clothing. "Okay, the jeans are good. Oh, good! Two pairs. I'll start with those."

"They might not fit," Melinda fussed.

"It's better if they don't. I don't want my dummies looking too neat," Wimsey said. "Oh, red suspenders! Those are good. And the belt. Oh, what a shirt!" She shook out a long-sleeved shirt printed with leaping bass. "That will do nicely. And this red checked shirt. That's really rather nice. A bandanna! Good. And a fishing hat! Oh, I'm loving this. Let's see what's in the other bag."

She reached over to open that one. "What—waders! Oh, this is too good." She continued digging through the clothing, but by now found only more of the same.

Wimsey paused over her selections. "All this is great, but I really need gloves, too."

Melinda offered, "I have some gardening gloves."

Wimsey accepted, "Those would work fine!"

So Melinda went to her laundry room to search around a moment, then returned with a pair of rarely used gloves. Wimsey appropriated them. "Okay, this will work fine. Now, what do I owe you for these things?" She stood over a pile consisting of the two pairs of jeans, two shirts, waders, hat, bandanna, belt, suspenders and gloves.

Melinda thought it over. "Fifty bucks," she decided.

Wimsey was a little shocked at the price, given that Melinda was about to throw the clothes away, but quickly wrote out a check to her. "There! Now, you and Tina-Marie be sure to come to my Halloween party. Wear a costume, if you like, but you don't have to. It starts at six."

"We'll come," Melinda said, holding the check.

"Great. Watch my front porch," Wimsey said, raking up her purchases. Melinda gave her a garbage bag to carry them in, and Wimsey went home with her booty.

Cootie greeted her without reproach to investigate all the interesting items she had brought home. Wimsey paused to eat a bowl of noodles, then set to work.

First thing, she retrieved her hardware purchases and her tool box. She installed one sliding bolt across the bottom of the French doors, and another in place of the flimsy chain lock on the front door. She tested the bolts to make sure they slid easily, then sat to wait impatiently for her dummies to be delivered. While waiting, she pulled out her sketchbook.

Flipping it open, she briefly regarded her murder-suspect diagram. "Was I ever dense," she muttered, ripping it out and wadding it up. She stuffed it into the kitchen trash can, then sat to plan her party. "This is going to be so much fun," she mused. Then, with a troubled sigh, she looked at her panting companion. "Normally, you'd love a party. But I can't risk it."

She fetched Cootie's leash and hooked her up. "Let's go for a walk, Cootie." The dog agreeably trotted down the front walk and turned west by habit, toward the pond. But Wimsey turned her back east.

They passed Melinda and Tina-Marie's house, then went up the front walk to Mrs. Rad's door. Wimsey rang the doorbell and waited. Sooner than expected, the door opened, and the occupant blinked out at her. "Good afternoon, Mrs. Rad. May I bring my dog in?"

"If you must," Mrs. Rad sniffed. *That's a good sign*, Wimsey thought. She led Cootie in and unhooked the leash. Cootie sniffed around the strange house.

Her owner turned to Mrs. Rad. "I'm having a party on Halloween to try to flush out Madelyn's murderer."

The other eyed her, uttering, "I thought that was the handyman. Theis."

"Wayne Theis was the tool—the hit man hired by the murderer. I think I know who that is. I'm going to try to find out Thursday."

Mrs. Rad shuffled on her cane to sit on the couch. "Who do you think it is?"

Wimsey hesitated, sitting beside her. "In case I'm wrong, I'd rather not say. Thursday should tell me one way or another."

"What do you want of me?" Mrs. Rad asked.

"I would like to leave Cootie here with you Thursday night. If all goes well, I will come get her no later than Friday morning. She's completely house-broken, and should only need to go out once before you go to bed. I will bring a bowl of her dog food, and her water dish, of course." Casually, Wimsey added, "She will bark at anyone who comes near the house."

Mrs. Rad shifted to look at the dog sniffing the bag of crumbs by the back door. Deliberately, she turned back around and said, "When you do come get her, you have to tell me everything."

Wimsey smiled. "It's a deal. Thank you." She reached over to grasp a gnarly hand, and Mrs. Rad squeezed her fingers.

While walking Cootie home, Wimsey saw the golf cart pull up in front of her house, and she laughed, breaking into a trot. Sitting primly in the back seat were her two mannequins. She hurried up to meet Carlos as he set the brake and climbed out. "Surely it's not six o'clock!" she said.

"No, ma'am, just half past four. But the manager came in and told me to go ahead and deliver 'em," he said, taking one under each arm.

"Great!" Wimsey hurried ahead of him to open the door, which she had left unlocked. She paused for a moment to unleash Cootie and let her run inside, watching her. Cootie went straight for her water dish, then the couch: no one else had been here.

Carlos asked, "Where do you want them, ma'am?"

"They'll be quite comfortable on the couch," Wimsey said with a nod. While he brought them in for Cootie to sniff, Wimsey went to her purse and pulled out a ten-dollar-bill. He set the dummies on the couch, pausing to cross the legs of one, and she pressed the bill in his hand. "Thank you."

He accepted the tip. "Thank *you*, ma'am. Have a good evening."

"I will." Wimsey let him out, bolting the door behind him just for the satisfaction of it. Then, with relish, she pulled out her clothing purchases and began to dress the mannequins.

The troll, she decided, would go on the front porch. The troll mask was not particularly frightening, just funny-looking, with a broad nose, heavy brow, and beady eyes under a shock of spiky black hair. So she put the bass-print shirt on one mannequin, following that with a pair of jeans, the suspenders, and the waders. (The clothes were about three sizes too big, which gave the dummy the slovenly look she required.) She pulled the troll mask down over the head, then placed the fishing hat atop it and regarded the result with pride. "You look adorable, Arnold," she christened him.

She brought an old wicker chair out of the second bedroom to put on the porch, then sat Arnold in this place of honor. She raised his fingerless hand in a friendly salute to the street, and positioned his waders in a nice masculine sprawl. Then she retrieved the motion-detector sound effects box, which she hid various places around him until finding the best spot for it to produce the sound at the right distance.

"What's this?" At the call, Wimsey looked back to the street, where Cliff sat in his pickup.

"Come here!" she replied.

Obediently, he hopped out of his truck and trotted up the walk. When he was about five feet from the porch, Arnold screeched, "EE HEE HEE HEYAH!"

Cliff stopped dead, then relaxed at Wimsey's laughing, "Isn't it great? I got it at the hardware store. I'm going to put another dummy on the back deck."

"Yeah, that's pretty good," Cliff wryly agreed.

"Listen, I'm having a Halloween party Thursday, starting at six. I want you to come. Bring anybody you want, but don't tell Sandy because I've got alcohol but I didn't get a 'permit,'" she said, enclosing the word in air quotes. "I sure don't want to rile her, or anything," Wimsey added mischievously.

"Sure," he said, grinning. "I'd be happy to come."

"Great. I've got lots of decorating to do. See you then." Wimsey turned to go inside and Cliff went back down the walk. Once again Arnold chortled, "EE HEE HEE HEYAH!" Cliff started, then shook his head and kept walking to his truck.

Wimsey sat to dress the other dummy in jeans, checked shirt, bandanna, and gloves. She paused over this mask, which was her favorite. The smiling, asexual face was not mutilated, grotesque, or even old, just—

unexpectedly sinister. The way the corners of the mouth turned up and the eyebrows turned down suggested dark plots and torture devices. And this one had long, flowing white hair, almost angelic in appearance, too pretty to be covered with a hat.

Wimsey placed the mask on the mannequin, which seemed to bring it to life. The two sat smiling at each other, and Wimsey murmured, "Let's do this, Camilla."

She pulled the Victorian gentleman's chair to sit right outside the French doors, under the protection of the eaves, and sat Camilla in the leather seat. She put Chas' boots on the feet, then experimented with various positions for it. Finally she settled on a rather superior attitude of arms flat on the chair arms and legs crossed. That done, she went inside to call Guy and invite him and his nephew Jay to her party.

Over the next several days, Wimsey invited everyone she met to come to her party. She made several trips around the pond in order to catch Doug and Amelie out walking, and invited them. She stopped strangers on the street to invite them, pointing out her house.

At one point—Tuesday, the 29th—she considered inviting Detective Lott. Then she decided against it. Not only would a cop spook her quarry, but Lott might get wind that she was up to something and interfere. So as long as he didn't call, she didn't call. But she decided to help him in advance with follow-up, and began a list of names, some with addresses or phone numbers that she could recall, but most without. And when she wasn't adding to it, she kept this list carefully hidden.

Every night, she bolted her front and back doors, and every time she returned after being out, she paused to see if Cootie reacted to foreign smells in the house. Every day that passed without incident gave her hope that the tool was waiting for Halloween, when she would have her home open and vulnerable.

She checked with the deli to make sure her hors d'oeuvres were on order for the 31st—carnitas, liver pâté, stuffed shrimp, and a fresh fruit platter to serve fifty, though she had no idea how many guests would come. As a bonus, the deli threw in orange party punch, complete with serving bowl, ladle and cups. The punch set would be picked up the following day, along with the table she was renting. She made another trip to the gift shop for decorated plasticware and napkins, and another trip to the grocery store for more alcohol.

During the week, she decorated her living area, kitchen, and front porch with her gift-shop decorations, and hung the treat-or-treating placard from Arnold's upraised hand. On the placard she had written, "Help yourself! Honor system—one each!"

She also found time to sit down with the Goodspeed once or twice. She knew that if she wanted to glean anything really helpful from it, she needed to pick a starting point and read straight through. But she couldn't help flipping open at random to read, because she always seemed to land on something that pierced her.

Wednesday she did this—sat on the couch with Cootie beside her, picked up the nondescript little book and read: "For we bring nothing into the world, and we can take nothing out of it. If we have food and clothing we will be satisfied. But men who want to get rich fall into temptations and snares and many foolish, harmful cravings, that plunge people into destruction and ruin."

She mulled over this passage for a long time, thinking about her previous life. Wealth was an insidious snare, in that she hadn't considered herself preoccupied with money. But now she realized how easy it was to get used to being *comfortable*—so comfortable that she hadn't noticed she was slowly being suffocated to death.

Thursday morning, Wimsey removed the sliding bolt from the back doors—but not the front. Then around noon, it suddenly dawned on her to try on her black widow's costume. So she did, turning this way and that in front of the mirror to study herself. This proved discouraging because she used to look fabulous in black. Now it made her look hard and old, despite the nice contrast of her silver hair.

"I'll need to take this in a little," she mused, gathering loose fabric at her sides. She studied the lines in her face and the bags under her eyes. "And buy makeup," she conceded.

Then she looked down at her legs—"and dark hose." She went foraging in her closet for black shoes, fortunately finding a pair of pumps that would work not splendidly, but well enough.

So she made another trip to the grocery store for makeup and hosiery. She found cheap mascara, foundation, and lipstick easily enough, but not hose. When she inquired at the checkout counter, she was dismayed to discover that they did not carry hose! Socks, yes; anklets, yes, but not pantyhose. There was no demand for it.

Wimsey almost panicked—her role required proper attire. Hopefully, she returned to the Halloween aisle of the hardware store. And there she found fishnet stockings, marked down. So her ensemble was complete.

She spent the early afternoon altering the black dress by hand. Following that, she took Cootie on a good walk to sufficiently evacuate before taking her over to Mrs. Rad's, along with her food and water dish. She gave her little pal a good squeeze before leaving her—this was also hard, but absolutely necessary.

Wimsey moved her CD player and speakers into the living area and stocked the CD changer with jazz. Then she changed into her black-widow's costume and made up her face. Studying the effect in the mirror, she smiled condescendingly at her reflection. "You look cheap and desperate."

At this point, she reconsidered: was it too much? Would the sudden personality change arouse suspicions? Then she decided, no, it wouldn't. She needed to convince her guests that she was the type of person to get plastered at a Halloween party. Those who would be shocked would just have to be shocked, and whisper that they had never guessed she was that type of woman.

Glancing at the clock, she checked her stock of beer, wine, and wine coolers in the refrigerator. She took out two coolers, opened them, and dumped out three-quarters of each beverage into the sink. She took a swig of the remainder, swishing it thoroughly around her mouth before spitting it out, to give her breath the right aroma. Then she refilled both bottles from the tap. One she placed in the washing machine, and one she left out on the counter.

By now it was 5:20. Her doorbell rang, and she opened it to receive her hors d'oeuvres from the deli. Two employees unloaded a folding table from a white van at the curb and brought it in to set up against the wall opposite the couch. They covered it with a white tablecloth festooned with fall foliage, then arranged the appetizer plates and punch service on it. The food was also decorated appropriately to the occasion, with little brooms for toothpicks and orange-colored pâté. Upon tasting everything, Wimsey was so pleased that she tipped the two deli workers fifty dollars.

After seeing them off, she had just enough time to put a bowl of candy in Arnold's lap, take a swig of her diluted cooler, and compose herself in the quiet house. She preferred the quiet; she wanted peace.

Then she heard Arnold cackle, and moments later the doorbell rang.

Inhaling, she murmured, "It's showtime."

Fifteen

Wimsey picked up the wine cooler and swung by the CD player to switch it on. With the voice of Harry Connick, Jr., filling the room, she opened the front door, cooler in hand.

Guy Krenkel and his nephew Jay stood on her porch, both wearing clothes they probably wore every day of the week. "Hello! You're the first ones here! You get a free beer!" she exclaimed.

"Thank you," Jay said with a nod, entering.

But his uncle lingered on the porch to point to Arnold. "Now that's the stupidest thing I've ever seen—him screeching like a banshee at us and all before we even get to the door. Somebody's going to take a chain saw to that thing."

"I'm glad you like him. I had so much fun putting him together," she said. "Come on in." By now it was just past sunset, so she turned the porch light on.

Guy entered, glancing around the room. "Where'd you say these beers are?" Jay asked, standing over the untouched punch bowl.

"In the fridge." Wimsey pointed with her cooler, so he made that his destination.

"Well now," Guy sniffed, "where's this fancy furniture you bought from Madelyn's boy?"

"Oh, that? Some of it I sold to a friend. But I still have the Messel side tables, and the sideboard in the second bedroom," Wimsey said, pointing. She paused at the door, seeing a pair of ladies come up the front walk. These two were her first costumed guests. One was dressed as a barmaid with a blond wig and black half-mask; the other wore a cheerleader costume.

"Hi!" Wimsey waved the bottle. "You look so cute, I may not let you in! Do I know you? I'm Wimsey."

Arnold let loose his cackle; the ladies jumped and erupted into giggles. The barmaid tittered, "I'm Babs, and this is my roomie, Shar."

"Well, come in!" Wimsey gestured with the bottle. "I've got two men here already." The old girls hurried inside, still giggling, to accost Jay.

Guy, standing over the Messel tables, nudged one with his foot and snorted, "These hoity-toity pansy tables with the lions is the dumbest stuff I've ever seen. What'd you pay for those?"

Distracted in trying to see that her new guests found the food and drink, Wimsey said, "Um, I bought the lot of Norbert's booth for nine hundred dollars."

"I wouldn't give a buck-fifty for 'em," he snapped. Apparently, seeing furniture purchased from someone else was enough to put him in a very sour mood.

"Go get a drink, Guy," Wimsey ordered.

But he sauntered out of the living area to look out back toward the lake. "Now why does a single lady need a house with a boat slip?" he asked.

Wimsey went to the refrigerator for a beer, opened it, and brought it to him. "I'll have you know that I'm thinking of buying a boat to accessorize it."

He quickly said, "I can get you a good deal on one."

Wimsey laughed, waving him away, and heard Arnold's cackle through the open door. As she went to greet a woman in a polyester pantsuit and fright wig, she glimpsed Guy heading down the hall toward the spare bedroom. But she didn't give it a second thought because from that point on, Arnold was emitting a constant chortle at the steady stream passing through Wimsey's front door.

The Lieberts arrived, Doug in prison garb and Amelie dressed as a cop. Wimsey pointed them to the fridge and the food table. A threesome arrived—two women and a man whom Wimsey had seen but never met. They were dressed as mobster and showgirls (the current terms which Wimsey would not think of using are "pimp" and "ho's"). She tried to catch their names, but Arnold screeched when Cliff came up the walk.

Wimsey ushered them inside as she greeted him, "Cliff! Glad you could make it! But couldn't you at least wear a sheet with eyeholes?" she chastised. Like Guy and Jay, he wore everyday jeans.

He looked sheepish. "Only sheets I have are way too dirty. But you look great."

"Sure." She waved it off. "Drinks are in the fridge."

"Thanks." He entered, then looked around in concern at the door standing open. "Where's your dog?"

"Oh, I boarded her for the night. She'd 've been a nervous wreck, running around and barking."

He was conceding that point when Arnold announced another visitor, and Wimsey looked down the walk at Chas approaching. She felt slight dismay at seeing the fistful of fresh flowers he carried. As far as a costume, he was dressed in subdued cowboy attire, probably straight out of his closet.

Reaching the patio, he glanced at Arnold in mild irritation, then extended the flowers to her. "Happy Halloween, Wimsey."

"Thanks." She accepted the flowers, gesturing inside. "Come get a drink."

"All right. Hey, I thought you were going to use my boots for that." He nodded down at Arnold's waders. Did he sound a tad jealous?

She laughed, "I had a better use for them! Come see." Leaving the door ajar, she swept back through the house, depositing the flowers in the kitchen sink. Chas followed, glancing at her wine cooler and her manner of displaying the flowers.

Before they could get through the living area, Guy appeared in her face. "Hey, that sideboard's a piece of junk, too. But I could use something like that, so I'll take it off your hands."

At once, she perceived that he thought it was genuine, as she had at first—or he thought it was close enough to genuine to sell as such. She told him straight up, "Guy, I'll be happy to sell it to you, but an appraiser came to look at it and told me it's fake." She started to move around him toward the back door.

Chafed at her taking his position, he stayed right in her face to insist, "That's what I'm telling you! It's junk." Chas was standing close enough behind her to inadvertently prevent her escaping Guy. It was most irritating. "But you're a nice-lookin' woman, and I like them black tights on you, so I'm gonna help you out with it." Guy started pulling his wallet out.

It took all of her self-control not to push him out of her face. "Sure. Tomorrow, Guy. I've got stuff in it that I need to clean out." Looking to slip around him, she wondered why Chas, hearing all this, did not intervene. He seemed the type to spring into action when a lady was being accosted—unless he was used to Guy's abrasive manner and assumed that she was, too. Then she appreciated Chas' letting her take care of herself.

Guy, however, would not be moved. "Well, go clean it out." He glanced up at her with the cold, shrewd eyes of a man who believed he was about to cheat someone.

All the rancor she held for liars and cheats rose up in her, so she leaned forward to say, "I changed my mind. I'm not selling it for any price." Then she rested the weight of one black pump on his toes.

With a strangled grunt, he moved out of her way. Wimsey regarded his look of black hatred before she proceeded to the back doors. Chas, behind her, noted, "Guy is a pain in the rear."

"I've handled worse," she said, flipping on the deck

lights and swinging open the back doors. "Here! This is Camilla. She's a great pal of mine."

Chas followed her out to the deck, eyeing the mischievous mannequin wearing his boots. A few other guests came out with them. "Hey, that's the chair you bought from Uncle Guy!" Jay said, beer in hand.

"Yes, and it makes a great throne. Don't you think?" Wimsey laughed.

"Umm," Chas grunted.

"At least she's quiet," Cliff observed.

Wimsey began, "Yeah, I only got one—"

A woman said, "Oh, what a nice night on the water. Say, can't we bring the stereo out here to dance?"

"What the hell, just turn it up!" Wimsey waved. The others laughed and Chas glanced at her. "You need something to drink," she decided for him.

"How much have you had already?" he asked.

"Mr. Chas, I'm nowhere near drunk," she scoffed, sweeping back into the house.

An indeterminate number of guests had arrived in the meantime, and Wimsey glanced in satisfaction at the food table being decimated. She opened the refrigerator, leaning in. "What'll it be, Chas?"

She felt his hand brush her back. He was getting a little bolder. "Ah, beer's fine. You got any lite in there?"

Wimsey took out a beer and thrust it into his hand. "I don't believe in lite. It's chicken. Whatever you're going to do, do it all the way," she said, lip curling.

He set the beer on the counter. "Could we talk?" he asked in a low voice.

"Sure! Wait a sec." She chugged the last half of the watered-down wine cooler. Cliff laughed in admiration and Chas' face went red. Wimsey tossed the empty bottle in the sink with his flowers and got another from the refrigerator.

As she was opening it, she saw a flash of white at the front door. A few people turned to look. And there appeared Tina-Marie in a perfectly gorgeous flapper dress all of white: sequins, fringe, rhinestone-studded headband with white feathers. She wore silver sandals, glittering white hose, and a white-feather harlequin mask. Melinda appeared at her side in a man's wrinkled suit and hat, with a painted moustache.

Wimsey dropped everything to go greet them. "Melinda! That's a nice suit." Wimsey recognized it from the bag of clothes that Melinda had been ready to throw out.

"Only one he owned," she said.

"How do you like Arnold?" Wimsey chuckled.

Melinda glanced back to the front porch. "Looks better than Hal ever did. Where's the rest of the clothes you bought?"

"On Camilla, out back!" Wimsey nodded. "You should go say hello to her." Then, for form's sake, she addressed the other: "You look lovely, Tina-Marie."

To Wimsey's startlement, Tina-Marie replied, "Thank you! It is a gay evening, is it not?" The voice was that of a sophisticated young woman who had lately learned English.

"Yes, it is! I do hope you enjoy my little party. May

I get you something to drink?" Wimsey asked, studying her. Tina-Marie's eyes were invisible behind the mask, but for the glitter.

"Oh, nothing now," Tina-Marie sang. "I just want to take in the lights, and the dancing!"

Wimsey glanced toward the back patio. "It looks like they are dancing out there. But do be careful; the anti-slip strips haven't been installed on the steps yet."

"What a lovely home you have!" Tina-Marie exclaimed, looking up to the ceiling. "Is the chandelier French?"

Several faces looked up to the ceiling, which boasted only contemporary recessed lights. Wimsey paused, then replied, "Yes. It's Baccarat."

"Oh, how marvelous!" Tina-Marie sighed. She inhaled a deep breath, and Wimsey saw her blackened lids close behind the mask. "Apple blossoms! How I love the spring. Are you pleased with your irises this year?"

Wimsey replied, "With the late frost, they won't win any awards, but we grow them for love." With these gentle replies, she knew that she was demolishing her party persona, thereby putting her plan at risk. But she could not bear to be a drunken ogre to this sad woman.

"How lovely. Oh, the Viennese waltz! Come dance with me, Roald."

Melinda took her arm protectively. "Of course, Tina-Marie." Then she led her glittering companion out through the back doors. Wimsey followed far enough to watch them descend the steps to the deck around the boat slip. There, within earshot of imaginary music, Melinda led her partner in a slow waltz around the slip.

A woman behind her giggled, "Oh, that was rich, the way you led her on! You're a mean bitty!"

Wimsey took a contemplative drink from the wine cooler. "That's right." And the other woman hurried off to whisper to her little group.

Chas, still at Wimsey's side, murmured, "Can we talk now?" No one else was nearby, which increased the risk of his telling her something she did not want to hear.

"About what?" she asked in a tone that warned him to stop.

"About us," he whispered.

She looked up at him. "I have guests, Chas." And she turned back at Arnold's screeching.

By now, approaching seven o'clock, the small house was full to overflowing; the refrigerator standing open to accommodate the constant demand; the food table in disarray. Wimsey looked over her party with a vague smile while Chas, in a momentary funk, went over to plunder the appetizers.

With no eyes on her at the moment, Wimsey set her still-full wine cooler on the kitchen counter and slipped into the laundry room. She took her hidden drink from the washing machine and unscrewed the top to guzzle from it as she sashayed out into the party.

More people entered; someone finally had enough of Arnold's cat calls and disconnected the sound-effects device. (Wimsey later found it broken on the porch. She also found the candy gone, as well as the bowl and

Arnold's fishing hat. But she never saw anyone trick-or-treating.)

People got loud enough to drown out the music even on full volume. Wimsey watched the barmaid Babs thrust out her hip in flirting with the mobster. *Old women dressing like teenagers; acting like teenagers— how pathetic can you get? Why can't we just grow up?* she thought dismally. Chas caught her eye from across the room, then turned his back pointedly to talk to another woman.

Wimsey inhaled with a certain reluctance. Her next move was going to be the hardest part of her performance. She didn't like creating spectacles. But she had to convince everyone here—at least, one person in particular—that she was blitzed.

So she took a conspicuous draft from her cooler and began heading toward Chas and companion with jealous fire in her eyes. He caught sight of her approach and turned expectantly. But before she reached him, Amelie stepped into her path. Surprised, Wimsey looked down at her (as Amelie was about two inches shorter).

"I don' appreciate whatchure doin'," Amelie declared, blinking heavily.

Wimsey was momentarily clueless. "What?"

"I know you're after my husban', and I wan' you to leave 'im alone!" the little wife declared, pink-cheeked.

Wimsey perceived that here was someone inebriated for real. But one opportunity for creating a scene was as good as another, so she huffed, "It's just harmless flirting! Don't be such a hen!"

"Oh! How dare you!" Amelie shrieked.

Wimsey laughed, taking another swig. So she was off-balance and not entirely prepared when Amelie flung herself upon her, fingernails extended. Wimsey managed to catch one hand, but the other raked across her throat and upper chest, inflicting light scratches.

"Here now! Ladies, ladies!" Doug chided, vastly pleased.

He separated the women, holding his wife's hands, and she burst into tears. "I can' stan' how they come on to you!"

"Hey, your husband's all over any girl he can get within reach of!" one woman in a fairy costume tittered, and Amelie turned to bawl her out.

Wimsey checked Chas, who was watching in disgusted disbelief. So she took advantage of the next opportunity to suffer more humiliation. "I don' want him!" Wimsey waved Amelie's husband off and tottered over to Chas on her sturdy pumps. She drew up close to suggest, "Wanna talk? Le's go back to th' bedroom."

Bystanders broke into laughing jeers—"What's he gonna do?" someone screeched. "He's got no blue pills! He can't *afford* 'em!"

At the uproarious laughter, Wimsey was momentarily aghast at her own lack of intuition. She had not realized that he was impotent. Was that what he had been trying to tell her—that he was interested only in companionship? She had never given him the five minutes required for him to say it. To deride a man for such a thing was contemptible, but only a sober person would understand that. She was pickled, soused, three sheets to the wind. So she got up in his face and laughed.

Crimson-faced, Chas put down his plate and made his way to the front door. Before walking out, he directed one last look to her: a promise that he would not forget this.

Wimsey eyed him, then chugged from her watercooler and raised her arms to shake her widow's fringe. "WOO-HOO!" Amelie rushed out in crying fits; Doug reluctantly followed. And this moment was the closest Wimsey got to betraying her disgust and shutting the party down.

But it raged on. By now there were people in every room of the house, doing heaven knows what. But Wimsey wasn't concerned about damage or messes; they were an incidental inconvenience inherent in the plan.

Between whooping it up and snatching bites from the food table to keep herself on her feet, she kept a calculating eye on all those who came and went from her party. The guests seemed to hold steady at around seventy—almost a third of the population of the village.

Melinda and Tina-Marie had disappeared, but other guests occupied the deck, some playing rowdy games around the slip. Wimsey began to worry about someone getting incapacitated enough to fall into the water. But then she saw Cliff out there with them, shooing them back from the deck's edge. Taking one old geezer firmly by the arm, Cliff led him to sit on the steps and made him stay there.

Watching, Wimsey nodded. "Yes. Good."

Then there was a sudden silence near the front door, Arnold having long ago ceased his vocalizations. Guests began scattering like juvenile delinquents upon the arrival of the cops.

This pretty much described the situation. A tall, broad woman in a business suit slowly made her way through the living area, looking around in outrage. Old people in silly costumes slipped out behind her in droves, the party having concluded. Wimsey glanced in mild concern at the clock. It was only eight-thirty.

The woman approached Wimsey to glare down at her. In response, Wimsey finished off her last diluted cooler. "Are you the resident? Wimsey Reade?"

Suppressing a giggled snort, Wimsey murmured, "Uh, yeah. Um hmm."

"Do you know who I am?" the woman asked threateningly. Cliff stopped behind her as other guests continued to flee.

"Th' Wicked Witch of the West? Great costume," Wimsey chortled. Cliff raised a hand to stifle a snicker.

"I am Mrs. Hansrote, the night manager. You have no party permit; you have no alcohol permit, and you have obviously exceeded the amount of alcohol allowed at a gathering."

Wimsey shrugged, leaning on the kitchen counter. She was now a sleepy drunk. "I wanted ever'body to have a good time."

"Do you know that many of these golden agers are on medications which preclude the use of alcohol?" the woman thundered.

"'Golden agers'? Doesn't that make us all adults?" Wimsey sneered a little too honestly. To cover her slip, she yawned.

Cliff interrupted, "Excuse me, Mrs. Hansrote. I was keeping an eye on Mr. Farley and Mrs. Ames. They didn't—"

She turned to him in wrath. "Your services are no longer required, Mr. Osborn! You will clean out your locker tomorrow morning!"

Defeated, he withdrew, and the last of the remaining guests escaped with him. Mrs. Hansrote turned back to the unrepentant sinner. "And you, Ms. Reade, are evicted from the village. You have two weeks to find another place to live."

"Whatever," Wimsey murmured, laying her head down on the counter.

"Oh! Village management will speak to you tomorrow!" Mrs. Hansrote declared. She stalked out, closing the front door firmly behind her.

In the stillness that followed, Wimsey raised up and looked around her trashed house: partly eaten food everywhere; the punch bowl upside down on the carpet; cans and bottles littering the floor and furniture; the decorations shredded, and the kitchen one big trash receptacle. "I needed more time," she murmured.

Was it enough?

Sixteen

Five hours following the unceremonious conclusion of the party, a figure stole up the steps to Wimsey's back deck. The deck lights were off, but the gibbous moon shone a pale light upon the back of the house. While the person's face was in darkness, the masculine clothes and strong stride suggested a man. In his left hand he carried a small leather case.

He ascended the steps carefully; mists rolling in from the lake made them slippery even on a cloudless night like tonight. Coming to the back doors, he glanced down at the grinning mannequin still seated in the broad leather chair. Then he studied the living area and kitchen through the door panes. All was dark and still.

He reached into his shirt pocket, then paused—the doors were open a crack. Obviously, the lady in residence had been too wasted to remember to lock them. He eased the door open and slipped inside. With the door cracked and the heating off, the house was cool.

Inside, he paused to make sure of his bearings in the darkness, then he trod quietly down the hall. Bypassing the second bedroom, he stumbled over something, but caught himself before falling. Reaching down, he discovered a woman's shoe in the middle of the floor. Its mate lay a few feet away, where it also had been kicked off.

Smiling, he tossed both aside before coming to the door of the master bedroom, which stood open. He stood still in the doorway, watching and listening.

No sign of the dog—good. The picture window blinds had not been closed, either, allowing the moonlight to shine in. He regarded the black fishnet stockings lying discarded on the floor. Apparently, they were uncomfortable enough for the lady to shed. He liked them, so he wadded them up and stuffed them in his jeans pocket. Then he looked at the figure on the bed.

She was lying on her side facing the window, hunched under the covers in the cool room. The mussed silver hair shone in the moonlight, obscuring her face. He could see that she still wore the black widow's costume, given that her shoulder and upper arm were just visible under the rumpled covers. At present, she was totally unconscious.

He sat gingerly on the bed and unzipped the leather pouch, from which he withdrew a small syringe. Tucking the pouch in his shirt pocket, he uncapped the syringe and reached for her nearest arm. Feeling in the covers, he paused, a look of confusion crossing his face. Something was wrong. He didn't hear her breathing.

"EEYAH HA HA HA!"

At the screeching, he flung himself off the bed

against the wall, dropping the syringe to clutch at his palpitating heart. Terrified, he gazed at the grinning demon with the long white hair at the door of the moonlit room, arms outstretched in a checked shirt and work gloves. It was the dummy from the back porch, laughing wildly at him.

"Wha—wha—" he gasped.

"I have a message for you, Cliff!" It advanced.

"No!" he cried. He braced against the wall, preparing to throw himself into a fight for his life.

"Yes!" the demon said. There was a flash of red in the moonlight, and a liquid blast hit Cliff in the face. He reeled back with a cry of surprise—then his eyes caught on fire, which engulfed his nose and mouth. Blind and coughing, he frantically tried to wipe the burning, massing foam from his face. "Cliff! Murder is not worth any amount of money!"

"Who are you?" he cried, tears pouring from his eyes and mucus from his nose.

"Blindness is better than hell, Cliff," it said, sounding human.

He coughed and spat, "Wimsey!" then lurched off the wall in her general direction, which only brought him closer for the next shot of mace in his face. Crying out, he dropped like cement, then rolled over to cough violently, dripping phlegm on the carpet.

The demon came to stand over him. "You're not listening, Cliff. You've been listening to a very evil voice," she said.

"I'll kill you!" he cried, reaching out to grab at the

boot nearest his face. While he flailed at it, the heavy boot caught him in the chest, rolling him over on his back. He clutched the ankle, gripping it with both hands. "I've got you now," he gasped.

The boot he held came down slowly on his diaphragm, rendering him breathless. Still he clutched it, reaching up the leg hand over hand, gripping the loose pants to bring her down.

"Cliff," a soft voice said. Gasping for air, he peered through fiercely watering lids to see the wicked grin in the shadows. "The love of money is the root of all evil," he heard whispered from behind the mask. And the next thing he saw was the red canister inches away.

"No," he groaned. He squeezed his eyes shut and turned his head, but that didn't prevent his taking a third shot of mace, this time at very close range.

When the sheriff's units arrived minutes later in response to the 911 call, they ran up the back steps of the floodlit deck to the lighted house. "Sheriff's department!" they shouted at the open doors.

"Come in," Wimsey said tiredly, pushing up from the kitchen counter. Over her phone, she told the dispatcher, "All right, they're here. Thank you."

The officers stared at her in oversized checkered shirt and pants. "He's in the back bedroom," she said with a nod. "Cliff Osborn. He came equipped with a syringe that's on the floor back there. I haven't touched it. But it's probably a dose of tranquilizer."

Two officers ran back to the bedroom while the third

took a notebook from his pocket. "You want to tell me what happened, ma'am?"

"Cliff Osborn broke in to finish the job that Wayne Theis botched," she said. "Actually, he just walked in; I had neglected to lock the door."

One officer frog-marched Cliff out, coughing, wheezing, with eyes swollen shut. "Ah, yeah, Sheriff; Burke's bagging a hypo and bottle of pills. Looks like he was going to make it look like a suicide or accidental OD. He's had the s—t maced out of him," the deputy reported, then glanced apologetically at her.

"I suppose so," she conceded, handing the sheriff the near-empty canister of mace.

Sheriff Jahns took it, glancing around the trashed living room. "Did he do this?"

"No, I had a party earlier," she said, yawning. "Sheriff, please tell Detective Lott to come to Mrs. Rad's house tomorrow morning at ten—she's in one-twenty-four—and I'll tell him everything I know. It involves Madelyn Treschler's murder. But right now—"

The remaining officer came out of the master bedroom carrying evidence bags and a grinning head mask with long white hair. "Was he wearing this?" he asked, holding up the mask.

"No," Wimsey said, taking it from him. "I was." They studied her and she said, "I'll explain everything tomorrow, and give the detective some leads to follow up. But I've been sitting out in the cold for hours, and I'm just exhausted. Have you got everything you need? Good. I'm going to bed."

Wimsey awoke—gradually—at the insistent ringing of her doorbell. Moaning, she raised up from the blanket on the floor of the second bedroom and looked around. "Oh, yes," she muttered. "They'll be a few people wanting to chit-chat this morning."

She staggered up to look at the computer clock: 8:50. Then her eye landed on the sideboard. In the morning light, she saw deep scratches scoring its top and front. Someone had taken a knife or screwdriver to it. She snorted, then collected herself to go to the front door.

When she opened it, the three people on the porch looked at her gravely. Wimsey knew she must look like a lunatic, wearing oversized men's clothes, with heavy makeup smeared all over her face. Sandy, the day manager, said, "May we come in, Ms. Reade?" The others, silently staring, were the deli manager and an employee.

Wimsey opened the door with a cordial wave, and the trio entered to look over the remains of the party. Wimsey told the deli manager, "The hors d'oeuvres were wonderful. I'm sorry; the tablecloth is stained terribly. It looks like the bowl and a few of the cups got broken. Oh, look! Here's the ladle, stuck in the couch."

The deli manager, a man in a village polo shirt, opened his mouth ominously, but Wimsey turned to Sandy. "It's a good thing we had our little arrangement —Mrs. Hansrote was not very happy with me last night! But about one o'clock this morning, Cliff Osborn broke in to try to kill me."

"No," Sandy whispered, her face paling.

"Yes, I'm afraid so. The sheriff's people came and got him last night—I mean, early this morning. They'll probably want to talk to you later. But I want you to know that I'm honoring our agreement: I won't say a word to anyone else, and I won't sue the village."

"Thank you," Sandy whispered, still in shock.

"Don't mention it. Listen, could you have someone come clean this up for me? I have to shower and go meet the detective. You're such a dear. Please excuse me. Oh, and don't worry about locking up—it's not necessary now."

Wimsey turned back toward the bedroom, then stopped to address the gaping deli manager. "Again, thank you. The food was perfect."

"You're welcome," he said mechanically.

Wimsey shut herself in the back bedroom to shed Camilla's clothes. The smell of mace had almost completely dissipated by now. In satisfaction, she eyed the faceless dummy in the silver wig and black costume resting undisturbed in her bed. "Wasn't sure I'd be able to pull that off," she murmured.

She showered, scrubbing her face thoroughly, then dressed in nice slacks and a sweater set. She retrieved the list from its hiding place to stash in her pants pocket. "I hope Cootie didn't give Mrs. Rad any trouble," she sighed. She missed her pal.

On her way out the front door, she encountered a cleaning crew coming up her front walk. "Thank you!" She waved, and they waved back.

She paused on the sidewalk, but there was really no way to avoid the coming unpleasantness. Might as well get it over with. So she turned west toward Shrewsbury Circle, and walked to the window of the coffee shop.

Chas was on duty today, as usual, and when he looked over and saw her, his face went rigid. Still, he managed to ask, "What will you have today?"

"I didn't come for coffee, Chas; I came to apologize. I'm very sorry for humiliating you last night—I never intended that to happen at all," she said.

"That kind of thing happens when you drink too much," he said stiffly.

"I wasn't drinking; I was only pretending to. But it worked. Cliff thought I was drunk enough to pass out, so he broke in early this morning to try to kill me," she said.

He stared at her as if debating whether to believe her or not. She leaned forward to look in the window. "Can you leave for a while? The detective in charge of Madelyn's murder case should be coming by Mrs. Rad's shortly, and I'm going to explain everything to him. In light of what you went through last night, I'd like for you to hear, too."

"Yeah," he said. "Okay. Just a minute." Taking off his apron, he went into a back room. Minutes later he came back out. "Okay, I covered it with the manager."

"Good." She nodded toward the door. They met up and began walking toward the lakefront houses on St. Mary Mead Lane. Chas looked deep in thought, every now and then shaking his head.

On the way up the street, they saw the Lieberts coming toward them for their usual walk around the pond. Wimsey slowed, prepared to eat another helping of crow. But Amelie waved in a most friendly manner. "Hello, Wimsey! Chas. Lovely party last night! We had a riot, didn't we? We must do that again."

Wimsey stopped, mouth hanging open. "I'm glad you had a good time," she said weakly, glancing at Doug.

He patted his wife on her rear. "Go on to the deli, sugar; I'll catch up." She nodded, cheerfully waving goodbye.

Chas and Wimsey looked to Doug, who explained, "She has two drinks, goes berserk, then passes out and forgets everything. It's something I let her do about once a month."

"I see," Wimsey said. Chas just looked shocked. Doug nodded good-bye and followed his wife, so the other two went on their way toward Mrs. Rad's.

Passing a long bed of daylilies, Chas couldn't stand it any longer. "Why would Cliff want to kill you? I can't make any sense of it."

"Long story. I'll explain everything when we get there, because I don't want to repeat myself over and over," she said.

When they went past Wimsey's house, she glanced at one of the cleaning crew bringing a vacuum cleaner up the front walk. "Your place was a mess," Chas observed.

"Yes, it was," she acknowledged.

They passed Melinda and Tina-Marie's house, and Wimsey made a mental note to check on her later. Then they turned up the walk to Mrs. Rad's front door. Even before Wimsey rang the doorbell, she heard Cootie whining and scratching on the inside. "Down, Cootie," she ordered, and the scratching stopped.

It took a few minutes, as usual, but they soon heard the lock turning. As soon as the door was open a crack, a white flash emerged out of the door. Rather than go to her owner, however, the dog ran straight to the flower beds to do long-held business.

"Cootie!" Wimsey exclaimed in horror. The dog was unapologetic, so Wimsey turned to Mrs. Rad. "I'm so sorry. I'll clean it up."

Mrs. Rad looked outside for a moment, then said, "I might get a dog."

"Oh." Wimsey refrained from smiling. "May we come in?"

Mrs. Rad shuffled back to the couch while Wimsey and Chas entered. Wimsey fetched Cootie's leash to walk her around out front until she saw the detective's county vehicle pull up to the curb. He climbed out, eyeing her. "Good morning, Detective Lott."

"I hear you've been busy, Ms. Reade," he said.

"We have a lot to cover," she admitted. "Let's go inside. I promised Mrs. Rad and Chas that I would explain everything to them, as well."

So he accompanied her and Cootie back into the house, where Wimsey introduced the detective to the others. Then they sat, and Wimsey began, "Well. The bottom line is that my ex-husband Greg hired Cliff to kill me."

"That's absurd!" Chas scoffed, and Wimsey stared at him. Since she was speechless, he went on, "I knew Greg Corrister for years. He's a fine man and a great businessman. Just because he's having this company trouble, you're going to accuse him of some kind of outlandish murder-for-hire plot? That's despicable."

Wimsey found herself unable to reply. Mrs. Rad said nothing. Cootie lay quietly at Wimsey's feet. Lott looked at her, then reached into his breast pocket for his notepad. "What's your name again? Your full name?" he asked.

"Charles R. Albers," he replied defiantly.

"All right, Mr. Albers," Lott said, writing. "How did you know Corrister?"

"He was president of Trident Insurance Brokerage when they arranged to cover my company, oh, fifteen years ago," Chas replied.

"Any big losses? Big payouts?" Lott asked, busily writing.

"I don't see the relevance," Chas huffed.

"'At's okay; we can get a court order for that information," Lott said.

"That's nothing short of harassment," Chas said, the color creeping up his neck.

"Not at all, Mr. Albers; I'm trying to conduct an investigation into a murder and two attempts. If Ms. Reade thinks she knows who's behind it and you indicate knowledge of the suspect, that sounds like probable cause to investigate you back to your diaper years," Lott said.

Chas stood. "You can talk to my lawyer."

As he headed for the front door, Lott called after him, "Don't leave the village, Mr. Albers."

He glanced back at the group on the couch before exiting, slamming the door behind him.

There was a moment of silence following Chas' departure. Wimsey, still stricken, looked at the detective and said, "Regardless of what Greg did for him years ago, Chas didn't have anything to do with this."

"Now why do you always go shooting down my favorite suspects?" Lott asked. Then he shrugged. "Eh, if you say so. But he wasn't willing to shut up and listen, and I want to hear this."

"He's jealous," Mrs. Rad said, leaning back. "And you've hurt his pride, somehow."

"Oh, you have no idea," Wimsey groaned.

"So talk, Ms. Reade," Lott said impatiently.

She inhaled. "I can't believe it took me so long to see what everyone else saw. . . ."

Seventeen

"And what was it you finally saw?" Lott prodded Wimsey.

"The resemblance between Madelyn and me. That was the key to the whole thing," Wimsey said. At Lott's doubtful look, she said, "Oh, I don't mean we look alike; I mean that we're both 'old ladies' with white dogs—as a matter of fact, the only dogs in the village. It was just coincidental that they both happened to be smallish dogs that were somewhat white."

Lott's face went slack in comprehension. Wimsey continued, "Something Cliff said last Saturday tipped me off. He asked what kind of dog Cootie was; I said, 'oh, she's just a mongrel,' and he said, 'yeah, the pound dogs are best.' Well, the fact that Cootie's a mixed-breed doesn't mean I got her from the pound—in fact, I got her from an individual who couldn't keep her anymore. But Greg never paid attention to the details of how I got her; he always called her 'that pound dog.' And he was the only one who referred to her that way.

"My daughter Tara knew this, so I asked her if she

had talked to anyone in the village about me, maybe to give them some personal history. Of course, she hadn't. So the only way I could see that Cliff would jump to that conclusion was if he had talked to Greg."

Wimsey paused; her listeners were silent. "I believe that Greg knew I was here from day one. I tried to keep it secret, but we had too many mutual friends who would let it slip without knowing they were doing anything wrong. So he had one of his people fish around the village for someone willing and accessible to be a tool—and they hit on Cliff. Lauren told me he gambled, which would make him constantly in need of cash. I believe Cliff was offered a great deal of money to kill me.

"But Cliff was too cautious to soil his hands directly, so he brought in Wayne Theis," she said. At this point, Lott began writing in his notepad. Wimsey continued, "Theis was not quite as bright as Cliff—moreover, since he had been in the village only days before I arrived, he didn't know everyone. I believe he was told that his target was an old lady with a white dog . . . which he found. And he murdered Madelyn by mistake."

Lott stopped writing. Wimsey pursed her lips and went on. "Theis, being clumsy and stupid, used a village wrench that Cliff had apparently been carrying around. So when the maintenance supervisor began an inventory, and told everyone to turn in whatever tools he had, Cliff was stuck with a set of wrenches—minus one that had been used to drown a murdered woman's dog. He couldn't turn them back in, so he started just throwing them out." Lott nodded contemplatively.

Wimsey continued, "Theis' mistake was disastrous, of course, because it brought the police on the scene, and Greg intended that it should look like an accident or natural death. Cliff almost panicked at this point, because he had already been paid, and had paid Theis. So Cliff began hovering to see how close he could get to me, and whether he could do the job himself. He was the one who trampled your mums looking in the window when I was here," she told Mrs. Rad. "But for whatever reason—I think he was too squeamish—Cliff could never put his hands on me.

"So Theis was given a second chance to earn his pay. Whether he broke into my house that Friday looking for photographs of me, or the disk with the evidence, or intended to hide there until I got back, I don't know. He is the one you saw on my deck," she said, nodding again to Mrs. Rad. "I still don't know for sure who broke into my son-in-law's office and copied the letter he had written to the village inquiring about security for me. But it prompted me to dispose of the book and the disk, which was imperative. I had no idea at the time what a close watch Greg was keeping on me."

Lott opened his mouth at this point, but seeing her eyes focused on something distant, did not interrupt. "The timing is what threw me off," she murmured. "I was stuck on thinking that he wasn't interested in harming me until he knew that I had sent the disk to the D.A. But my son-in-law's office was ransacked in the early morning of the day I moved here. Greg had only been waiting for me to leave my daughter's house. She's his daughter, too, and he did not want anything to happen to her, or his granddaughter."

Wimsey stopped, looking down at her hands to compose herself. Lott glanced away; Mrs. Rad kept her faded eyes locked on Wimsey. Clearing her throat, Wimsey lifted her head and continued, "So Theis made his third attempt the following Monday, coming to my house posing as Guy Krenkel's nephew Jay. Since I shut him out then, he made his *fourth* attempt the following Thursday, when he came to the back door with a 'message.' I am sure that message was from Greg, and I could probably come up with something close to it," she said wryly.

"But you knocked him out cold and he fell down the steps and drowned," Lott could not resist adding.

Wimsey nodded. "This left Cliff no choice but to finish the job himself. He became almost annoying in 'keeping watch' over me. He said he felt responsible; I realize now he was looking for the right opportunity. He almost had it last Friday—it was overcast, and I was out at the pond alone with Cootie. But then Chas showed up and ran me home in the rain. If he had been Greg's tool, he would've taken that opportunity to complete the job. But he didn't. Not only that, if he were taking money from Greg, he wouldn't need to work in a coffee shop. Even if he enjoys it, it's murder on his feet!" she said with a sympathetic laugh.

In an aside, she added, "Just because Greg hated me doesn't mean he couldn't be nice to someone else. He liked being a 'good guy.' It's entirely conceivable he did a good turn for Chas in his business, earning his lifelong gratitude. Even an evil person knows how to be good occasionally, when it suits him."

Lott cocked his head. "What if Chas is the one reporting your movements to your ex?"

"What if he is?" Wimsey replied with a shrug.

"Then I'd charge him with conspiracy to solicitation," Lott replied.

Wimsey shook her head. "He didn't know anything about that, Detective. If he told Greg anything, it would be because Greg asked him as a favor to keep an eye on his wife, who he still loved, to make sure she was doing all right."

"Probably," Lott allowed.

"Now about this party," Mrs. Rad said as an instruction to continue.

"Yes," Wimsey exhaled. "I had to give Cliff a safe opportunity to 'off' me. So I threw the party so he'd see me getting drunk, without my dog in the house. I bought two mannequins at the hardware store, dressed them up, and set one on the front porch and one on the back. I put a sound-effects device on the one in front—as well as a sliding bolt on the door—because I wanted to make sure he wouldn't come in that way. I wanted him to come in the back.

"It worked better than I could have imagined. Cliff followed me around all during the party, except when he was on the deck around the boat slip trying to make sure nobody else drowned so the police wouldn't be called.

After Mrs. Hansrote broke up my party, I changed places with the dummy in back. I put the dummy in the black widow's costume in my bed, and I sat in the clothes and mask by the back door.

"I sat there for *hours*—I was so afraid of going to sleep. But he came. So I slipped into the bedroom behind him and scared him half to death. Then I emptied a can of mace at him. What was in the syringe he had?" she asked the detective.

"Phenobarbital," Lott said casually, leaning back. "Same as the pills. He was out to make it look accidental, again."

Wimsey nodded. "So that's it."

A moment of silence followed, then Mrs. Rad said, "Where is the connection with your ex-husband, other than a chance phrase?"

"Oh, yes," Wimsey said, as if remembering something. She withdrew the list from her sweater pocket and handed it to Lott. "That's what I was hoping to use the detective for. Here are all my husband's close associates, other than his lawyers. I believe he would have used one of them to make the initial contact with Cliff. I've included phone numbers when I could remember them, but they've probably changed. If you can establish phone contact between Cliff and any of these people, that should do it."

"Sure," he said cheerfully. "That'll be useful in getting ol' Cliff to spill his guts."

"That was very foolish and dangerous," Mrs. Rad said to her.

"Well, of course it was," Wimsey agreed. "But now that it's all said and done—" She stifled a yawn. "I'm sorry, I'm exhausted. Thank you so much for keeping Cootie for me. I think we'll go nap now."

Detective Lott stood. "I'll give you a lift. Mrs. Rad," he nodded to her.

"Hmph," she said.

Outside, Wimsey glanced at the car. "Detective, it's easier for me to just walk Cootie two houses down than try to get her into a strange car."

"Then I'll walk you," he said, detouring to the sidewalk. On the way back to her house, he said, "Why didn't you call me?"

She winced. "Would you have let me go through with it?"

"No way. But it was a good plan. I'd 've been the one sitting out back," he said.

She flashed a tired smile at him. "And had all the fun of seeing Cliff wet his pants? No."

Lott grunted in acknowledgment, then they were silent the few minutes it required to reach her door. Pausing on the porch, she said, "Thank you, Detective."

He nodded. "I'll call you with what we find out." He patted the list in his pocket.

"All right," she said, studying his subdued expression. Then she and Cootie went in to a nice clean house. She locked the doors for form's sake, stretched out on the bed beside the dummy, and slept for the next four hours.

The bleating of her phone woke her. Groaning, she

looked at the display and murmured, "Hello, Detective."

"Ms. Reade. Did I wake you?"

"Yes, but that's all right. I needed to get up anyway." She pushed herself up to a sit. Cootie, beside her, stretched and yawned. "What is it?"

"Okay, well—" At his reluctant tone, she came fully alert. "All right, Cliff Osborn has been charged with attempted murder. He's been fully cooperating—he gave us his phone, and indicated the number of the man who called him to solicit your murder."

He paused, and she said, "Who was it?"

"Well, Cliff said he called himself 'John.' The number is evidently that of a disposable cell phone—it's untraceable. Osborn said he met 'John' once, in order to receive one hundred thousand dollars in twenties. Twenty thousand he gave to Theis for his services. We're still trying to trace the serial numbers of the bills, which appear to have come from an offshore bank.

"Osborn couldn't describe John at all, and he was really trying. He said he wore a devil's head mask and gloves. Osborn was pretty sure he was a white guy, about six foot, maybe two-hundred-forty pounds. John told him your name and that you were about to move into the Old England Retirement Village."

"When was this?" Wimsey asked.

"Ah, Osborn said the meeting was Wednesday, October ninth. He said he got the initial call early that morning from someone who knew about his heavy gambling debts, offered him a way out. Those were the only two times Osborn had contact with him."

"And Greg's name never came up," Wimsey said.

"No, it didn't," Lott confirmed.

"Surely there was mention of Cootie. What did 'John' say about 'a pound dog'?" she demanded.

She heard him flipping through papers. "I don't see any specific mention of that," he finally said.

Wimsey leaned back on the headboard contemplatively. "Then Cliff is lying," she said softly. "He knows more than he's telling, but he's more afraid of Greg than the police. I underestimated him"—and she wasn't referring to Cliff.

"Are you *sure*—?" The detective aborted his standard question to say instead, "I would like to put you under a protective watch."

She looked out the window to the lake shimmering in the afternoon sunlight. "What about Norbert's lawsuit?"

He adjusted to the change of topic. "Ah, what I hear is that with Osborn's arrest, the judge has summoned lawyers for the dog association and the kids to see if they couldn't work something out."

"Norbert included Trentham and Michelina as plaintiffs?" she asked.

"Yes, on the advice of counsel," Lott said.

"I underestimated him, too," she murmured.

"Ms. Reade, we really need to talk about your protection. Corrister is going to try again," Lott said.

"Thank you for your concern, Detective. And thank you for keeping me informed. I really need to get Cootie out now. Bye." And she terminated the call. But before doing anything else, she played with the phone until she figured out how to change the ring tone. The new ring she selected consisted of the first few measures of Beethovan's Fifth.

She put on a coat, for the day had become blustery, and walked Cootie for several miles around the lake. She turned a brief eye upward at the migrating geese, only vaguely noting the magnificent fall color of red oaks and birches. The wind blew the lake into choppy peaks that sent cold spray inland, so she turned her collar up to keep walking. And she ruminated.

If Greg was determined to kill her, any protection Detective Lott offered would be inadequate. Lott did not know Greg like she did, and yet he still surprised her. So she had to watch out for herself . . . and be ready for the consequences should she fail.

When she contemplated dying, her hand crept to the pocket of her coat, but she did not have the Goodspeed in this pocket. It was at home. All she had was her phone. She was somehow not surprised that it suddenly played Beethovan while her hand was on it. She brought it out of her pocket to look at the display: Unknown Name, Unknown Number. And suddenly she knew who that was. She answered, "Hello."

"Hello, Wimsey. It's good to hear your voice. How are you?"

"Doing well, Greg. How did you get my number?"

"Oh, an old friend who's in Des Plaines now, I believe. But you probably don't remember Artie," he said.

"Of course I do," she said, unruffled. With his contacts, Greg could have gotten her number from numerous sources, inside or outside the village. She knew that Artie had not betrayed her simply because the Dallas District Attorney had, in fact, received the disk. But Greg had put two and two together to figure out—or find out—who had helped her send it. He knew all along that it had come from her.

"Well, I had just been hearing about some break-ins down your way, and I wanted to make sure you were all right," he said.

"Thank you for your concern; I'm fine," she said.

"Well, that's good to know. I want to do as much for you as you have done for me." Master of communication that he was, there was not a trace of sarcasm in his voice.

"Greg, you've always taken excellent care of yourself. You've done a far better job of it than I could. And I'm sure you will justify your faith in yourself during this present inconvenience."

"Don't be sarcastic, Wimsey; it's unattractive."

"So sorry," she deadpanned.

"Anyway, I just wanted to make sure you're all right . . . and that you stay that way," he said.

She perceived the threat clearly. "Don't worry about a thing, Greg."

"I won't. Good-bye, Wimsey."

She closed the phone and pocketed it thoughtfully. "Time to go home, Cootie," she murmured.

At the fall of twilight, the air got considerably cooler. Wimsey hurried back to the boardwalk, and from there even Cootie was straining at the leash to get home. With newly installed anti-slip strips underfoot, they clambered up the steps to the lit back deck. Wimsey, hands shaking for the cold, unlocked the door and bent to unhook Cootie from her leash.

The dog stopped, growling, and Wimsey froze. Slowly straightening, she looked around the dark house. She had left the living area lights on; she was sure of it. Then she spotted a paper on the kitchen counter.

She went over to pick it up and read: "Mrs. Reade. We were laying the strips when we noticed one of your ceiling lights was out, so we brought in the ladder and changed it and turned off the lights. So if you turn out the lights when your gone the bulbs will not burn out as quick. Thx, Hy Eckwert, Main. Supr."

"Oh," Wimsey exhaled. Cootie, having expressed her disapproval of the unauthorized entrance, trotted over to wait by her food bowl. Wimsey turned on all the lights, relocked the doors, and poured Cootie's dinner.

She pulled out a frozen dinner for herself, then fetched the Goodspeed to the bistro table to read while she waited for dinner to heat. Having disciplined herself to read from beginning to end instead of just flipping, she opened to the bookmark in Acts, where she had left off. And she read:

"Men of Athens, from every point of view I see that you are extremely religious. For as I was going about and looking at the things you worship, I even found an altar with this inscription: 'To an Unknown God.' So it is what you already worship in ignorance that I am now telling you of. God who created the world and all that is in it, since he is Lord of heaven and earth, does not live in temples built by human hands, nor is he waited on by human hands as though he were in need of anything, for he himself gives all men life and breath and everything."

Something about the passage prompted Wimsey to look up and admit, "I'm afraid. I'm afraid that, as usual, Greg will get his way."

But . . . if she took this God seriously, He would give her life and breath. She looked back down at the page and continued to read: "While God overlooked those times of ignorance, he now calls upon all men everywhere to repent, since he has fixed a day on which he will justly judge the world through a man whom he has appointed, and whom he has guaranteed to all men by raising him from the dead."

Wimsey, considering herself a good person, wondered what it meant "to repent." "What have I done that I should change?" she mused. And since she asked, the answer came.

She wilted at the thought, then the oven timer dinged. So she was able to eat her dinner to avoid the repentance presented her—temporarily. If she meant what she said about taking this God seriously, then she had to prove that by doing what He said. You did not ignore someone you professed to take seriously.

Groaning, she pulled out her phone and placed a call. It was answered, "Mom! Hi. What a privilege that you call instead of me having to call you."

"I don't know where you get the sarcasm, Tara."

"Sorry," Tara chirped.

"All right. Well, I guess it's time to tell you about the little adventures I've had here." And Wimsey recounted to her everything about Madelyn, Theis, Cliff, and her suspicions about Greg—including the last conversation.

With Tara's questions, plus the interruption of having to tell her husband and daughter to go ahead and have dinner without her, it took a half hour to cover it all. Then Tara said, "Mom, how could you not tell me any of this before?"

"Oh, Tara, I—didn't want you to worry. There's nothing you could do. And . . . whatever Greg is, he's still your father, and I didn't want—"

"The s.o.b.," Tara said, and the phone went dead.

Wimsey looked at the phone in surprise; Tara had never been angry enough to hang up on her before. Mildly perturbed, Wimsey put the phone down on the table and continued to read.

About an hour later, when she had a cup of hot cocoa in hand and her Tchaikovsky CD in the changer, Wimsey heard her phone play from the table. She answered, "Hello, Tara. Listen, honey, I'm so sorry—"

"Okay, Mom. Do you remember Randy's friend in the FBI I told you about?—David?" Tara said briskly.

"I believe so," Wimsey replied.

"Okay, Randy called him with what you told me. David's going to take it to his boss and ask for a warrant to tap Daddy's phone. If he tries anything else, they'll know it."

Wimsey's jaw dropped. "But—there's no hard evidence—"

"There's probable cause, and that's all they need. They *are* the FBI," Tara pointed out.

Wimsey sat back. "Actually, that's . . . that's a great relief, Tara. Thank you, honey."

"I guess it's just as well you didn't tell me before now," Tara said to Wimsey's surprise. "The fact that you were right about this handyman, and that he did try to kill you, makes your story a lot more credible than if you had said something before anything happened. I just thank God you're okay."

"Me, too," Wimsey murmured.

"Okay, gotta run. Halle is pestering me to read her a story."

"All right. Good night, Tara."

"G'night, Mom."

Over the next several days, Wimsey's life settled into a routine of walking Cootie, reading, visiting with Mrs. Rad and Melinda, and researching the wildlife around the lake. On her walks, she discovered herself suddenly the most popular person in the village, as resident after resident approached with congratulations on her party and eager questions as to when her next would be. She always demurred.

When Wimsey and Cootie were returning from one such walk, Melinda came out to meet her on the front sidewalk. "Good afternoon! How are you?" Wimsey asked.

"All right," Melinda said. "I was just wondering what you're going to do with your dummy." She gestured to Arnold, still sitting rather askew on the front porch.

"I don't know. I guess I need to get rid of him," Wimsey mused.

"In that case, I'd like to buy him," Melinda said. When Wimsey looked at her in surprise, Melinda admitted, "He reminds me of Hal, a little."

"Oh, well, take him," Wimsey said.

Melinda looked a little anxious. "I'd rather buy him. You bought the clothes from me."

"So? You'd be doing me a favor to take him off my hands. I'm glad you didn't ask for Camilla, because I'm keeping her!" Wimsey laughed.

"Camilla? Where?" Melinda asked curiously.

"By the back door, dressed just as she was for the party," Wimsey said. At Melinda's quizzical look, Wimsey invited, "Come see."

She unlocked the front door and took Melinda to the back deck where Camilla, redressed in her original outfit, was seated in the Victorian gentleman's chair. "I bring her in when it rains," Wimsey confided.

Melinda looked concerned. "I thought that was one of your guests."

"No, she's a resident. So's Arnold. Take him," Wimsey insisted.

So Melinda lugged the dummy to her house next door, and Wimsey replaced the wicker chair in the second bedroom. Then her doorbell rang. She opened it to Melinda on her porch again. "I don't want to take the dummy for nothing, so. . . ." She handed Wimsey a man's walking cane with a beautiful silver eagle's head for a handle.

"Melinda, this is gorgeous. It's too valuable for me to take in trade for Arnold," Wimsey protested.

Melinda looked at the cane. "It was Hal's, when he couldn't fish any more, and I . . . don't like remembering how he was when he couldn't fish."

She turned quickly off the porch and Wimsey called, "Thank you!" She brought it inside with some bemusement. "What am I going to do with a cane?" She tapped the silver head in her palm. "Hey, you could really hurt someone with this." So she stowed it in the second bedroom, next to the defaced fake sideboard.

As the next few days passed, Wimsey continued to read her Goodspeed, usually at night right before she went to bed. She tended to postpone reading it during the day because it made her uncomfortable, in that she perceived the power behind the words and the authority they carried. As long as she had been in ignorance, God had passed over her disobediences; but the more she knew, the more she was accountable for. But she couldn't go to sleep without opening the little book.

But . . . things were coming to a head; she could feel it. Having gone this far, Greg would not give up now, which was the point of his phone call. The pressure of waiting to see what he would do finally compelled her to reach more desperately for the consolation at hand.

The Wednesday after her Halloween party, she

broke with habit and sat down with the Goodspeed in the early afternoon. It was one of those glorious, golden Hill Country fall days, so, mistrusting herself to pay attention to what was most important, she sat in the living area to read, turning her back to the beckoning view of the lake.

She read through the Letters quickly until coming to Paul's first letter to Timothy. And she read: "Charge the rich of this world not to be arrogant, nor to set their hopes on such an uncertain thing as riches, but on God who richly provides us with everything for our enjoyment. Charge them to do good, to be rich in good deeds, open-handed and generous, storing up a valuable treasure for themselves for the future, so as to grasp the life that is life indeed."

She felt almost hilarious relief reading this—"Since I'm not rich, it doesn't apply to me, and I don't have to worry about it."

Her phone warbled classical music, and she put down the New Testament to look at the phone display. "Hello, Detective Lott. How are you?"

"Fine, Ms. Reade. How are you?"

"Never better, thank you."

"May I come over, Ms. Reade?"

"If you like, Detective."

"Thank you. I'll be there shortly."

About fifteen seconds later her doorbell rang. Cootie sprang to the door barking, and Wimsey opened it to the detective standing outside. "I appreciate your calling first," she said, glancing at the county car parked at the curb.

"You're welcome. May I come in?" He was carrying a manila folder.

"Yes, certainly." She stepped back, then watched in concern as he limped in. "Detective, whatever did you do to yourself?"

"Ah, too much walking," he grunted. "They're telling me I need knee replacement surgery, and I don't want it. I got too much to do."

"Detective, you can't—" She blinked in shock at the sudden, obvious solution that occurred to her.

"I can do whatever I dam' well please," he said.

She turned on her heel and went to the second bedroom, then came back with the silver-headed walking stick. "Try this," she instructed.

He took the stick, glancing at her, then placed its tip to the floor and began walking. "Wait." She stopped him. "Which is your worse knee?"

"The right," he grumbled.

"Okay. Hold the cane in your left hand. Now take a step with your left foot. When you step with your right, bring the cane forward at the same time. Yes. Try that for a while," she said.

He walked around the living area with the cane. "I think it's a little long."

"It may be, but try it out for a while before you have it cut down any," she said.

"Uh, yeah. Okay, what do you want for it?" he asked, bringing out his wallet.

"Detective, I will not let you pay me for it—"

"Ms. Reade, we've been over this before—"

"—because it was a gift and I do not turn gifts into income opportunities," she said coolly.

He looked at her, then muttered, "We'll see."

"What is that?" She nodded at the manila file.

"Well, we'll cover that in a minute." He used the cane to get back over to the couch and sit, throwing the slender folder on the glass coffee table. "I wanted to let you know a couple things. Ah, Madelyn Treschler's case file has been closed: murder by the deceased Wayne Theis. And the judge in Norbert's case just issued a ruling in his favor. Her estate will be split three ways among her children. They, in turn, have agreed to a memorial gift of fifty grand to the dog association."

"That's interesting," she said, sitting up.

"Yeah. Normally, you know, the legal will of a competent woman would never be overturned, but Norbert had a sharp attorney who not only dredged up Dickers' trust funds, but also produced a witness to Madelyn's cheating at the dog shows. The association was anxious to avoid bad publicity, so was glad to take what it could get. And don't ask how I know about this, because the proceedings were sealed," he said.

"I see," she murmured.

"And . . . Cliff Osborn was killed yesterday." With that, he opened the manila folder. "Here is the report." His voice was heavy.

Her hands went cold. "What happened?"

"Ah, he was being transported to Huntsville to await trial and he—it appears he jumped out of the van into traffic. Pretty messy," he said, grimacing.

"What do you mean, 'it appears that he jumped'?" she asked.

He shrugged. "Ah, just that . . . we only have the transport guard's word for what happened, so we're . . . watching his bank account."

Wimsey looked thoughtful. "You may have more evidence than that. The FBI got a tap on Greg's phone. Let me check to see what they might have heard."

While Lott watched with mouth slightly ajar, Wimsey phoned her daughter. "Hi, Tara—oh, is that Halle I hear crying? I'm sorry; I won't keep you. I just wanted to ask about that FBI wiretap that Randy's friend was going to arrange—"

She stopped to listen, then said, "Okay, that's fine. Thank you, Tara. Tell Halle I miss her, too, and I'll come visit shortly."

She closed her phone while Lott watched patiently. Then she cleared her throat and said, "Um, my son-in-law has a friend who's with the FBI. He's . . . submitting paperwork to have Greg's phone tapped. Tara is sure it won't take more than another week."

Lott nodded. "FBI. Yeah, that's good. They'll be good protection."

"Yes," Wimsey agreed, observing how despondently he studied the silver head of the cane. *He doesn't believe what he just said. He doesn't think they'll be able to do anything to protect me from Greg,* she realized. In her heart rose the plea, *God, if you are really there—*

Her doorbell rang, and Cootie sprang off the couch to answer, as usual. When Wimsey opened the door, a courier held out an electronic clipboard. "Wimsey Reade?"

"Yes."

"Sign here, please."

She did, and he handed her a large cardboard envelope. Lott watched tensely while she shut the door and came back to sit on the couch. "Where's it from?" he asked.

"Zurita's," she murmured. She opened the envelope to withdraw a check. At her sudden intake of breath, he quickly looked over her shoulder.

"Nice," he said.

She was staring at a check for $381,400.00 for the auction proceeds of the rug she had bought off Norbert. Before she could feel guilty for any possibility of having cheated him, she recalled the news of his inheritance. He would never miss the rug.

Then the Scripture she had just read came back to her, and she knew that receiving this check was not coincidental. A question seemed to hover over her: *You were about to ask for something?* She was holding her breath.

"What're you gonna do with it? Take a cruise?" he asked, twirling the cane. He looked as though he was getting quite used to it.

Blinking, she asked, "Detective, what's the best charity you know of?"

"Ah, probably the Salvation Army. Yeah, that's a good idea. Making a donation will help with the taxes on it," he said.

"May I borrow your pen?" she asked. When he pulled it out for her, Wimsey flipped the check over and wrote on the back, "Pay to the order of the Salvation Army," and signed it.

While he gaped, she handed it to him. "Can you see that they get it, Detective?"

"Ms. Reade—the whole thing? You can't—"

"I can do whatever I dam' well please," she replied.

"Giving it all away?" he cried. "Why?"

"Because—" How could she explain it without it looking like payment to God for protection? "Because . . . if you want a relationship with someone, you take seriously what they say. And I—I don't believe in doing anything halfway."

He studied her, then glanced down at the open New Testament on the table. Comprehension spread across his face, and she knew that at one time in his life, he had been a church-goer. He cleared his throat and said, "In that case, I'd better hand-deliver this check right away."

"I'd appreciate it," she said.

With the assistance of the cane, he rose from the couch and started for the door, taking tentative steps. Then he glanced back, lifting the silver head. "Thanks again."

"You're welcome."

He departed down the walk toward his car at the curb while she watched from the front window. He handled the cane as if it were already a part of him, tossing it affectionately on the passenger seat before sitting behind the wheel.

Seeing him drive off with the check was like seeing light and color for the first time, or hearing a symphony after a lifetime of deafness. Something had happened in cutting off her right hand: she was no longer afraid. The Unknown God just became a little clearer.

Wimsey's phone played its music from the coffee table. She turned from the window to eye it, then picked it up. Glancing at the display, she saw, "Unknown Name, Unknown Number." So she answered, "Hello, Greg."

Eighteen

"Hello, Wimsey." She picked up on the strained tone of her ex-husband's voice instantly. It sounded different, as if he was trying to affect a nonchalance he did not feel. Since Greg was a master at conveying just the right impression, Wimsey pressed the tiny phone closer to her ear to catch every inflection.

Before she could speak, he continued with a light laugh, "You're an amazing woman, Wimsey. I never gave you enough credit. Listen, I've been—I want to apologize for behaving like such a jerk. You were a good wife, and you deserve more than you got for putting up with me. I'm a little strapped with legal bills, but, I could probably swing two hundred grand. How would that be?"

At first, she was speechless. "You want to give me two hundred thousand dollars?"

"Yeah. Yes, I do," he said in warm satisfaction. It was the good-guy Greg talking, the Greg who earned the eternal devotion of people who barely knew him, like Chas.

But Wimsey knew him. She recognized an attempted buy-off, which made her wary. So she casually replied, "I just gave away almost twice that."

"Oh, you did," he said just as casually, but she detected the undercurrent of rage in his voice. He had always been the Moneymaker, the one who earned so much more than she. This indication of her sudden financial superiority was more than he could swallow. It made her suddenly very glad for having given away every dime from the sale of that rug.

"Besides," she went on, "what makes you think you can make everything right with money?" Her thoughts ran, *What is this all about? Why would he be attempting to bribe me this late? I already sent the disk; what more could I possibly do to him?*

"All right, then, what do you want?" he snapped.

Her confusion deepened. "I don't want anything from you, Greg."

"Oh, so you're not satisfied. What will it take? Me admitting that you're scaring me to death with your little joke? Okay, you got that. Ha, ha, you're scaring the s—t out of me. Is that what you wanted to hear?"

Her mouth went dry. "I . . . don't know what you mean, Greg."

"Oh, right," he said sarcastically. "That's part of the joke—to be all, 'I don't know what you mean, Greg,'" he said in a mocking falsetto. "Well, if that's how you want to play, I'm game. I've already called my attorney, who's calling the cops. This harassment isn't going to get you anything but jail time."

"What harassment? What have I ever done to you?" she cried.

"What have you *done*? The sweet, cheated-on little wife?" His attempt at sarcasm hit a slightly hysterical note. "Okay. Make me spell it out. Sure, if that makes you happy. This little jokester you hired to harass me. Showing up at court, on the street, in the restaurant, everywhere I go, leering at me with that—that *face*, behind that ghastly long white hair."

Her heart lodged in her throat. "Camilla?" she gasped.

"Oh, so you do know who I'm talking about!" he said, bitterly victorious. "Well, you have crossed the line sending her to my house, looking in through the windows! I don't know how you found out where I live —but—that is an invasion of privacy that I won't stand for. You won't call her off? Fine. I'll get you, Wimsey; as God is my witness, I'll—"

He broke off and she listened over the pounding of her heart. Then he cried, "There she is again, at the window! Ha! Whatever you paid her, you're going down for it, Wimsey!" His voice was high and hysterical. "Ha! You—you—no! Stay out! You can't come in here! No! Go away!" he screamed.

"Greg!" she cried.

She heard a clattering, as if he had dropped his phone. Still, she heard his screams subside into a low, pleading moan, "No, oh, God, no. . . . Stay away from me. Leave me alone. What do you want—Ungh!—" He uttered a strangled cry that suddenly ceased.

Wimsey continued to clutch her phone as best she could with trembling fingers. Then she heard a nondescript voice say softly: "Good-bye." And the connection went dead.

Though her hands shook violently, Wimsey managed to close the phone. Then she looked down at Cootie, who had buried herself, shaking, in a corner of the couch. Wimsey dropped to the couch to hold her.

She did not know how long she sat there clutching her dog; she was only vaguely aware of the shadows cast by the autumn sun tracing their way across the clean beige carpet of her little living area. The light made the golden lions on her Messel tables blaze and shimmer. Focusing on the rampant lion that faced her finally brought her out of her shock, somewhat.

Her phone sounded its music; she picked it up to look at the display: Unknown Name, Unknown Number. With a resolute calm, she pressed the talk button. "Hello."

"Who is this?" a male voice asked.

She cleared her throat and lifted her head. "This is Wimsey Reade."

"Greg Corrister's ex-wife?"

"Yes. Who is this?"

The voice softened. "Sorry. Had to make sure I had the right party. This is Detective Grant Cowell of the Dallas Police. I'm sorry to tell you that Mr. Corrister is dead, ma'am."

She gasped, "I didn't do it! I don't know who was

harassing him—I—I didn't pay anyone to kill him! And I don't even know where he lives—"

"Excuse me, ma'am," he interrupted. "Mr. Corrister died of a heart attack. I'm at Baylor Medical right now. They just pronounced him dead, and I wanted to let you know before you heard it on the news. Ah, this is his phone I'm talking on. Looks like you were the last person he talked to."

"Heart attack?" Wimsey whispered. "Are they— sure? He's never had heart trouble, to my knowledge. Not even high blood pressure."

"Yeah, they're sure. No entry wounds," he said dryly, then added, "I guess the strain of, ah, recent events caught up with him."

"But—are you *sure*? Where was he when it happened?" she demanded.

"He was in his office at home. Scheduled to appear in court for sentencing next Monday. His wife heard something from another part of the house and went to check on him. Found him on the floor; no respiration. So she called nine-one-one, but the EMTs got no vitals and no response."

"There was . . . no one else with him?"

"No, ma'am," he replied. "The house was secure; the burglar alarm set. The lab rushed a tox screen and there was nothing in his system but traces of a prescribed sedative. He died from a massive myocardial infarction." After a pause he asked, "You okay, ma'am?"

"Yes." Her voice cracked, and she cleared her throat. "Yes. Thank you for calling."

"You're welcome, Ms. Reade. Have a good afternoon—er, anyway."

"Thank you. Good-bye." She closed the phone and looked down at Cootie, who climbed out of the sofa cushions yawning and shaking herself. "Let's go for a walk, Cootie," Wimsey murmured.

At the back door, she hooked Cootie up to her leash. Stepping out, she froze beside the mannequin still seated in the chair. Holding her breath, Wimsey crouched to look it in the face and touch the canvas arm. Nothing strange here. It was just—a mannequin: a mask and man's clothes over a stuffed canvas form.

She straightened to take Cootie down the steps and off the boardwalk to the edge of the lake. Here, the dog strained at the leash, so Wimsey reached down and unhooked her to let her run freely along the shore. Wimsey could do this only because Cootie was good enough to not run off, and to come back when she was called. They understood each other; they had a relationship.

With the glinting lake, the golden trees, the placid ducks all mingling in her blurring vision, Wimsey dropped her head under the weight of awe. "Have mercy on him," she whispered. "He just could never understand. . . . *I* don't understand how, or who . . . but I don't have to understand. You have freed me from many things, especially, from . . . being a slave to money. Thank you. Thank you."

Raising her head again, she saw Mrs. Rad sitting on her back deck with binoculars in hand. Wimsey stopped trembling. Mrs. Rad acknowledged her, so Wimsey lifted a hand and began climbing up to the boardwalk, getting sturdier with every step. "Cootie! Cootie! Let's go hear what Mrs. Rad has seen today."

The dog pricked her long white ears and sprang up the shore to follow.

Books by Robin Hardy

>   (continued on the next page)

Sammy: Arenamania
Sammy: In Principle
Sammy: Grave Agreement
Sammy: Love Shouldn't Hurt
Sammy: The Consolation of Bucephalus
   (Sammy and Marni's story continues in the Sammy/ Streiker Salmagundi, below.)

The Idecis
Unknown Name, Unknown Number: A Wimsey Reade Mystery
Padre and its sequel *His Strange Ways*

The Sammy/Streiker Salmagundi
   If Only for This Life
   Abby's Monsters (coming 2015)

Edited by Robin Hardy

Sifted But Saved: Classic Devotions by W.W. Melton